"Do you remember when we used to—"

"—sled down this hill?" The memory sparked a laugh in Holly. "We were crazy."

Leaving the trees behind, Holly stepped into the hayfield at the top of the ridge. Mac followed close behind as she walked to the summit and studied the view before them.

Mac came up beside her. The touch of his shoulder against hers sent an electric shock through her body.

"Holly."

Holly focused on the mountains in the distance, covered in haze, and ignored the burn where his arm touched hers. "Hot today," she said. "I can't imagine sledding in weather like this, can you? I wonder if the kids—"

"Holly." The gruffness in Mac's voice brought her up short, but she refused to meet his eyes.

"Mac, I can't—"

Mac reached out and pulled her closer. "The girl I knew didn't have *can't* in her vocabulary."

Dear Reader,

First of all, thank you for picking up this book. The journey to publication has been long and I have learned so much in the past few years. All of which goes to prove you're never too old to learn. Thanks to all who have offered advice and encouragement along the way. Special thanks to the crew at Harlequin who worked to bring *Wanted: The Perfect Mom* to print. This book is my first with Harlequin. I am honored to be included in the diverse and talented group of Harlequin Heartwarming authors.

This story is about family—the one we're born into and the one we create. Both have tremendous impact on our lives. Family dynamics are a living, growing thing. Sometimes, as in Holly's case, there comes a time when our place in the original has morphed into something unrecognizable. Creating a new family seems an impossible dream. Holly must find her way in the unfamiliar territory between the two.

She figures it out. We all do. Eventually.

Enjoy the read.

T.R.

HEARTWARMING

Wanted: The Perfect Mom

———

T. R. McClure

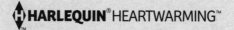
HARLEQUIN® HEARTWARMING™

Recycling programs
for this product may
not exist in your area.

ISBN-13: 978-0-373-36794-8

Wanted: The Perfect Mom

Copyright © 2016 by Tanya R. Schleiden

All rights reserved. Except for use in any review, the reproduction or
utilization of this work in whole or in part in any form by any electronic,
mechanical or other means, now known or hereinafter invented, including
xerography, photocopying and recording, or in any information storage
or retrieval system, is forbidden without the written permission of the
publisher, Harlequin Enterprises Limited, 225 Duncan Mill Road,
Don Mills, Ontario M3B 3K9, Canada.

This is a work of fiction. Names, characters, places and incidents are
either the product of the author's imagination or are used fictitiously,
and any resemblance to actual persons, living or dead, business
establishments, events or locales is entirely coincidental.

This edition published by arrangement with Harlequin Books S.A.

For questions and comments about the quality of this book,
please contact us at CustomerService@Harlequin.com.

® and TM are trademarks of Harlequin Enterprises Limited or its
corporate affiliates. Trademarks indicated with ® are registered in the
United States Patent and Trademark Office, the Canadian Intellectual
Property Office and in other countries.

HARLEQUIN®
www.Harlequin.com

Printed in U.S.A.

T. R. McClure wrote her first story when she was ten years old. A degree in psychology led to a career in human resources. Only after retirement did she pick up her pen and return to fiction. *Wanted: The Perfect Mom* is her first novel with Harlequin.

T.R. lives in central Pennsylvania with her husband of thirty-seven years. They share their country home with one horse, one cat, four beagles and Sunny the yellow lab. T.R. is always up for travel adventures with her grown twin daughters.

Visit the Author Profile page
at Harlequin.com for more titles.

To Grandma McClure, who always had a bag of sugar cookies in the freezer for hungry grandchildren. On lazy summer walks, she shared with me the magic of the touch-me-not flower. Thanks to her for happy childhood memories on the farm.

CHAPTER ONE

ONE SHOT.

Dark, viscous liquid poured into the glass. With the final drops, golden crema swirled.

Pour into a warmed china mug. Add the perfect measure of aromatic vanilla.

And then the pièce de résistance...perfectly steamed whole milk.

Holly Hoffman stood back from the shiny new commercial espresso machine and let loose a deep sigh as the aroma of fresh ground beans surrounded her. She grabbed a damp cocoa-brown bar towel and wiped the steam wand.

The first vanilla latte purchased in The Wildflower Coffee Bar and Used Book Store was a veritable work of art, as it should be. Holly had been working toward this May 1 opening for six months. Six months of visiting coffee bean suppliers in the Strip District in Pittsburgh, training with the espresso machine company and dealing with her loving but definitely opinionated family.

The shop had been open ten minutes and already the line stretched out the door. Who would've thought so many coffee aficionados lived in the little central Pennsylvania community of Bear Meadows?

As Holly frothed a pitcher of nonfat milk, she looked around the comfortable surroundings created with the help of her sister-in-law, Carolyn. Four brown-and-yellow-plaid armchairs surrounded a low table in the corner. A matching couch and coffee table stretched along the wall lined with bookshelves.

Louise, Holly's best friend since kindergarten, was intent on the cash register. She tapped up, down and across like a virtuoso pianist. Mrs. Hershberger stood on the other side of the gleaming white counter, squinting through rimless glasses at the extensive menu over the back bar.

"What's the difference between a latte and a cappuccino?" Mrs. Hershberger asked. The recently retired teacher had already ordered a vanilla latte with whole milk…but she liked to learn new things. The summer before, she'd gone on an excursion to the Antarctic.

Behind her, Wendy Valentine gripped her

briefcase to her suit jacket and drummed well-manicured nails on the leather. Smoothing her black pageboy, the local television star glared at Mrs. Hershberger as if staring would help her sort the coins she'd scattered on the countertop as she paid for her drink. But anyone who'd had Mrs. Hershberger for first grade—pretty much everybody in town under the age of fifty—knew the teacher didn't like to be rushed.

Holly steamed milk in a shiny metal pitcher. The low rumble joined the buzz of conversation in the shop. Wendy would order nonfat milk, no doubt about it, which was why Holly had the milk almost up to temperature.

Behind Wendy was Holly's landlady, Mayor Gold. She eyed the furnishings and lodge-like decor, probably wondering if she was asking enough rent. Carolyn, standing shoulder to shoulder with Holly, was already steaming soy milk. Everyone had heard Mayor Gold's speech on eating lower on the food chain. Behind her, mailbag slung over his shoulder, stood Bill the mailman in his khaki shorts.

"Vanilla latte," Holly shouted, unable to keep the sound of triumph out of her voice.

Mrs. Hershberger, standing with her back to the espresso machine, jumped. "You don't need to shout, girl. I'm not deaf, you know."

"Sorry, Mrs. Hershberger, that's just how we announce your drink's ready." Holly smiled and lowered her voice. "Here's your vanilla latte. You enjoy, now." Apparently her parade-ground voice, courtesy of the military, was a bit too loud for the confines of The Wildflower. She would have to watch it.

Mrs. Hershberger gave her a wink, patted her hand and headed toward the tables along the windows.

Louise grabbed a ceramic mug and wrote *V C N F* on a yellow sticky.

Holly faced the espresso machine, feeling like Marshal Dillon on Main Street in Dodge City during the opening credits of *Gunsmoke*. She knew *V C N F*. They had been practicing all week.

Vanilla cappuccino, nonfat milk.

She glanced at the counter to her left, where Louise arranged cups with the precision of a drill sergeant. At least ten mugs with sticky-note orders in coffee shorthand sat in a row. Their eyes met over the mugs.

Louise's red lips curved in a smile.

Holly knew what she was thinking.

They were officially in business.

JOHN "MAC" McANDREWS sat in his patrol car across the street from Holly Hoffman's new coffeehouse. A line of people stretched out the door and down the boardwalk, which ran from Megan Martin's Hair Today to Sue Hunter's The Cookie Jar. Not even eight o'clock on a Monday morning and a newcomer would think Bear Meadows was a bustling community. He sighed and rubbed his forehead where the pain of a caffeine headache lurked.

Mac debated getting in line. Up at five, he had left the house without making coffee, responding to a reported break-in. The Smith brothers again. Hawkeye had decided to visit the family hunting camp to get an early run at some turkeys but neglected to tell his brother. Skinny Smith, hearing someone walking around outside in the darkness, called the police on his cell phone. By the time Mac arrived, the seventy-year-old twins were already in the woods, the cabin empty.

Through the large windows, he observed Mrs. Hershberger set her cup on a table, then wave cheerily. Too bad she had retired. One of the few people in town not to have had her as a teacher in first grade, Mac had still, through a confluence of events, managed to be a recipient of the woman's high expectations. Where would he be now without her influence? Probably in jail. He waved back.

Mac thought back to his last year of high school. He often sat with Chris Hoffman and the rest of his family as they cheered for Holly during the girls' volleyball games. Mac would watch entranced as Holly made point after point, game after game.

She was a firecracker. Setter and team captain, Holly would prop her hands on flexed knees and fix her gaze on the ball as the opposing team prepared to serve. When the ball went into play, she hustled about the court, energy pouring out of her, dark ponytail flying. Nothing compared to her intense concentration. He remembered being the object of that concentration once. Her intense focus was hard to resist, all the more reason to keep his distance. They had both moved on after high school, he to the army, she to the air force.

His temples were throbbing, and when he glanced across the street, the line out the door of The Wildflower had lengthened. A large, tiger-striped cat peeked around the corner of the beauty shop and scurried under the porch. He should call animal control but he had work to do. The cat would have to wait.

Mac turned his key in the ignition and shifted the SUV into Drive. He would get a coffee at the gas station on the edge of town.

He didn't need Holly Hoffman's fancy coffee. He just needed some caffeine.

A LULL FINALLY came at three o'clock. Carolyn, Louise and Holly collapsed in the cushioned chairs. Crumbs of blueberry scones and bagels littered the surface of the shellacked wood table and the rug. Holly picked up a crumb and inspected it. "Five second rule?" She shot a glance at Carolyn and Louise.

"More like five hours." Carolyn groaned. "You need a mat at the cash register. My feet are killing me." She threw her legs over the arm of the chair and leaned her head back, closing her eyes. Loosening the clip holding her hair, she ran her fingers through curly locks and sighed.

"Well, you're no spring chicken, honey." Carolyn's husband and Holly's oldest brother walked in. In each of his big hands Sonny carried three Wildflower mugs. "Your cups are all over the front porch. How are you keeping track?" He set the cups on the counter with a clang and then sat heavily on the arm of Holly's chair and threw his arm along the back. At six foot two and 250 pounds he sat pretty much wherever he wanted to.

"Any chance of getting a cup of coffee?" He grinned. Three pairs of eyes glared.

"Get your own coffee," Holly said. She leaned back and brushed her bangs from her face. Despite the air-conditioning, a bead of sweat rolled down her cheek.

"You opened a coffee shop. You better get used to serving customers on demand or you'll be out of business and living on the street in no time." He tugged a hank of her hair.

"Stop it." Holly slapped at his hand. "At least the orders will be from paying customers. Besides, we're beat."

Sonny pulled her ear. "Welcome to the real world, little sister. Need I remind you of our deal?"

Holly frowned at her brother. Despite his teasing, he'd always supported her. "You're right. I wouldn't be here if it weren't for you." She sat up and fixed her gaze on Carolyn and Louise. "Any of you. Thank you for your help."

"Don't be ridiculous," Rose Hoffman said. "We're family. Of course we'll help." Holly's mother came out of the back room and dropped a clipboard on the counter with a clatter. "I'll bring you a cup of coffee. Would you like regular or decaf?"

"The strongest she's got, Mom. What's the point in drinking coffee if you can't get a buzz?"

"Mom, sit down," Carolyn said. "You've been working all morning. He's got two legs. He can figure out how to get coffee." Carolyn glared at her husband and whispered, "She's sixty-two years old, Sonny."

Rose's voice drifted over the counter. "I may be sixty-two but I'm not deaf, dear, and I think I can manage a cup of coffee. Haven't you heard? Sixty-two is the new forty-two." She set the large mug down on the table and put her arms around her oldest son's neck, squeezing tightly.

"You need a haircut. Your hair's longer than mine." Rose ran her fingers through her son's unruly black hair—the same shade as her own, though hers was threaded with strands of silver. "Why don't you stop over and I'll give you a cut later?"

Holly smiled at the pained expression on Sonny's face. "Good idea. Why don't you let Mom cut your hair, bro?"

"Mom, stop, you're choking me." Sonny gagged as he pulled away but only succeeded in losing his balance and sliding down on top of Holly.

"Oh, for goodness' sake," she said, "you're smashing me." Holly slid out of the chair and landed on the floor. Pain radiated from her hip. A bruise for sure. Her brother sat comfortably in the chair that had been hers just moments before. She threw a scowl his direction.

"Thanks, sis." He reached for the mug his mother had set on the table and slurped. "Your coffee's good and strong, just how I like it." He shot a sideways glance at his wife. "That's how I like my women, too."

Carolyn aimed a kick but missed as he jerked his leg away. "Don't you have some work to do?"

"It's not strong…" Teeth clenched, Holly pulled herself up from the floor. "It's bold." Limping to the front window, she rubbed the stinging spot on her behind.

Resting his head on the back of the chair, Sonny wrinkled his brow. "I smell—" he sniffed "—gerbils and cedar chips." He shot Holly a look of concern. "Are you sure the pet store got everything when they cleared out of here? I think I just saw something run under the couch."

Holly crossed her arms. "This place was spotless before I moved the furniture in. And you know it."

Laughing, Sonny reached in his pocket as his phone trilled. Further discussion of the previous tenants was forgotten as he launched into a description of materials for a project on the other side of town.

Holly caught Carolyn's eye. "How can you think when he's on the phone? He's so loud."

Carolyn shrugged. "Welcome to my world. Now I know why your family didn't mind that we married right out of high school. They wanted him out of the house so they could hold a conversation without shouting."

Holly chuckled. She had to admit, when her father, whom everybody called Fritz, and older brothers, Sonny, Thomas and Chris, were in a room, the noise level quadrupled. As the youngest, she had to fight for the slightest attention.

If she leaned against the window and looked down the street, she could just see the Victorian house her parents had bought two years before. The tiny window in the attic belonged to Holly.

The sound of boots thumping on wooden planks drew her attention and, pressing her cheek against the window, she chilled at what she saw. With a cowboy swagger, minus the accompanying jingle of spurs, Mac McAndrews strolled in the direction of Holly's shop.

She pressed her forehead against the cool glass and closed her eyes. What was he doing here?

The thumping of the boots came closer.

Mac McAndrews. She hadn't seen him since high school graduation...*his* high school graduation, which just happened to coincide with Chris's graduation. Otherwise Holly wouldn't have been within a mile of the high school.

Jump, Frog, jump. The second half of eighth grade, when every cookie she ate went to her expanding middle. Schedules changed and a tenth-grade boys' class shared the gym with Holly's eighth-grade girls' class. Holly had stayed away from the trampoline after that.

She'd been back in town for six months and she hadn't seen him until this very minute. She didn't care if she never saw him again, if they somehow coexisted without ever crossing paths. So why did he have to show up on opening day?

Holly retreated behind the counter and placed the china mugs her mother had washed on top of the espresso machine to keep them warm.

The bell jingled over the door.

Sonny raised his arm. "Mac. Hey, buddy."

Holly peered around the edge of the espresso machine.

John "Mac" McAndrews, all six foot two of masculine authority, stood in the doorway of her coffee shop.

"Sonny." His voice was deeper than she remembered, more gravelly.

Sonny strode over to Mac and clasped his hand. "Have you come to check out little sister's foray into the business world?" He shot Holly an evil grin. "She's still trying to keep up with her big brother."

Mac's gaze swiveled in the direction of the counter. "Holly."

Still partially hidden by the espresso machine, Holly closed her eyes and took a deep breath. They were kids then. Surely he had changed. Or maybe not.

When Holly opened her eyes she found herself staring at a pair of dark glasses. Mac stood waiting just on the other side of the counter.

He'd been tall and lanky in high school, but he had filled out nicely. Holly's eyes traveled up the black uniform pants to the heavy black belt with a holster carrying a Smith & Wesson .38. A trim waist expanded to broad shoulders. She continued past the collar brass to a chiseled jaw. The unruly light brown hair streaked blond by summer sun was gone, rendered nondescript by a buzz cut. *Figures*.

The old anger stirred deep in her belly, boiling, growing.

When Mac had started calling her names, every boy in the class took up the chant. *Jump, Frog, jump*. But they were all smart enough not to use the nickname when Chris was around.

She wasn't that embarrassed little girl anymore. She gripped the edge of the counter and took a deep breath to calm her nerves. "John? John McAndrews? I didn't know you were back home." So she told a little white lie. The family didn't know she knew. She had been crazy busy the past six months.

"I came back last fall. Personal reasons."

"I'll bet Mac would kill for a shot of your heavy-duty espresso, Holly." Sonny leaned on the counter. "I heard the Smith boys had you up and around pretty early this morning."

Mac nodded at Sonny and then turned back to Holly. "How have you been?" His gaze drifted upward. "You cut your hair."

Holly ran her fingers through her hair and lifted her chin. "A long time ago." Propping her hands on her hips, she stared at the dark glasses. "I'm doing great. How are you?"

Mac pulled off his shades and Holly's stomach plummeted at the sight of the dark blue eyes. His body had changed, his hair was different, but the soft blue eyes were the same.

One corner of his mouth curved up, as if smiles were at a premium. "It's nice to see you again." He reached across the counter.

Holly hesitated, and then stretched out her hand and allowed him to wrap his fingers around hers.

He wanted a shot? She'd give him a shot, all right.

One shot was all she needed to repay him

for making eighth grade miserable, for taking away Chris, her closest brother and confidant. She wasn't a little girl anymore. She could take anything he dished out and feed it right back. After all, she was a veteran of the United States Air Force.

She met the gaze of the boy whose sudden appearance at Bear Meadows High School had changed the course of her teen years.

Jump, Frog, jump.

CHAPTER TWO

"WOULD YOU LIKE a shot, Officer?" With no little effort, Holly pulled free from Mac's tight grip and returned her hand to her hip. She gave him the same chilly smile she'd given the young lieutenant who thought he could ask enlisted staff to bring him coffee.

"Black coffee is fine, if it's no trouble." Mac's gaze drifted to the menu behind her. "I usually get my coffee at Charlie's gas station on the edge of town." He smiled. "Only fifty cents a cup."

Holly narrowed her eyes. The man dared to compare her special blend gourmet coffee to the stuff at Charlie's gas station? Mac hadn't changed at all. "Your first cup is on the house." With effort she kept the smile on her face. "Wouldn't want to break the bank, would we?"

Sonny straightened, spread his hands on the counter and stared at her as if she'd lost her mind, which perhaps she had. "Why don't you just get the man a cup of coffee, Holly?" He grimaced before turning to Mac. "You should know, sis, being a *business owner*, Mac is the chief of police now. You never know when you might need his assistance, now that you *own a business*."

Her back to the counter, Holly's shoulders stiffened as she drained Wildflower Special Blend into a take-out cup. She took a deep breath. "Chief of police? Congratulations. That was quick." She flipped the spout closed and reached for a plastic lid. Pressing the lid onto the cup, she turned and set the coffee on the counter, finally meeting Mac's eyes. "You can't have been on the force long. You must have impressed somebody."

Mac wrapped his fingers around the cup, then met Holly's eyes. "Chief Stone died in January. He had a heart attack while he was out shoveling snow. The choice was me or Moose Williams, and he's just out of the academy."

Once again Holly's stomach dropped. If she kept this up, she would need surgery to reattach the organ to her middle. Had she been so busy researching business requirements last January she had missed the man's death? Chief Stone had been around forever.

"What a shame," she said. "He was a great guy." She smiled at the memory of the antics she and Louise and her brother's friends had dreamed up. "Kept us out of trouble, didn't he?"

Mac pursed his lips and nodded. "He certainly did." He reached for his back pocket. "What do I owe you?"

Holly raised her palms. "Like I said, the coffee's on the house, Mac." She couldn't resist an added jab. "Since my coffee is out of your price range."

"Thank you." Cup in hand, Mac walked across the wooden floor. At the door he turned, lifted his cup to Sonny and with a brief glance at Holly, left. As he slammed the door, the bell rang once and fell to the floor.

Holly gaped as he passed the front windows. After he was out of sight, she eyed the little silver bell in the middle of the floor. The silence brought her back to her spot behind the counter. Four pairs of eyes zeroed in on her.

Sonny slammed a fist on the counter. "What's wrong with you, girl? The man just moved back to town after losing his wife. You were downright rude."

"He insulted my coffee." She lifted her

chin high and returned her brother's glare. "Would you mind hanging up my bell?"

OUT OF SIGHT of the coffee shop, Mac sat in a wooden rocker at the end of the strip mall, leaned his head back and shut his eyes. He hadn't been the nicest to his best friend's little sister when they were kids. Apparently she remembered, as well. Holly, the precious, youngest girl of the big, happy Hoffman family... Well, she'd just happened to be in the way. Always underfoot.

He opened his eyes and took the lid off his cup. Steam wafted upward and he breathed deeply. Smelled a lot better than the unknown substance he'd bought at Charlie's gas station earlier.

Across the street the bank president exited the building. With a wave at Mac, he walked to the adjacent parking lot and got into a late model sedan parked under a cherry tree. Pink petals flew into the air as the dark blue car pulled out of the lot and roared down the street.

Next to the bank, Joe Miller, a bag of mulch slung over his shoulder, left the hardware store, followed by his hugely pregnant wife and a toddler. He tossed the bag into the trunk of a car parked at the curb as his wife settled the toddler into his car seat. Joe helped his wife into the car, trotted around to the driver's side, got in and drove away.

Mac sighed. The Millers were the picture-perfect American family. They probably had a dog at home, too. At one time, he'd had that life.

Three years later and he was back where he'd started and life was all about work. As he stared at the cherry tree across the street, the thought struck him that he would have been married nine years this month, nine years May 15. Where had the time gone? Mac rubbed his hand over his face and sipped his coffee. *So many changes...*

He turned as a brand-new four-wheel drive truck roared into one of the slanted parking spots next to the strip mall and jerked to a stop. A group of teenagers spilled out of the pickup and jumped onto the boardwalk. Chattering excitedly, the two boys and two girls didn't even notice Mac sitting in the chair. They sauntered down the walk and disappeared into the coffee shop.

School was out for the day.

Mac heaved himself out of the chair and crossed the street to his police car. Setting his cup on the roof, he paused, taking in the vacant lot between the hardware store and the old library, now empty. Holly's shop was one of five occupied storefronts—a beauty salon, a computer store, a used clothing store and a bakery. The boardwalk, with scattered benches, rocking chairs and potted plants, invited customers to stroll and shop. Across the street were the bank and the hardware store.

He studied the vacant lot again. Although a trash can stood not fifty feet away, the ground was littered with candy wrappers and cigarette butts. At the squawking of the police radio, he shook his head, grabbed his coffee and settled behind the wheel. He had other fish to fry. The vacant lot was someone else's problem. Just like the cat.

HOLLY WAS SAVED from her brother's wrath, at least temporarily, by the noisy arrival of four teenagers. Two girls entered first and the tallest, a blonde, headed for the couch. She collapsed, propped her flip-flop-clad feet on the coffee table and waved at the boy leaning on the counter. "I want a nonfat mocha."

"Just get me anything with caffeine." The second girl, short and slight but with pretty light brown hair, whispered in the other boy's ear and followed her friend to the couch.

Holly was about to ask the blonde to take her feet off the table when she noticed her mother heading toward the pair.

"You're Edie Black's granddaughter, aren't you?" Rose perched on the edge of the coffee table, causing the girl to drop her feet to the floor. "I haven't seen your grandmother in ages. How is she?"

Holly grinned as she turned her attention to the two boys. After raising four children, her mother was skilled in getting people of all ages to do as she wanted without causing a confrontation.

"What can I get for you boys?" Holly asked.

The first one, tall and lanky, grinned at her. "Two mocha lattes, one nonfat and one—" His green eyes flicked up to the menu board and then back at Holly "—fat."

Holly bit back a smile as she glanced at Carolyn, already pulling milk from the refrigerator underneath the espresso machine. "One skinny mocha latte and one fat mocha latte, Carolyn."

She didn't miss a beat as she poured whole milk into one pitcher and nonfat milk into the other. "Coming right up." Carolyn slipped the first pitcher under the wand and the burble of milk steaming filled the room.

After paying with a polite "Thank you, ma'am," the tall teenager moved to the end of the counter. The second teen stared at the board, his gaze flicking back and forth from the board to the wallet in his hand. "Two black coffees."

"Would you like our special house blend, the Colombian, or the Kenyan?"

The boy continued to stare at the menu board.

"I recommend the Wildflower Blend. If you like you can add some cream and sugar at the condiment table."

The teen nodded and laid a five-dollar bill on the counter. "Thanks."

"Thank you."

Holly poured the coffee into ceramic mugs just as Carolyn handed the lattes to the tall teen. Holly came up behind her sister-in-law. "Do you know them?"

Carolyn crossed her arms and studied the four teens surrounding the coffee table. "The tall one is Tom Johnson's son." She leaned back, her lips inches from Holly's ear. "You know, the bank president."

Of course, Holly thought, that explained the expensive jeans and the confident attitude. Money did that for a person. "What about the other one?"

Carolyn thought a moment and then waved a finger in the air. "Matt McClain's boy."

Holly watched the muscular boy sitting quietly while the Johnson boy and the Black girl talked animatedly. Not as tall as the bank president's son, the McClain boy was dressed in a T-shirt and jeans.

"Matt works at the electronics factory, right?"

"Not anymore. The plant shut down just before Christmas and he got laid off. They have four kids. I think this one's the oldest."

"Huh. Good-looking kid. He's built like a wrestler." Holly grabbed a bar towel and wiped up a spill. She noticed a ceramic bowl by the cash register. Bright yellow letters spelled out *Tip Jar*. A yellow slipper-shaped flower grew between the two words. "Where did this come from?"

Carolyn tilted her head. "I made it in my kiln."

Holly raised her eyebrows and gave her sister-in-law an appraising glance. "Aren't you the creative one?"

Carolyn smoothed the front of the chocolate-brown apron with the Wildflower logo on the front. "I'm an art teacher. I hope I'm creative."

A memory of Carolyn, eight months pregnant with the twins and accepting her college diploma, flashed into Holly's mind. How did she do it? "Well, if we ever get any tips, you three should divide them. Bad enough you're working for free."

"Just for a couple months till you get on your feet. No worries, sis-in-law. But I should go pick up the twins. They had a scout meeting after school and if I leave now, I should get there just in time." She untied her apron and pulled it over her head, dislodging a clip. Curly chestnut hair spilled over her shoulders.

Sonny came around the end of the counter and clasped his wife around the waist. "Oh, I like it when you let your hair down, baby." Fourteen years of marriage and three children had done nothing to cool their obvious affection. High school sweethearts, Sonny had waited for Carolyn to graduate while he'd started a construction business.

Holly pushed the couple toward the seating area. "Staff only behind the counter."

Sonny backed away slowly, his arms still

locked around his wife's waist. "I'm staff. Who do you think built this counter, girlie?"

"I know you did, all great and powerful contractor brother." She turned at the sound of the bell over the door.

A willowy blonde woman entered, looking as if she'd just stepped off the pages of a fashion magazine. With her hair in a French twist, she wore a navy blue pantsuit with a pale blue shell.

Holly returned to the cash register and studied the new arrival. Somehow she knew the woman wasn't a local.

She tried to catch Carolyn's eye as she hurried toward the door but instead caught Sonny's.

He pointed a finger at her as he held the door for his wife. "I haven't forgotten about that other deal, Holly. I'll be back."

Holly stuck her tongue out at her brother but pulled it back just as the blonde approached the counter.

"I'll have a nonfat cappuccino, extra hot, ma'am." The woman's Southern accent was slight but recognizable. Diamond studs twinkled in her ears.

Holly pulled the milk from the refrigerator and poured. Lifting the metal pitcher to the wand, she puzzled over her customer while keeping watch on the thermometer. Probably visiting family. Tom Johnson's sister worked down South somewhere. She frothed the milk and, with her other hand, pulled a shot of espresso. Giving the concoction a quick stir, she set the cup in front of the woman who had placed a few bills on the counter.

"Keep the change, honey." She walked to one of the chairs, her high heels tapping, and she sat, set the cup on the table and pulled a laptop out of a large leather purse.

Holly couldn't take her eyes off the woman. She rested her hands on the open drawer of the cash register. The woman sat with her legs crossed at the ankle so just a portion of red sole showed.

"Well, are you?"

Holly jumped when she discovered her mother at her elbow. "You scared me to death, Mom. I thought you were in the kitchen."

"I was." A crease appeared between Rose's brows. "I asked you a question and you were miles away."

Holly's hands were still resting on the drawer. What was she doing? *Change. Keep the change.* She removed three quarters from the drawer, edged around her mother and dropped the change in the tip jar with a clang.

Her mother pursed her lips, closed the cash drawer and eyed her steadily.

Holly rested her hands on her mother's shoulders. "Sorry, Mom. I was thinking. What were you saying?"

Rose's face relaxed and she wrapped one arm around Holly's waist and pointed to the display case with the other. "We're completely sold out of whoopie pies and no bakes. Did you order more for tomorrow?"

Holly peered into the display case. "I don't believe it," she said. "You'd think people would want something like scones and biscotti. No bakes are so simple. One minute on the stove, plop a spoonful on waxed paper and you're done. I can't cook but even I can make no bakes."

"Buying is easier." Rose took a crumb-covered plate from the case. "We still like our old-fashioned goodies but nobody bakes anymore. People are busy, and making cookies is just too much work." She reached into the open case.

"Mom, I'll do that." Holly put a hand on her mother's back.

Rose waved her off and said, "I'm fine.

Why don't you talk to Sue at the bakery? She might have to hire more help." Withdrawing her head from the case, her mother put a hand on her hip and smiled. "Now, isn't that nice? Your business is providing work to people in town."

"Tell that to Dad," Holly said.

The four teenagers had finished their drinks and were heading for the door. The only other customer was the blonde woman, who appeared content with her cappuccino and laptop.

"Now, Holly…"

"Okay, I'll be quick."

"Take your time." Louise came out of the kitchen and headed for the cups left by the teens. "We're all caught up. We can handle things. How about it, Rose?"

Holly smiled at her best friend. "Have I told you how much I appreciate your help with this venture?"

Cups in hand, Louise rolled her eyes. With a glance at Holly's mother, she lowered her voice. "Think you can handle seeing Mac around? That stuff happened a long time ago."

Louise had been Holly's most ardent defender when the older boys would start their taunts. As small as she was, they just laughed at her attempts to quiet them. Holly shrugged as she picked up the tip jar and jingled the change inside. She didn't care to think about Mac's reappearance in their lives. "He insulted my coffee."

Louise smiled. "Your coffee will win him over, just like everyone else in town."

"Everyone except my father," Holly said. "Chris is the only one who has traveled. He's used to places like this. But the others still think coffee should cost a quarter."

"They're a minority. Stop worrying."

"What if they're right, Weaz? I've invested my life savings in this shop, not to mention the loan from my parents and your free help. If the business goes under, I'll have nothing to show for it. My father will never let me hear the end of it."

"If you wanted to be safe you would've stayed enlisted. But you took a chance. If it doesn't work out, you're young. You'll find something else."

"Let's hope everyone in town doesn't share McAndrews's fifty-cents-a-cup attitude." She peered into the tip jar. "We got tips." Holly dumped the change in her hand and counted out fifteen dollars and fifty-two cents. "Somebody put in their two cents' worth, most likely my brother, who thinks he's funny."

As Louise started to back through the swinging door into the kitchen, she said, "Add the cash to the register."

"No way. You, Mom and Carolyn get the tips. It's the least I can do." Dumping the change in the jar, Holly pushed back her guilt that no one was accepting a paycheck yet. She needed to start making a profit soon. By fall, when everyone returned to their usual duties, she would need an employee or two.

"What else would I be doing?" A resigned smile graced her face before she disappeared into the kitchen.

Holly could hear her loading cups into the dishwasher and her heart went out to her brave friend.

Kneeling by the display case, Rose caught her gaze. "I think working here has been good for Louise. She seems more like her old self. You go on, we're fine."

Holly untied her apron and hung it on the hook next to the kitchen door. Thinking of Louise's tragedy, she realized her own memories of being teased in gym class couldn't compare. "Okay, I'm out of here. I hope you don't get a busload of senior citizens while I'm gone."

Holly left the shop and stood outside, savoring the fresh spring air. For a minute, she allowed herself to visualize The Wildflower as a success. A comfortable spot where locals came to relax and visit. A hangout after Friday night football games at the high school. After all, she had duplicated the school colors in her shop.

The Bear Meadows Cubs were expected to win the state title this year. Her shop could even be a stopover for fans traveling through town on Saturdays on their way to Penn State football games in the fall. Then maybe her father would come around. Not that she ever expected him to say he was wrong.

Holly stretched her arms over her head. Her back cracked loudly. "Ah, that feels better." She shrugged her shoulders, took a few steps to the right and glanced in the window of the beauty salon. Seeing the proprietor with a customer, she stuck her head in the door. "Hi, Megan. Hi, Mrs. Fleck."

Mrs. Fleck brought a hand out from under her drape and waved at Holly. Pieces of her hair had been pulled through a foil cap. "I'm getting highlights. What do you think, Holly?

Maybe I'm too old for this nonsense. I've never dyed my hair."

"You'll look great. You music types are always at the forefront of fashion."

Mrs. Fleck blushed and waved away her compliment. "Before I started teaching, I was in a girl band, believe it or not."

Holly leaned against the doorjamb. "I always figured you for a wild woman, Mrs. Fleck."

Her own long dark hair caught back in a ponytail, Megan wiped some white paste on a lock of hair and flashed a smile. "Hey, I like having you right next door, Holly. Your caffeine helped me through two dye jobs and a three-year-old's first haircut."

"So I heard. These walls are thin." Holly laughed. "Glad to help. See you later." With a wave, she left and entered the computer shop.

Pierre Lefonte stood behind a glass case sorting boxes. "Holly. How are you, mademoiselle? How is your system working? Good, I hope."

Holly leaned on the counter. "So far, so good. Thank you, Pierre. You didn't come over for your free coffee."

Pierre flipped a lock of hair out of sparkling brown eyes and grinned at her. "You were busy, no? Perhaps tomorrow. And I would prefer a double espresso. None of your weak American coffee for me."

"We'll convert you one of these days." Holly straightened and wagged a finger. "I will hold you to it, then. One double espresso. Au revoir."

"Au revoir, mon amie." Pierre went back to sorting as Holly left the shop and continued on the boardwalk.

She peered through the window of the used clothing store. Seeing no sign of the extravagantly dressed Cheri, she continued to the bakery, where the scent of fresh bread lingered in the air. "I love the smell in this place." She leaned on the counter and smiled at the short, heavyset woman standing at the open cash register. "The flowers by the door look nice. Did you put the pot together?"

Periodically licking her thumb as she counted one-dollar bills, Sue peered at Holly over horn-rimmed reading glasses. "Cheri seems to think flowers will draw in more customers. Tell her to put the pot in front of her door. I don't have time to fuss with flowers." She banged a roll of quarters on the edge of the cash drawer. "Did you let yourself into the shop yesterday after I closed?"

Holly straightened. "Of course not. I'd only use the key you gave me in case of emergency." A flicker of unease caused her to look around. "Why do you ask?"

Sue stopped counting and rested her hands on the open drawer. Glancing at the filled racks, she shook her head. "I could have sworn I made more peanut butter cookies yesterday." She resumed counting. "I don't know. Ever since Brad started this midlife crisis nonsense I haven't been able to think straight." She pressed her lips together and her eyes glistened.

"I'm sorry, Sue." Holly's heart went out to her new friend. Everyone in town knew Brad's midlife crisis involved another woman. "Did you tell anyone about the missing things?"

"I called the police station. Now I wish I hadn't. Chief McAndrews will think I've gone off my rocker if I say somebody's been stealing cookies." She tucked a few strands of dyed blond hair behind her ear. "Forget I said anything, Holly. Did you make any sales?"

"Did I make any sales? Do owls hoot? We sold out of whoopie pies and no bakes."

Sue's hands stilled and her head jerked up, blue eyes wide. "I thought you had more than enough. I thought you had too many, in fact, and they would go stale. I thought—"

"You've got to think positive, Sue." Holly couldn't remember the last time she'd seen a smile on the baker's face. She had known Sue first as a volunteer at school functions. Ten years later, no trace of that happy woman remained. "No chance of your baked goods going stale. I'm here to order more."

"Dot McClain asked me if I needed any help," Sue said. "Her husband just got laid off. Working here won't replace her husband's pay but some money's better than nothing."

Holly thought about the boy who'd ordered two black coffees. So times were tight at his house. She glanced at the racks filled with bags of fresh bread and boxes of old-fashioned cookies. "How has business been?"

Sue counted the ones, then returned them to the drawer. "Business is good on the weekends but not so great during the week. I'm thinking of opening just two days a week. I saw in the paper the retirement home is looking for a cleaning lady for second shift."

Holly pressed a hand to her chest. "What about me?"

"I'll still provide you with baked goods."

Eyes narrowed, she peered over her glasses as she pulled out the fives. "What else do I have to do with my time?"

Holly racked her brain for a subject to pull Sue from her dark mood. "Do you see Josh often? He's in the army, right?"

"I haven't seen him since I moved out of the house." She shook her head. "I like keeping busy. Besides, your little coffee shop is saving my bakery…such as it is."

Despite Sue's negative attitude, a warm feeling swept through Holly as she realized that her mom had been right. Her coffee shop was helping create jobs. She just hoped her business continued. Holly glanced up at the cookie jar clock over the counter. "Oh, my goodness, is that the right time?"

Sue answered without looking up. "Yep."

"I've got to run." Holly backed toward the door. "What time can you have the cinnamon buns ready in the morning?"

"How early do you want them?" Lips tight, the baker slammed the money drawer shut.

"Is six forty-five too early?" Watching her friend's face, Holly groped behind her for the door handle.

"Not for a baker." Sue patted the front of her apron, flour dust surrounding her in a cloud. With just the trace of a smile, she waved goodbye. "Thanks again, Holly. I appreciate your business. You're a lifesaver."

With an answering smile and a final wave, Holly reached for the door. She had been gone too long already.

CHAPTER THREE

MAC COULD SEE HOLLY, arm outstretched, backing toward the door. Realizing she was coming through that door with no idea someone stood on the other side, he stepped away just as the door burst open. Everything would have been fine if someone hadn't left a flowerpot sitting in the middle of the walkway. With the heel of his boot catching the edge of the pot, Mac found himself cartwheeling toward the edge of the porch.

He had to give Holly credit for a quick reaction. She grabbed the front of his shirt and reversed his momentum. "A little clumsy this morning, Chief."

The mischievous grin left her face as Mac's backward motion transferred to forward motion and she found herself pressed to the wall of the bakery. Mac's hands landed on either side of her head as he tried to prevent himself from smashing into her.

Her expression a mixture of surprise and

alarm, Holly shoved at his chest. "What the heck, McAndrews?"

Hands still pressed to the wall, Mac stared at Holly. Her green eyes locked on his face, her lips parted. Mac's memory brought up a picture of a fifteen-year-old Holly, holding an orange flower in the palm of her hand, smiling up at him. He took a slow breath. "Are you—"

"Get off me, McAndrews. You're squishing me."

This time Mac's jaw dropped. "*You* grabbed *me*." He backed up a step. "And may I remind you who just came plowing through that door like a runaway horse?"

"Did you just call me a horse?" Holly brushed off his hands and pushed past him. "You haven't changed one bit."

She stalked down the boardwalk toward the coffee shop. When she reached her door, she turned and shot him a laser beam of a look that sent a shiver up his spine. What was her problem?

He escaped into the bakery and shut the door with a sigh of relief. Holly wasn't fifteen anymore. She had grown into a strong, smart woman, just as he always knew she would.

And if she didn't like him very much, well, that didn't come as a surprise.

He glanced at Sue, expecting a smile. Instead, she crossed her arms over her chest and raised an eyebrow. "Well, did you find anything out?"

His eyes lighted on the cookie jar clock, hoping against hope it was quitting time.

It wasn't.

And who was he kidding? No such thing as quitting time for the chief of police.

HOLLY RACED INTO the shop and slammed the door. Striding over to the counter, she leaned on it and took a deep breath. Why, after six months, was that man suddenly underfoot? She closed her eyes.

She had liked him at first, when Chris brought the new kid to the family Christmas party. Then when she saw him in gym class, everything changed. He was nowhere near the nice, polite boy who helped her father set up the Christmas tree that had fallen victim to one of her brothers' all-too-common tussles. He had everybody fooled. Everybody except her.

She slapped a hand over her chest and belatedly looked around the room, hoping no customers had observed the owner's brief foray into madness. No one had. The teens were gone, the blonde was gone and apparently her mother and Louise were gone. Her pounding heart slowed. "Mom?"

A voice wafted from the far corner of the store. "Over here."

Holly went around a wall divider and peeked into an alcove stacked with books and magazines. Her mother lay sprawled on a beanbag chair, studying a business magazine. Holly propped her hands on her hips. "Comfortable, are we?"

Rose laughed as she struggled to rise from the chair, which kept collapsing as she pushed on it. She reached out a hand. "Pull me up, honey."

Holly gripped the outstretched hand and pulled. "What were you doing?"

Rose straightened her apron and returned the magazine to a neat pile on a shelf. "I was straightening up this area and I happened to see an article on bed-and-breakfasts. I had to read it."

"Of course." Holly followed her mother to the counter. "You should head home anyway. Dad's probably waiting for his dinner." She drummed her fingers on the counter as her mother removed her apron. "What's he up to today?"

Her mother folded the apron into a small square of fabric before answering. "When I left this morning he was putting the finishing touches on the backyard gazebo. He's always doing something, you know. He can't seem to sit still." She rested a hand on Holly's shoulder. "I'm sure he'll be down soon, honey. He's proud of you."

"He's so proud of me he refused to offer me the same terms as Sonny and Thomas because he thinks I don't have business sense." Her father would rather do hard labor than visit Holly's coffee shop. He had told her in no uncertain terms that leaving the air force was a mistake, that she should "tough it out."

"Oh, Holly."

She squeezed her mother's hands. "Thank you, Mom, for your help. I wish I had the money to pay you."

Rose laid a hand on her cheek. "Of course, sweetheart." She carried the folded apron into the kitchen. When she came out she had two paperback books in her hand and her purse looped over her shoulder. "You don't owe me anything. Look at all the free books I get to read."

Laughing, Holly propped both elbows on the counter as her mother passed with a wave. "Wonder who the blonde lady was." A stranger in their little town stood out and usually ended up being someone's relative.

Rose paused, her hand on the doorknob. She turned, brow wrinkled in thought. "What did you say, dear?"

"The blonde who was drinking a cappuccino, working on a laptop. She doesn't look like a local."

Rose leaned against the open door and put a finger to her lips. "You know, if I didn't know better, I would've guessed she was Mac McAndrews's wife. But of course she can't be. His wife passed away three years ago."

"How do you know what she looked like?" Holly's antenna emerged. Mac was married to a woman who looked like the blonde cappuccino-drinker?

"Chris showed me a picture once. She was on the cover of an equestrian magazine." Rose turned in the doorway, hands clasping her books to her middle. "Beautiful woman. Bye, dear."

With a backward wave she was gone, leaving Holly to wonder: after he'd been married to a woman like that, who could possibly meet Mac McAndrews's standards? She pitied the next woman to fall under his spell.

Holly looked up as the bell over the door jingled. "Mom, did you forget—"

Instead of her mother, Holly was greeted with the sight of Sonny, the expression on his ruddy face intense. He flipped her sign to Closed and locked the door. "Mom's halfway home."

Holly held up a hand like a stop sign, her eyes closed as she anticipated her brother's wrath. "Whatever you're going to say—"

"I'm not saying anything. Carolyn said you might need help cleaning up." He walked behind the counter and stared at the dual coffeemaker. "Is it okay if I turn this off and empty the pots?"

Holly stared at her brother, momentarily taken aback at the offer of help. *Go figure. I can't even understand my own brothers half the time. Men.* "Sure, just dump the coffee in the sink and rinse with water." She tapped her fingers restlessly on the counter. "Thanks."

Sonny grabbed a container and easily lifted the heavy pot to the drain board. "No problem."

"Mom already covered the pastries so I guess I'll—" she looked around the room at the crumb-littered tables and chairs moved about "—wipe everything down and put things back where they belong."

An hour later, the counters sparkled, the floor was mopped, and Sonny and Holly stood on the front porch. The sun was poised on the tops of the distant mountains, as if protesting its coming demise.

"Thanks, bro." Holly wrapped an arm around her brother's waist and squeezed. She started down the steps.

"Hold on. I'll give you a ride. My truck's right here." He pointed to his dust-covered white pickup with toolboxes and a ladder rack in the bed.

"Okay." Holly opened the door of the big truck only to find a bag of power tools on the passenger seat.

"Let me do some rearranging." Sonny grabbed the bag and stuck it behind his seat. "How's that?"

"Fine. Now all I need is a step stool to get into this thing." Holly reached for the hand-grip and hoisted herself onto the seat.

Sonny slammed his door with a screech and backed out of the parking spot. "The girl I knew jumped onto the back of a sixteen-hand horse with no problem." He glanced at her, his eyes squinting in the glare from the setting sun.

Holly nodded and waved as they passed Mrs. Hershberger, planting pansies by the front stoop of her small ranch house. "A lot can change in ten years."

Sonny didn't answer as he pulled into the long driveway of the Victorian house her parents had converted into a bed-and-breakfast. When they'd first purchased the fixer-upper, Holly thought the old house was a dead ringer for the Amityville Horror house. She'd had her doubts about the wisdom of turning it into a B and B, but unlike her father, who had repeatedly advised her against leaving the military, Holly kept her comments to herself.

Her parents and Sonny had been able to see something else and after a summer of renovations, the bed-and-breakfast was now one of the most popular stays in the area. It was only May and they were booked solid for every weekend Penn State was playing at home. A sign on the manicured front lawn said Flowers Bed and Breakfast. He cut the engine and the two sat in silence. "You were a little prickly with Mac earlier. How come?"

Holly picked at a chunk of chocolate syrup stuck to her jeans. She wasn't sure herself why the sight of Mac McAndrews stirred up such conflicting emotions. "It's a long story." Not wanting to see the look on her brother's face, she continued to work at the stain. Sonny had been in the military the year Mac started coming around. He had no idea the turmoil the newcomer had caused and she wasn't about to tell him.

"And you didn't know Chief Stone died? You were home at Christmas. He died the beginning of January."

"I was either running to Pittsburgh researching supplies or working at the store. I didn't know which end was up. I hardly ever saw Mom, and I for sure wasn't reading the obituaries." Holly glanced into the neighbor's yard, where their obviously pregnant black Lab entertained herself with a stick. "I didn't know Daisy was having puppies. I thought Fran just wanted one litter."

"Don't change the subject. What about Mac? Why were you so rude? When you're in business, Holly, you have to be polite to everyone, even if you feel like tossing them out the door."

"Quit treating me like I'm an imbecile. You think you're the only one who can run a business?" Holly shifted on the hard vinyl seat. When Sonny didn't respond, she continued. "Besides, like I said, I've had a lot on my mind. When I heard the pet store closed and saw the vacant storefront at Thanksgiving, I made up my mind to leave the military. Everything happened so fast."

Sonny pulled two pencils, a small tablet, assorted business cards and his phone out of his pocket and tossed them in the center console. "You sure did make a lot of changes in a short period of time." He caught her eye. "But you still haven't explained why you were so hard on Mac this morning. You haven't seen the guy since high school and if something happened back then..." Sonny peered at her in the gathering darkness and his voice took on a serious note when he asked, "Did something happen back then?"

Holly forced a laugh. "Nothing bad happened. We just didn't get along."

"That's kid stuff, then. But whatever had you so fired up this morning, you need to let go. Mac's had some rough times since he left home." Sonny punched her in the shoulder. "Any regrets about the coffee shop?"

"Ouch." Holly rubbed her shoulder. Her brother didn't know his own strength. "So far, I have no regrets whatsoever." She sighed.

"But if I don't pay Dad back by the end of the year I'll never hear the end of it, not to mention losing all my savings. Then I'm sure I'll have plenty of regrets."

"I don't know why Dad is pressing you for such a quick turnaround. Thomas and I both had three years to show a profit." Sonny pushed open his door and stepped out.

"No kidding."

"Maybe you should serve soup and sandwiches for lunch."

"I don't cook. Remember?" Sonny's habit of making business suggestions was okay but sometimes she just wished people would mind their own business. *Soup and sandwiches? I barely have the espresso recipes memorized.* She slid down from the seat, slammed the door and said, "Maybe. Someday."

Leaning on the open door, he gave her an appraising look. "Hey, you got your first day in. Congratulations. Let's see if Dad left anything from dinner."

Holly followed her brother to the side door. "I knew you had an ulterior motive. Didn't you already eat?"

"Scout night means slim pickings at my house. I'm starved."

Holly slapped him on the shoulder as they entered her mother's kitchen and were greeted with the lingering smell of pot roast. "You're always starved." As annoying as Sonny could be, Holly had to admit she'd missed teasing and being teased by her brother. That was one thing that hadn't changed since she'd been gone.

CHAPTER FOUR

FRIDAY MORNING, MAC decided to patrol the outskirts of town. An out-of-towner's hunting camp had been broken into. The only damage was a shattered window and the disappearance of some canned goods, but he still wanted to check it out. Passing Holly's shop, he noticed a line out the door. Coffee would have to wait.

A short while later, he found himself crossing the suspension bridge over Little Bear Creek. Halfway across he stopped just in time to see a sleek brown trout jump in the fast-moving stream. On the bank, the green of late spring had rapidly covered the dead brush of winter. He continued on and turned left onto a macadam road that paralleled the stream. Coming to a freshly plowed field, he slowed and studied the white house at the end of a long lane.

Gravel crunched beneath the tires of Mac's patrol car as he eased down the driveway of the Smith farm. The twins were the third generation to live on the two-hundred-acre farm. They no longer worked the land but instead rented out the fields to younger farmers who needed more land but couldn't afford it. He stopped the car at the foot of a long flight of steps leading up to the front porch. A garden surrounded by a wire fence sat off to the right. A long row of green onion tops peeked through dark, rich, freshly turned soil.

The homestead, where the twins and their sister had been born and raised, had to be at least a hundred years old. A fresh coat of white paint glistened on the two-story structure. The new metal roof sported a satellite dish.

Mac leaned back in his seat and stroked his chin, remembering the last time he'd been to the farm. Shortly after his return to Pennsylvania, he and Chief Stone had visited some of the neighbors in the area. Then, the house had been badly in need of a paint job.

He should've shaved this morning. Instead, he'd invested those extra five minutes in chasing much-needed sleep. Sleep that still refused to come. He'd lain in bed thinking about Anne, about Riley and what his wife would think of their current living arrangements.

"Are you gettin' outta the car or are you just gonna sit there and gawk?"

Lanky as his nickname implied, Skinny Smith stood not five feet away, dressed in clean but faded bib overalls and a red plaid flannel shirt. A large black dog lounged at his feet, his graying muzzle forming a perfect circle as he gave a low woof. Mac jumped out of the vehicle and thrust out his hand. "Sorry, Mr. Smith, I haven't been here for a while. I was admiring the work you've done."

Skinny gripped Mac's hand. After a brief squeeze, he wrapped his fingers around the overall straps, tilted his bald head and squinted at Mac. "You're the one who came out with Chief Stone that day. You just got back from livin' down South for a while, ain't that right?"

"Yes, sir." Mac's stomach flipped as he remembered the reason for his sudden return home. They had put it gently. *We have to let you go.* But he knew he had lost his edge. Coming home was an attempt to get his life back in order. Now his former in-laws had been pressing him to take his little girl for the summer.

Between the guilt and the never-ending decisions he sometimes questioned his sanity. His forehead was throbbing and he realized he had again skipped coffee. The double bourbon the night before hadn't helped, either. He caught Skinny shooting him a puzzled look.

Skinny started toward the steep porch steps and waved a hand at Mac. "Come on in. Hawkeye's makin' French press coffee. You look like you need some."

Mac's jaw dropped. French press? Apparently the townspeople weren't the only ones to have become citizens of the world in his absence.

Watching the dog make his way up the steep steps, he followed and caught the screen door just before it slammed shut behind Skinny. The farmer continued through a long, dark hall lined on one side with stacks of boxes.

"We have company, brother. Grab another cup."

When Mac entered the kitchen Skinny was opening a pink bakery box. His brother, identical in every way, except his shirt was blue plaid, poured coffee out of a glass container. He pushed a china cup and saucer across the table and motioned for Mac to sit.

"Mother always said things taste better

if they look nice. We still use the china set she got for her wedding. Kind of silly, I suppose, for two old bachelors. How about it, brother?" Skinny chuckled, a deep rumbling in his chest.

Hawkeye nodded as he continued to pour. "Yep."

His forefinger threaded through the small, circular handle, Mac lifted the cup and toasted the two men. "Gentlemen, this is a welcome— unexpected, but welcome—surprise." He held the cup under his nose and inhaled the rich, heavy scent before sipping the hot brew. "Ah, perfect."

"Fair trade organic." Hawkeye finished pouring and set the French press on a pad in the center of the Formica table. "We farmers have to stick together."

A black cat clock, its eyes darting back and forth, ticked noisily above the sink as the three men enjoyed the coffee. Between the two farmers, the hound thumped his tail in anticipation as Hawkeye reached for a scone from the box. Breaking off a corner, he presented the morsel to the dog, who mouthed the treat daintily from the old man's hand. "Good boy." He petted the dog.

Skinny bit off a piece of muffin. He winked

at Mac as he chewed. "Buddy's the best dog we ever had. He's a black-and-tan coonhound. Got him from up toward Erie. He chases raccoons mostly, but he'll go after a squirrel or a rabbit. When we're ready to go, he's right beside us." He gave another bite to the dog. "Not so much anymore, though. He's getting old, like us."

"So he is," his brother added, crumbs littering the table in front of him.

Mac eyed the bakery box, and when Hawkeye pushed it closer, he helped himself to a chocolate cookie sandwich with white cream oozing out of the middle. "I haven't had a chocolate gob in years." The first bite melted in his mouth, followed by the rich coffee. He swallowed. "Where do you guys find this stuff?"

"Over town. Those things are called whoopie pies in these parts." Skinny seemed surprised at his question. "We stop at The Cookie Jar and then, since the Hoffman girl opened up her place, we bought our special beans from her. Saves us from driving all the way to State College, what with the price of gas such as it is."

Mac looked around the kitchen at the modern appliances and wondered how two old farmers afforded updating the homestead, much less buying fair trade organic coffee. He emptied his cup and stood. "Thank you, fellas, I needed that." He brushed a crumb from his uniform jacket.

Skinny leaned back in his chair. "You sure did. You looked a mite peaked when you got out of your car. You got some color in your face now. You should stop at the coffee shop mornings, get yourself goin'." He chuckled. "And the Hoffman girl's not too bad to look at, either. How about it, brother?" He nudged Hawkeye.

"Yep." His brother smiled into his coffee cup.

"If I was forty years younger…" The talkative brother led the way back to the front porch.

Mac grinned. He agreed with the two men. The Hoffman girl, his best friend's little sister, had grown from a gawky teenager into an attractive woman. And he owed that woman an apology. He just hoped she accepted the long overdue request for forgiveness.

How could he have been attracted to two such different women? Holly and Anne were night and day. Refined and delicate, Anne's pale complexion and fine blond hair had placed her on the cover of many local equestrian magazines. She was the cool balm he'd needed after the heat of the desert, when his overseas duty finally came to an end. Holly, while she had never graced the cover of a magazine, was known for her phenomenal times in barrel racing. She was all darkness, energy and heat.

Following his host, he passed the living room at the front of the house and caught a glimpse of a flat screen television. Ahead of him Skinny held the screen door, his bright eyes watchful.

"Thanks again, Skinny." With his stomach full of whoopie pie and his head mercifully pain free, Mac shook the man's hand and clumped down the steps.

"Anytime, Chief McAndrews, anytime." Skinny stood on the porch, his fingers wrapped around his overall straps. In his rearview mirror, Mac saw him still watching as he drove slowly up the drive.

APPROACHING HER STORE from the alley, Holly paused as she neared the back door. A tiny corpse lay right in the middle of the threshold. Sonny's teasing about gerbils echoed in her head. But peering closely, she discovered the victim was a mouse, courtesy of the brown cat she had glimpsed earlier, she guessed. Scooping the creature onto a scrap of cardboard she deposited the lifeless body in the Dumpster, then unlocked the back door of the coffee shop. She would have to return the favor.

She set a milk-filled bowl outside the back door just as the brown tabby appeared. He sniffed the bowl and walked away.

"Not a milk drinker, eh?" Holly shook her head. "Maybe you'll change your mind."

She walked through the gleaming kitchen and into the quiet storefront, where she unlocked the front door and flipped her sign to Open. Although she didn't expect any business at seven o'clock on a Saturday morning. After a hectic opening day on Monday, and being reasonably busy the rest of the week, Holly figured most people would sleep late today. She expected Louise at nine. In the meantime she would get the coffee going, make some iced tea and uncover the pastries in the display case.

She scurried around, humming a tune from her high school days, and readied the shop for business. She glanced in the tip jar. *Empty.* Even Sonny's two cents were gone.

"Goodness, I forgot to open the cash register." She popped into the kitchen, where the green money bag protruded from her purse. Returning to the cash register, she punched in the code and the drawer opened. Withdrawing a wad of cash, she proceeded to fill the drawer.

The bell jingled over the door. "You should keep your door locked when you're handling that much cash. No telling who might wander in."

Holly jerked her head up to see Mac McAndrews's tanned face and blue eyes. "You're telling me."

His answer was a faint smile. Instead of his uniform, Mac was dressed in faded jeans, a black T-shirt and sneakers. Keeping his mouth pressed in the familiar straight line, he stood in the open door, as if uncertain of her welcome.

"Come in." Holly sorted the coins and thought about Sonny's words the night he had helped her to close. They were just kids back then. "Would you like a cup of coffee? On the house."

The bell jingled as the door eased shut. She glanced up quickly, unsure if he was inside the store or had decided her brand of welcome wasn't worth the aggravation. Mac approached the counter and leaned one elbow on the surface. "Will you have one with me?"

Holly flipped down the money holders and slammed the drawer shut. Turning her back, she retrieved two mugs from the tray. "I suppose I have a minute for a cup of coffee." Her heart beat a little faster, presumably at the thought of caffeine. *Why else?*

Rounding the end of the counter, she carried the cups to the low table with the four cushioned chairs. Perching on the edge of one, she tilted her head toward the door. "Cream and sugar on the condiment counter."

Mac settled onto the opposite chair and reached for the cup. "Black is fine." He leaned back in the chair, cup in hand, and surveyed the shop. "Besides, good coffee doesn't need to be doctored."

Holly smiled at the unexpected compliment. "Do you drink your gas station coffee black?" Eyes lowered, she took a sip of her rich, special blend coffee, her first of the morning.

Mac laughed loudly. "Lots of milk and sugar to disguise the taste." Silence stretched between them.

Searching for a topic of conversation, Holly drummed her fingers on the arm of the chair. "Would you believe I own a coffee shop and half the time I forget to drink a cup?" She scooted back and rested the cup on the arm of the chair.

Mac propped his ankle on his knee. "I'm not surprised. Wednesday I drove by and your line was so long I ended up getting coffee at the gas station. Again."

Holly made a face. "So you said. I figured you aren't particular when it comes to coffee."

"I was in a hurry." Mac patted his knee and threw her a look. "I can appreciate quality."

Wondering if he was still talking about coffee, Holly shivered. "I'm afraid business might slow once people get over the novelty of having a coffee shop in town." While he read her menu board she studied him. He looked less severe than he did in uniform, more like the boy she knew in high school. Even his close-cropped light brown hair showed hints of the blond streaks she remembered. Suddenly he turned his head and caught her watching him.

"I was thinking about our encounter the other day."

Heat crept up Holly's neck and onto her

cheeks as she remembered her rudeness. "I apologize, I—"

"I'm the one who should apologize." Cup clasped in both hands, Mac leaned forward. "I wasn't very nice to you when we were kids."

She sipped her coffee, let the hot liquid lie on her tongue before swallowing. Over the rim of her mug, her eyes met his. "Really? I don't remember."

Did he know she was lying? Of course she remembered. The incident in eighth grade was one of those memories that stays with you forever. It's bad enough to think everybody is laughing at you. In Holly's case, she had *known* they were. Thanks to Mac and his timely, loud and accurate insult.

Mac kept her gaze as if trying to read her. Balancing the coffee cup on his knee, he took a deep breath. "We moved here two weeks before school started, two weeks before I entered the tenth grade. Chris was one of my first new friends. But then Chris was friends with everybody." Mac stared into his coffee cup. "The first time he invited me to your place was for a family Christmas party."

Holly had a clear picture in her mind of fifteen-year-old Mac coming in the door with

Chris. "That was the year Thomas and Sonny got into a fight and knocked over the Christmas tree."

"Never a dull moment at your house," Mac said, grinning. "We moved here because my mom wanted to be near her sister."

"Who was your aunt?"

"I doubt you knew her. She worked for the federal government. Three months after we moved here she got a promotion in Maryland. She left and we were back to not knowing anyone in town."

"Until you met Chris."

A ghost of a smile lit his face, then quickly disappeared. "I spent a lot of time at your place. Mom started nursing school. She was hardly ever home."

"I can't believe you preferred the chaos at—"

"There's no excuse for the way I treated you, the things I did." Mac shook his head. "I'm sorry."

His shoulders were set and he couldn't meet her eyes. Apparently his apology hadn't come easy. Although moving to a new school didn't entirely explain why he'd singled her out for his verbal attacks. Maybe she would never know. But then, he had always been a mystery. "No worries, Mac. You were going through a hard time."

He shrugged. "Being with your family helped."

"I'm glad."

"I remember you riding your bay horse all the time, running barrels in the field. What was his name?" Mac pulled a paperback from the shelf and studied the front cover.

"Twister." She had avoided Mac through the end of eighth grade and all through ninth, but in tenth grade, things changed. She shot up five inches, thinned out. Part of the reason she'd begun competing in barrel racing was Mac's constant presence at Chris's side. Even then, she'd sometimes see Mac leaning on a fence post, watching. When she caught him watching her, he'd walk away. Riding Twister had built her confidence. The trampoline incident faded. "I haven't ridden in years."

"Too bad. You were so good." He returned the book to the shelf.

Holly drummed her fingers, wondering how the old gelding was doing. "He was a good horse."

"So what possessed you to open a coffee shop in Bear Meadows?"

She leaned forward. "Walking around European cities all those years, visiting cafés, I always thought, *I can bring this home*, this feeling of carefree abandon. I want this, but at home." She looked around the shop. Her shop. The comfortable chairs, the used books, the menu on the back wall. Her gaze returned to Mac, who was watching her, his blue eyes alert. "Why did you come home?"

With a quick look at the clock, Mac stood and carried his empty cup to the counter. "I've got to run."

Grabbing her own cup, Holly followed more slowly. She might have bought his answer if she hadn't seen the brief flicker in his eyes. Fear? Embarrassment? She couldn't tell. She studied his broad shoulders. Whatever emotion she'd seen, it reminded her that there were two sides to Mac McAndrews. One very sweet…and one very ugly.

CHAPTER FIVE

THE BELL OVER the door jingled.

Mac's large frame blocked her view of the door, yet Holly breathed a sigh of relief at the interruption. Until the person walked up to the counter.

"Are you busy?" Her father glanced from her to Mac and back again.

Holly wiped sweaty palms on the front of her apron. "Hi, Dad. What brings you here?"

Ignoring her question, Fritz faced Mac. The two men were about the same height. Chin thrust out with a hint of challenge, the older man eyed the younger.

Mac stretched out his hand. "Good morning, Mr. Hoffman. Nice to see you."

Fritz's hand came up slowly, then tightened around Mac's. "Chief."

The refrigerator pump kicked on. A batch of ice crashed down into the ice machine. Holly looked from one man to the other. A current sizzled between them.

Holly wasn't sure what was going on, but she couldn't let it continue. "Do you want a cup of coffee to go, Mac?"

Her father finally released Mac's hand and, without a word, wandered over to the alcove.

Mac watched him go, and then lowered his voice. "No more coffee today, thanks, but before I go I wanted to mention something. Remember the day you ran into me coming out of The Cookie Jar?"

Holly's eyes narrowed. "Are you referring to the day you tripped over the flowerpot?"

Mac threw a half grin her direction before continuing. "Anyway, the day we ran into each other, Sue asked me to come in because she thought she was missing some things."

Her arms erupted in goose bumps. Sue couldn't afford to miss anything. If Sue went out of business, Holly might, too. "Missing what things?"

Mac glanced toward the pastry case. "Well, she thought somebody was taking baked goods."

Holly followed his gaze. She suddenly realized nobody was taking inventory of her own baked goods. She could be missing food and not even know. "Is she missing anything else?"

"She left her change at the store a couple nights last week and took the cash upstairs. When she came down in the morning the drawer was cleaned out. I looked around but saw no sign of a break-in." He slid his empty cup across the counter. "Have you noticed anything missing?"

Holly motioned toward the cup. "My mug inventory is dwindling. But they're not stolen, they're kind of borrowed long-term. When the store is crowded, people take their coffee out on the porch and then keep right on going."

"I'm sure they'll all plead innocent. You should charge them for the cup when they buy coffee." Mac chuckled. "Maybe Sue put the change somewhere and then forgot. She hasn't been herself since, well, you know." He glanced toward the alcove where her father could be seen looking out the window. "I wanted to give you a heads-up about the possible thefts."

She set her cup next to his. Mac caught her arm. Her skin tingled where his warm hand wrapped around her forearm. Looking up, she saw concern in his eyes.

"Just be careful, okay? I got notice this morning someone robbed the bank's branch office in Shadow Falls. That's fifty miles from here but still, who knows what's going on? The culprit might be one person, or a gang."

Holly licked her dry lips and said, "Don't worry, Chief, I can take care of myself." She pulled out of his grasp and rounded the counter. Pausing across from him, she reached for the empty cups.

Mac wrapped his fingers around her wrists. "I'm sure you can, but all the same, I'll have Moose Williams stop by every once in a while, just to see what's going on."

The touch of his warm hand sent tingles up her arm and managed to scramble the neurons in her brain. She met his gaze and, like one of her many tumbles from the back of her horse, found herself unable to breathe.

Between Mac's touch and her father's unexpected appearance, Holly's brain seemed to be misfiring. Her father chose that moment to return. His gaze lighted on Mac's hands circling her wrists. Holly pulled her hands back across the counter. "Would you look at that? I forgot to uncover the pastries."

"Thanks for the coffee, Holly. I'll see you around."

Mac disappeared through the door with a

jingle. Silence returned to the coffee shop. Fritz strolled around the tables, walked past the shelves of books and then returned to the counter. "I can't believe what people pay for a cup of coffee these days."

"What was that about?" Holly tossed the wrappings in the garbage.

"What do you mean?"

"That thing with Mac. You looked like two big dogs, sizing each other up."

Her father chuckled. "Ask him." He studied the menu board. "I remember when coffee was a quarter."

Holly took a deep breath. Looking down at the embroidered flower on her apron, she let out the air slowly. "Well, you're in luck. You get the family discount."

Her father shot her a look. "Discount? I figured I'd get coffee for free." He finally smiled.

Holly reached for a ceramic mug and then hesitated. "Did you want your coffee to go?" Although her father's first visit to her new coffee shop was a momentous occasion, she couldn't imagine he actually planned to hold a conversation.

"Well, I do have a project back at the house." He glanced at the pastries in the case.

"Oh, what the heck. I can spare a couple minutes. Go ahead. I'll take one of those bear claws, too. Sue is quite the baker. She's probably half the reason you get people in here, just for her baked goods."

Holly shook her head. She didn't bother to remind her father that if people wanted the baked goods they could walk down the boardwalk, buy a box and take them home. The Wildflower provided a destination with ambience. She set the cup on the counter, then retrieved a bear claw from the case.

Carrying her father's order to the low table, she set down the coffee and pastry and sat, waiting for her father to finish his inspection.

Her dad settled into the chair opposite and picked up his cup. He sipped, set down the cup and forked off a bite of the breakfast treat.

"Do you like the coffee?" Holly had spent days finding the perfect blend for her signature coffee, with just the right amount of acidity and strength. She was proud of her creation.

Fritz held the cup under his nose and sniffed. "Strong."

Holly pursed her lips, biting back the immediate retort that came to mind in favor of a more diplomatic answer. "The proper terminology is *bold*."

"If you say so." Fritz stared out the front window. "I still can't believe people in this town will pay the kind of money you're asking, especially when so many are out of work."

"Thanks for the encouragement, Dad."

He finally looked directly at her. "Encouragement has nothing to do with it. You either make it or you don't. You have to understand business."

"You don't have a business degree. Sonny and Thomas don't have degrees." Leaning forward, Holly propped her elbows on her knees and clenched her hands into fists. It took everything she had not to blow up at the man. "Are you afraid I won't pay you back at the end of the year?"

Fritz set down the cup with a clatter. "I have to stop at the hardware store." He wrapped the half-eaten pastry in a napkin and shoved the package into his shirt pocket. "Thanks for the coffee."

And ten minutes after he showed up at her shop for the first time, Holly's father disappeared out the door.

Holly dropped her head in her hands. What

happened to the father she knew and when had he become so darn difficult?

BEFORE LONG, MAC was stopping at The Wildflower every morning for a cup of Holly's special blend. The caffeine helped him function and he was supporting a local business. Right?

He didn't know if his simple apology would be enough, but her animosity had lessened. So he arrived promptly at seven, got a mug of coffee and chatted with whoever was working. Sometimes her mother, sometimes Louise and sometimes Carolyn stood behind the counter while Holly busied herself in the kitchen or storeroom. On Saturday mornings, Holly would sit with him and share a coffee and the local news. Then he would grab a coffee to go and continue about his day.

The Friday before Memorial Day weekend, Mac paid for his coffee and ran into Chris Hoffman on his way out the door.

Chris slapped his shoulder. "Hey, man, long time no see." Tall, thin, with stylishly cut jet-black hair, the thirty-year-old turned as many heads now as he did in high school.

"Look at you," Mac said, "you're the poster boy pilot." He gripped Chris's outstretched hand. "Where have you been, Chris? Or should I say, where haven't you been?"

"Flying right seat with the big boys. I just got back from LA." Chris laughed as he shut the door and looked around the shop. "I'm on a ten-day break and I thought I'd check out baby sister's business venture." He turned at the sound of the kitchen door banging open. "There she is—the family entrepreneur."

Holly paused when she caught sight of Mac and Chris. Just a few days ago she would have been irritated at the sight, remembering how often Mac had inserted himself between her and her closest brother. But since Mac's disclosure, she'd started to let go of that old hurt.

"Hey, bro, welcome home." She shot a look at Mac. "Good morning, Chief McAndrews."

Mac smiled and said, "Good morning, Ms. Hoffman." He tore his gaze from Holly's bright green eyes and slapped Chris on the back. "Let's get together while you're home." He reached for the door.

Chris's face lit up. "Why don't you join the family Monday afternoon at the farm? Thomas is burning burgers."

"Sounds good, Chris. I look forward to catching up."

"And bring your mom and your little girl."

The words were a bucket of ice water on his thoughts of spending time with Holly away from the shop. "Mom is on a bus trip and my, um, Riley is still in North Carolina with her grandparents."

"Another time, then." Chris grinned.

Without a backward glance, Mac left the coffee shop and paused on the porch, taking a deep breath of the cool morning air. The tempting aroma of fresh-baked bread reached him and he glanced down the boardwalk toward The Cookie Jar. There had been no more instances of disappearing change or baked goods. Maybe Sue had been confused, after all.

Across the street, Tom Johnson waved as he got out of his car and walked toward the bank. "Beautiful day, Chief," he said.

Mac nodded and held up his cup in a wordless salute. Tom disappeared into the bank, locking the door behind him. No banker's hours for Tom, Mac mused as he clattered down the steps to his police car. He didn't regret coming back here. Bear Meadows was made up of good people, salt of the earth. But he had no social life. Any high school friends had either moved on or were busy with families, as he had once been. He pushed thoughts of his daughter out of his mind. Her grandparents would entertain his daughter over the holiday better than he ever could. He liked talking to Holly, but she scared him. She always had. Mac backed out of the parking space.

He took a swig of coffee and headed toward Shadow Falls for a visit with their police chief. The bank branch had been robbed again the previous day, only this time the culprits, a man and a woman, were caught on a surveillance camera. Seemed like the perfect distraction.

"WHEN DID YOU get in?" Holly wiped the counter, where a dried glob of chocolate syrup resisted her efforts. Mac's daughter didn't live with him. Interesting. He must know as much about childcare as she did.

"Late last night. We're staying in the Daffodil room."

Holly paused. "I never took Valerie for the B-and-B type. For a woman you met over a glass of pinot noir at the San Francisco Airport, I'm surprised you convinced her. How does she like sleeping in a room where everything is yellow?"

Chris settled onto the stool at the end of the counter. "The Jacuzzi Dad installed makes up for the over-the-top cheerfulness. And she wanted the baby to be around her grandparents. Harley just started to walk last week." He leaned on the counter. "You don't mind my asking Mac to come over, do you? You two weren't exactly friendly back in the day."

Holly frowned as the last trace of chocolate disappeared into her cloth. Chris had been home with chicken pox the day Mac had turned Holly into a laughingstock in gym class. He had never mentioned the incident and she doubted any of his friends dared to tell him about it. "He made some comments I wasn't happy about."

Chris shrugged. "We were kids. Boys pick on girls. That's our raison d'être."

Holly sighed, feigning nonchalance. "In response to your question, no, I don't mind. The more, the merrier."

"Good," he said. "Is your business doing well?"

"Her business is doing as well as can be expected. She's only been open a month." Carrying a plate of cookies, Rose came out from the kitchen and kissed her son on the cheek. "Was your room to your liking?"

"Great, Mom," Chris said.

"Good." Rose patted him on the shoulder. "Your sister works too hard. She hasn't done anything fun since she left the military."

"Well, that was fun. Leaving the military, that is." Holly shared a smile with her brother.

"You know what I mean. Movies, shopping, going out to dinner." Her mother opened the pastry case and added cookies to the plates inside.

"How do you know?" Holly paused in her cleaning and eyed her mother. "I have lots of fun."

Emptying the plate of cookies, her mother straightened and closed the pastry case. "I know you're either here or in the attic."

"You make me sound like an eccentric aunt." Chris looked pointedly at the top of her head. Lifting one hand, Holly discovered Carolyn's hair clip attached to her short hair. Belatedly she remembered finding the clip in the kitchen and sticking it in her hair while she unloaded the dishwasher. She sighed and changed the subject. "Let me guess. You want a—" she stared up at the ceiling as she analyzed her brother's espresso preference "—skinny amaretto latte, *affogato* style."

Chris pursed his lips and said, "Sounds good." Their mother filled the containers on the condiment counter. "You know, Mom has a point. All work and no play… What happened to the woman who took spur-of-the-moment vacations in Mexico?"

Holly groaned as she took a mug off the top of the espresso machine. She pulled a container of milk from the fridge. "I've had enough trips to last a lifetime."

"Don't you miss the traveling?"

"Sometimes." Holly peered around the machine, eyes flitting from her mother to the temperature gauge on the steaming milk. She moved the wand so the burbling grew louder and she raised her voice. "What would Valerie like, Chris? I'll make her a drink."

"She's a simple woman, Holly. Just make her a double shot skinny vanilla latte. And don't think I didn't notice—you're trying to get rid of me already. But I think I'll enjoy the ambience of your little coffee shop before I head back. Valerie won't be up for another hour, at least."

"Who's watching the baby?"

"Dad."

Grinning at Chris calling his stylish wife a "simple woman," Holly set the cup on the counter. "One skinny amaretto latte, *affogato* style." At the same time she wondered how her brother had persuaded her busy father to babysit.

Chris reached for the cup, eyebrows raised. "Nice, sis." He sipped the frothy drink. "Good job. Thank you."

Holly flashed her brother a smile and breathed a sigh of relief. Chris had traveled as much as she. His approval was a good sign.

Chris wrapped his fingers around the brown mug and took another sip. "So, Mom, what do you suggest we do to get Holly out of her rut?"

"Oh, for goodness' sake…" Holly muttered, reaching for the peach tea bags.

"It would be nice if you had a date with some young man but that doesn't seem to be happening." Rose sprayed the front of the display case with glass cleaner. Ripping off some paper towels, she attacked the glass.

"Whatever happened to Nick?" Chris asked.

Pouring milk into the pitcher, Holly glanced at her brother. "I told—"

"He was such a nice man," her mother continued as if Holly hadn't spoken. "Polite and so handsome in his uniform." She turned back to the display case and spritzed the other side.

Chris strolled toward the bookshelves, his voice rising as he walked away. "I don't think he tripped Holly's trigger, Mom."

"Hel-lo-o. I'm standing right here." Holly lifted the milk to the steamer wand and soon the burbling filled the room. Nick. He had looked good in his dress blues. Great build, dark brown hair, brown eyes, flashing white teeth. He could have posed for a recruitment poster. They both could have, which was the root of the problem. Nick wanted a military wife. Too bad she didn't realize the truth until she had invested four years of her life. *Men and their motives.*

"Maybe she can go shopping with Valerie while you're home," her mom said. "All she wears are air force T-shirts."

"All I need are air force T-shirts." The burbling ceased as she pulled the milk pitcher from the wand.

"My point exactly."

Annoyed at the ongoing discussion of her personal life, Holly ripped open the box and tea bags flew across the counter and landed in the sink. Throwing the destroyed box in the trash, she shot her mother a look.

"Mother, stop. I don't need fun. I don't need dates. I don't need clothes. I need to stay in business so Dad can't walk in here and say 'I told you so.'"

Her mother stood openmouthed in front of the pastry case, paper towels in one hand and spray bottle in the other. Her brother leaned on the end of the counter, staring into his coffee mug.

"Methinks she doth protest too much," Rose said and disappeared into the kitchen.

Gathering up the scattered tea bags, Holly added six to a pitcher of hot water and set the timer, irritation prickling between her shoulder blades. Maybe she shouldn't have returned home. All this familiarity was getting on her nerves.

Between her confusing reaction to having Mac's hands around her wrists, her father's lack of enthusiasm and her mother's insistence that she have fun, Holly had had about all she could take.

She reached for the nonfat milk for Valerie's skinny latte. The sooner Chris went on his way, the better. Then her mother wouldn't have anyone with whom to discuss Holly's private life.

Holly pumped sugar-free vanilla into the

cup, pulled two shots of espresso and added the milk, steamed extra hot to survive the short trip home. "One double shot skinny sugar-free vanilla latte, extra hot, brother." She set the cup in the center of the counter and smiled.

"Okay, I'm leaving." Chris waved a paperback novel in the air. "Borrowing."

"Bye." Holly threw the bar towel on the counter and shook her head.

Chris opened the door, then turned and threw her a sympathetic grin. "Hang in there, sis. You'll be fine."

CHAPTER SIX

ON MEMORIAL DAY, Holly closed the shop at noon. *It's fine*, she told herself, *everyone's having picnics or spending the weekend at the lake.*

Heading for her own family picnic, she shoved some stale cookies into a tin, hurried home and changed into a pair of old shorts and an air force T-shirt. Then she loaded her mother's cooler packed with salads into the trunk of her tiny sports car.

"Ready, Mom?" Holly stood at the kitchen door of the bed-and-breakfast. One thing about her mother: she didn't hold grudges. Their earlier disagreement was forgotten as they gathered supplies for the afternoon picnic at the farm.

Rose glanced around the kitchen and held up one finger. "Let me grab a book, in case I get a minute to myself."

Holly went out to the wide back porch and sank onto the swing. Bright green tufts of lettuce grew in her mother's kitchen garden, along with a few shoots of just emerging onions. Brilliant pink peonies, blossoming in full glory, lined the paved walk leading to the gazebo in the far corner of the yard. Holly breathed in their heady scent.

Book under her arm, Rose pulled the kitchen door shut and wiggled the knob to make sure it was locked. A bag of potato chips dangled from her fingers.

"More chips?" Holly rose from the swing.

"I had an extra bag. Those boys eat like vultures."

"The backyard looks nice, Mom." Holly opened her car door and sank into the driver's seat. Her mother placed the chips on the floor and then, holding tightly to the handgrip, lowered herself onto the passenger seat.

"Thanks, honey. The gazebo your father built adds a nice touch. He's working on a covered bridge for the little stream out back. That man works too hard."

Holly eased down the long driveway and looked both ways before turning left and heading toward the farm.

The only place to park was the lawn. Holly gingerly pulled her low-slung car onto a patch of grass next to her parents' SUV. She popped the trunk, grabbed the cooler and followed her mother to the back of the house.

When she rounded the lilac bushes, Holly skidded to a stop. The patch of concrete that had served as a back porch all the years of her childhood was gone, replaced by decorative slate stretching the length of the old farmhouse. At the far end Thomas grilled hamburgers in a new outdoor kitchen area. The only thing Holly recognized was the hand pump and square cement basin. She rested the cooler on the edge of the trough.

Bestowing kisses on one of Sonny's twins as she passed, Rose continued to the screen door. Holly prepared to heft the heavy cooler when a voice stopped her in her tracks.

"Looks different, doesn't it?"

She turned and stared into Mac McAndrews's warm blue eyes. The farm hadn't been his home, but he was around often enough to understand the memories that had disappeared along with the destruction of the old porch. "I'm shocked." She looked around to see if anyone heard.

Mac took the cooler from her and walked to where her mother waited with the door open. "Hi, Mrs. H."

Rose patted Mac on the shoulder as he

passed her and disappeared into the kitchen. "Thanks, Mac, honey."

Holly sank onto the concrete edge of the trough, her gaze on the lights and slow-moving fans hanging from the new porch ceiling. Her brother had created a Southern plantation feel with his remodeling. Gone were the rafters with the peeling paint, where her swing had hung. On a rainy day she would swing bare toes in and out of the falling rain. She reminded herself the farm was Thomas's now—Thomas and Beth and their two little boys and soon another little boy or girl.

She followed the scent of barbecuing meat to the grill. "Hey, what's happening?"

"I wasn't sure you were coming." Thomas rubbed a patch of dark whiskers at his chin.

"Why wouldn't I?"

"You haven't been out here since Christmas." Wiping his fingers on the front of his Kiss the Cook apron, Thomas gave her a sidelong glance as he flipped a burger. He slammed the lid as steam rose in a cloud.

"I've been busy with the coffee shop." She pretended to be absorbed in watching one of the twins playing with a gray cat. "You've made a lot of changes."

Easing the lid open, Thomas added hot

dogs to the spaces between the hamburgers. "Does it bother you?"

"Of course not. Why would it?" Holly gave her brother what she hoped was an encouraging smile. She'd thought she was coming home after she put in her papers. Instead when she came back at Christmas her trophies and ribbons had already been boxed up and moved to the attic. She'd known Thomas would take over the farm someday. She just hadn't expected the transition to be so soon.

"By the way, I made elderberry wine last fall. If you want any there's an open jug in the wine cellar." After loading the cooked burgers and wieners onto a plate, Thomas disappeared into the kitchen. "Catch ya later, sis."

"You have a wine cellar?" Holly crossed her arms and studied the young girl with curly hair the same chestnut shade as Carolyn's. "Let's see. You're Rachel."

Trailing a piece of yarn in front of the transfixed cat, Holly's niece giggled and shook her head.

Seeing her nieces and nephews once or twice a year, Holly wasn't surprised the girl was shy. She tried for a giggle. "How about Rosa Lou? That's it, right?"

The girl's pale eyebrows shot up. "Aunt Holly, I'm Rosalyn. Don't you remember?"

"Just kidding." Holly worked the pump handle and washed her hands under the sudden stream with a bar of soap left on the edge. She elbowed her niece as she dried her hands on her shorts. "Of course I know who you are. You're my favorite niece, and you'll be turning double digits next month."

Leaving the girl entertaining the cat, Holly entered the kitchen to find everybody talking. She stood in the doorway and took in the chaotic scene.

"I didn't expect to see you today. I thought you'd be at the coffee shop." Fritz Hoffman appeared from the hallway to her left and squinted. "Did you have much business this morning?"

That made two family members who hadn't thought she was coming. Holly straightened as she addressed her father. "I closed at noon."

He pressed his lips together, as if trying to hold in his retort. Naturally, he failed. "Are you sure that was wise? You've got to make hay while the sun shines, you know."

"Everybody's having picnics—" She inclined her head toward the crowd in the kitchen "—like us, Dad. No one wants to hang out in a coffee shop today."

Running a hand through his thick white hair, Fritz nodded. "I suppose you're right." He eyed the women clustered around the counter. "Too many cooks in here. I think I'll disappear until the food is on the table."

A smile lit his face as he pushed through the door. "I see my A-student granddaughter."

Holly clenched her teeth. Of the four children, she was the only one to be the lucky recipient of her father's opinion on her life choices. Sonny, Thomas, Chris…all three had questionable moments in their pasts. Had her father said anything? No.

Holly surveyed the scene. "Disappearing is the best advice you've had yet, Dad." She eased past the open refrigerator, where her mother withdrew bowls of potato and macaroni salad, passed through the living room and exited by the front door. She wasn't surprised to see the front porch had been redone as well, with a pair of comfortable chaise lounges flanking the door and three pots of geraniums anchoring the wide stairs leading to the lawn.

In the front yard, picnic tables were already covered with bright tablecloths. Holly stopped for a moment to take in the familiar view of the far-off mountains.

She counted the number of children sitting at the kids' table. The twins, their seven-year-old brother, Freddy, Thomas's two boys—five-year-old Jeremy and three-year-old Justin—made five, which left room for Holly, the designated adult. She had spent time in a war zone. She should be able to handle the kids' table. No sooner had Holly filled a cup with iced tea from a large thermos and claimed her spot, than the family converged on the tables.

Thomas came around a corner of the house holding a platter of hamburgers and hot dogs. "Come and get it." His voice, conditioned over the years to rise above the sound of machinery, could have carried to the next farm.

Valerie placed Harley's high chair at the end of the children's table and sat at the end of the adjacent table. Though her straight, light brown hair was clasped at her neck, she still managed, as usual, to look elegant in a long pale blue skirt and white top. "Holly, would you get Harley a hot dog?"

"I've got her, Val. Enjoy your lunch." Holly slapped a hot dog in a bun and set the sandwich on the tray. The baby pounced on the food immediately.

"Oh, heavens, no, Holly." Valerie snatched the hot dog and Harley wailed in protest. "She might choke." Discarding the bun and dropping the wiener onto her plate, she cut off a slice, then cut the circle into four small pieces. She set the meat in front of her daughter, who ceased her wailing as she fisted a piece to her mouth.

"Sorry. I didn't know." She had learned a lot in the military, but she didn't remember any training on how to feed hot dogs to babies. She glanced around the small table of chattering nieces and nephews and wondered if she was endangering any other children.

Valerie patted her back, then sat down to resume eating. "She's fine, Holly. You wouldn't know. You haven't been around children."

Beth patted her protruding belly. "Good thing you don't have to worry about providing grandchildren. Your brothers took care of that."

"She's commanded troops. I'll bet she could figure out kids. If she wanted to." Plate in one hand and cup in the other, Mac winked at Holly as he passed Beth.

Holly caught her father's eye on her, but a second later he turned away.

She forced a laugh. "Men can be babies at times." Holly had considered having children when she and Nick were engaged, but she wasn't even thirty yet. Her family's assumption they knew what was in her future annoyed her, but then a lot of things had been annoying her since her return home.

Lunch continued with the only incident being a spilled glass of lemonade. After helping to clear the tables, Holly escaped, but not before grabbing a handful of carrots from the vegetable tray. She walked up the lane toward the pond.

Holly patted her stomach, full of her favorite foods—grilled hamburgers, her mother's potato salad and Carolyn's double chocolate brownies. The excited mealtime chatter, with everybody talking at once, had been a bonus. In her travels with the military, she had missed many of the family get-togethers, watching nieces and nephews grow, keeping up with life's changes...

She rounded the barn to say hello to her horse. Standing under an apple tree in the middle of the field with the others, the gelding pricked his ears at her appearance. With a snort, he trotted over and nudged her with his nose.

She reached up under his long forelock and gave him a scratch. "Hey, Twister, buddy. I've missed you." Ever since Mac had asked her about Twister at the coffee shop, she'd been thinking about how much she'd loved to ride. Of all her siblings, Holly was the only one who had continued riding through high school.

The other horses came closer. Holly reached in her pocket and withdrew four carrots. Ridden by her siblings in their youth, the horses lived at the farm in a kind of semiretirement. Holly wondered if any of the grandchildren had caught the riding bug. Noting the round bellies on the horses, she didn't think so.

"Who's this?" Holly started as another soft muzzle appeared along the fence. "Just in time, stranger." She broke the last carrot in half. "You almost missed out." She placed a carrot piece in each palm and fed one to the miniature, Streak, and one to the newcomer, a young, cream-colored gelding with a dark mane and tail. "Aren't you handsome? You must be one of the boarders."

The previous summer Thomas had built

a six-stall horse barn and had talked about boarding horses in the two free stalls. Holly scratched a spot between the pony's blue eyes and, after giving each horse a complimentary scratch, continued up the lane. The horses trailed along until they gave up on the carrots and wandered farther into the field.

A few minutes later, she saw Mac and Chris skipping stones into the pond. "Hey, you two. Catching up?"

"I was just telling Mac we haven't talked in a long time." Chris skipped a stone across the water. "Not since I flew out of Raleigh."

Holly tossed a pebble into the pond and studied the expanding ripples. "Are you walking to the ridge?"

"Sure. I haven't been up there in ages." He picked up a flat rock and leaned sideways, skipping the stone across the pond.

Holly sat at the top of the bank leading down to the pond and leaned back on her arms. "I'll bet you can't get five skips."

Chris shot her a look. "You talkin' to me or Mac?"

"Both. As I recall, neither of you were very good at this." Her comment brought roars of laughter from both men as they picked through the stones littering the bank, searching for the perfect rock.

"Prepare to be amazed, little sis." Chris drew back his arm.

"Uncle Chris." One of the twins stood a few yards down the lane.

Chris climbed the bank. "What do you need, honey?"

"Aunt Valerie wants you."

Chris looked over his shoulder at Mac and Holly and made a face. "I have been summoned."

Holly stood. "We'll walk down with you."

"No, you two go ahead. I'll take a rain check."

A bead of sweat rolled down Holly's forehead and she wiped it away with her hand. "Do you feel like a walk, Mac?"

"Absolutely. I don't often get homemade food so I'm afraid I ate too much. I'm more of a fast-food kind of guy."

Holly smiled. "I can relate. Although my food is even faster. Protein bars." She climbed the slight rise to the lane and turned toward the woods.

Mac walked alongside her. "This is the first we've met outside of your shop. Weird, huh?"

Holly nodded, sticking her hands in the back pockets of her shorts. "Dad thinks I should've stayed in. He thinks opening the shop was a risk, but—" she turned and looked at Mac straight on "—I was so tired of taking orders. Do you know what I mean?"

Mac chuckled. "You don't need to explain to me, Holly. I got out after four."

"I have to admit, though—and if you ever tell my father, your free coffees are history—it's a bit daunting to be totally responsible for my own success or failure. At least in the military multiple people are responsible for a task."

"Hey. I pay for my coffee. At least my take-out coffee. I'm sure Fritz just wants what's best for you." He pointed to a squirrel peeking from the side of a maple tree. "I haven't been up here in years. Do you remember when we used to—"

"—sled down this hill?" The memory sparked a laugh in Holly and she took in the gradual slope with the occasional surprise rock. "We were crazy."

Leaving the trees behind, Holly stepped into the hay field at the top of the ridge. The recently cut grass rose in a gentle incline.

Mac followed close behind as Holly walked to the summit and studied the view before them.

The hay field continued for a short distance before again becoming forest, a carpet of green composed of white pine, red oak and silver and sugar maples. Far below the sun sparkled on the waters of Little Bear Creek, winding its way through the floor of the valley.

Mac came up beside her. The touch of his shoulder against hers sent an electric shock through her body.

"Holly."

Holly focused on the mountains in the distance, covered in haze, and ignored the burn where his arm touched hers. "Hot today," she said. "I can't imagine sledding in weather like this, can you? I wonder if the kids—"

"Holly." The gruffness in Mac's voice brought her up short, but she refused to meet his eyes.

"Mac, I can't—"

Mac reached out and pulled her closer. "The girl I knew didn't have 'can't' in her vocabulary." He stroked her cheek with one finger. "Do you remember that day everybody was making hay and I found you along the lane?"

An odd mixture of dread and anticipation coursed through her body, igniting a curious sizzling in her veins. The moment seemed suspended in time—the buzzing bees, intense sunlight and the heavy scent of fresh-cut hay. And just like that, she was fifteen again, kneeling by the side of the lane when Mac had driven up and stopped next to her. Up until then she had kept her distance from Chris's best friend, but this day everyone was at the farm working together to get the last cutting of hay before rain set in. He had gotten out of the truck.

Leaves crinkled underfoot and the smell of damp vegetation surrounded them.

"Do you know what these are?" Holly had looked into Mac's smiling blue eyes as she cradled the delicate orange flower in her palm.

"Jewelweed?"

"My grandma called them touch-me-nots. She showed me this little trick. Look, this is cool."

Holly had bent over the waist-high plants and motioned for Mac to come closer. Placing thumb and forefinger around a plump, delicate green seedpod, she had grabbed his hand. "Easy, just a little pinch."

At their touch, the seedpod had burst open, scattering tiny ivory seeds on the ground, its insides curling into translucent bits of green matter. "See, didn't that tickle your fingers?"

Laughing, Holly had turned to catch Mac's expression but instead found him staring at her, his lips curved, the muscle in his jaw twitching. "Mac?"

The tingle from the exploding seedpod had traveled up her arm and into her chest as she straightened and Mac placed his hands gently on her shoulders. He brushed back a dark tendril from her face. "You're so cute, Holly."

Holly had pulled her gaze from his and stared at the hay field on the other side of the small stream.

Mac had put a finger under her chin and gently pulled her around to face him again.

Blood had pounded in Holly's ears, blocking out the sound of the farm equipment in the fields and the voices on the back porch. Her first kiss? With Mac? No way, no—

Mac's lips had landed on hers like a butterfly on a finger. He had pulled back, his warm butterscotch-scented breath on her lips, until he tilted his head and returned—for more.

Holly had leaned forward, increasing the pressure, and touched his arms tentatively.

Her fingers gripped his biceps beneath his shirtsleeves.

No boy had ever tried to kiss Holly Hoffman. Half of them were scared of her and the other half she had trounced in grade school. If they weren't afraid of Holly, they were afraid of her older brothers. So when Mac McAndrews actually kissed her within shouting distance of her entire family, and despite the incident in eighth grade, Holly had been pleasantly surprised.

Holly's eyes had remained closed as Mac had pulled away, and the scent of fresh hay and dry leaves filled her senses. Although the air had been cool and crisp, the sun warmed her skin.

"Holly?"

She opened her eyes. That wasn't the sun warming her skin—Mac's hand was on her arm. Like an observer, she waited as Mac leaned toward her, pulling her into an embrace. His lips brushed hers.

The sizzling in her veins burst into flame and she wrapped her arms around Mac's neck, drawing him closer as their kiss deepened, and she tasted the faint tang of elderberry wine on his lips. No more butterscotch, and she suddenly realized history was repeating itself, only now instead of being an innocent fifteen-year-old, she was a mature woman with responsibilities.

Holly pulled back. Mac looked as surprised as she was.

"Well." Mac's arms dropped to his sides and he backed up a step.

"Well." Still immersed in the moment, Holly stared at the man in front of her. For a second, she thought she saw a flicker of guilt pass across his face. "It's been a while."

Mac grinned, his eyes squinting in the glare of the sun. "Ya think?"

"We should get back." Holly started down the incline toward the woods. So far the day had not been one of her best.

But now? She cast a glance at Mac striding beside her. She should never have allowed the memory of their first kiss to intrude into the present and definitely never should have allowed this kiss. Her business demanded long hours, leaving little time for fun. Even with Mac.

CHAPTER SEVEN

TUESDAY MORNING HOLLY was inundated with customers, most of whom weren't happy about returning to work after the long weekend. Despite their crankiness, Holly was relieved. She'd been worried that with the onset of summer, her business, and thus her revenues, would decline. Standing behind the espresso machine turning out drinks, Holly saw Mac at the counter. He gave her a wink before slipping out the door with a large coffee.

The rest of the week—the last week of school—continued to be busy and Holly had little time to think about Mac. Twice Moose Williams had filled the doorway as he scrutinized the customers in her store before buying a large coffee to go. Louise thought he was cute, which Holly found interesting. Louise hadn't found anyone cute in a long time. The fact that she noticed the hulking, monosyllabic, barely-out-of-school police officer gave Holly some concern. Moose and Louise had nothing in common.

Friday afternoon the same group of teenagers entered the store and ordered frozen coffee drinks, all with an extra shot of espresso. Tempted to tell them they didn't need so much caffeine, Holly was silenced with a warning look from Louise.

They carried their drinks to the alcove, where the girls occupied the window seat and the boys sat cross-legged on the large beanbag chairs. They leafed through magazines and the few comic books on the shelves.

"Well, at least they're reading instead of on the internet." Rose tilted her head toward the alcove, where only the two girls were visible. "I'm taking a break, dear."

Just as she settled into a chair with a cup of coffee and a new paperback, Valerie and Chris showed up and joined her. Harley played with blocks on the rug, and Holly wiped off the tables.

"I like your place, Holly." Valerie perched on the edge of the chair, her hand protectively on Harley's head as she hung on to the low table.

"Thanks," Holly said. "Carolyn did a lot of the decorating. Not my strong suit."

Chris caught the toddler as she started across the floor.

"Why don't you buy matching shirts for your staff? A cohesive look would set things off."

Holly glanced at the blue sleeves of her air force T-shirt sticking out from the brown apron, then at Valerie's ivory linen pants and silk shirt. "I haven't given it much thought."

"The baristas in the city do. It would give you an air of professionalism."

"I suppose. I am kind of tired of the uniform thing, though."

Valerie nodded. "I suppose."

"We're not exactly the big city, Val. We're just simple folk." Chris rolled his eyes as he picked up his daughter. Holly was about to call him on his attitude when an older woman with short blond hair with frosted tips came in and approached the counter. Holding tightly to her hand was a little girl clutching a quilt. Louise had disappeared into the kitchen.

"Duty calls." Holly trotted behind the counter. "What would you like?" The woman looked familiar, but as with so many of her customers, Holly couldn't place her. Ten years had passed since she'd spent any amount of time in town, and she had given up trying to match names with faces. If they knew her, they would say something.

"I'll just have a cup of coffee. What can I get for my granddaughter? Do you have anything without caffeine?" The woman studied the menu board.

The girl pulled on her grandmother's hand. "Can I have a latte?" A plastic hobbyhorse band held her fine blond hair in a high ponytail.

Holly laughed at her request. "You're a little young for espresso, kid."

The girl peered over the counter, frowning at Holly's response.

Oh, boy, I've got to read up on communicating with the under-six crowd. "How about a fruit smoothie?"

When the girl spoke, Holly saw that she was missing her two front teeth. "Can I have strawberry banana?"

Before answering, Holly glanced at the older woman, who nodded. "Coming right up."

"Erma, is that you?" Rose waved. "Come over here and have a seat."

Holly returned the woman's change and handed her a mug of coffee. "Go ahead. I'll bring the smoothie over."

Grabbing the blender, Holly watched the woman and her mother greet each other. Still the woman's last name failed to come to mind. She shrugged and reached for the smoothie mix.

Then the girl began pulling paperbacks off the bookshelf and stacking them on the floor. "Mom."

Her mother continued to talk.

"Mom." She must have used the parade-ground voice because all three froze and stared at her. She motioned toward the child. "Can you ask her not to put the books on the floor?"

"Riley Anne, what on earth are you doing?" The grandmother knelt on the floor and re-placed the books on the shelves. "You sit on the couch, young lady. You know better."

Holly carried the smoothie over to Riley, who was sitting with her knees to her chest, thumb in her mouth. "Hey, here's your strawberry-banana smoothie." Holly set a napkin on the coffee table before putting the drink down. The child didn't respond.

Holly returned to the work area and rinsed out the blender. Well, it wasn't as if she'd lost a customer. Riley wouldn't be drink-ing coffee for at least ten years. She set the blender upside down to drain and went into the kitchen to empty the dishwasher. By the time she returned, her mother's acquaintance had set the empty cups on the counter and was at the door.

Erma motioned to the little girl. "Riley, let's go. Thank the lady for the smoothie."

With a backward glance at Holly, Riley ran to the door, then addressed Rose. "Bye. Thanks for the smoothie." She shot past her grandmother and disappeared onto the porch.

Holly leaned on the counter by the cash register, watching the two walk past the front windows toward the bakery. "I don't think she's used to discipline."

Rose leaned on the counter across from her. "It's understandable, I suppose."

Holly frowned and asked, "Is Erma a friend from school?"

Rose wrinkled her brow. "You haven't been gone that long. You must remember Erma. We worked together at the hospital."

"She does look familiar."

Awareness lightening her eyes, Rose nodded. "That's right. When you knew Erma, she weighed a good sixty pounds more. After she retired last year, she joined the gym. Working as a psych unit nurse had to be stressful and then she lost her husband at such a young age. Eating was probably her outlet. But she seems happier now, and she looks great, doesn't she?"

"Attractive woman." Holly tugged her mother's sleeve. "So who is she?"

Rose laughed. "She's Mac's mother, Erma McAndrews."

A lump formed in the pit of her stomach. Knowing the answer before she asked the question, Holly asked anyway. "Then who's the kid who pulled all the books off the shelves?"

Rose gave her a smile. "Mac's daughter. She's a little overactive, but she's been cooped up in a car for five hours."

When Holly was seventeen, she had run barrels on her horse, Twister, at the county fair. She'd kicked the gelding to go faster after the second barrel and the pair had raced for the third—except something happened as they came around. Her knee might have bumped the container, or Twister's hoof... They never figured it out, but as the gelding rounded the final barrel, Holly's feet had come completely out of the stirrups. She'd flown into the air and landed on her back in the soft dirt of the arena. The churned-up soil had saved her from broken bones, but the air whooshed out of her lungs, and she remembered lying there staring up at a summer blue sky wondering if she would ever breathe again.

That's exactly how she felt now. Find time for fun? With Mac? Who was she kidding?

Holly's heart sank into her toes. "I thought she lived with her grandparents in North Carolina."

"Not anymore." Rose smiled.

MAC PARKED THE patrol SUV in front of the bank. With school nearly over, high school and college graduations days away and the sudden onset of nice weather, the little town had been bustling. Moose had been called out for several fender benders and Mac had received word of stolen copper from a utility station just outside Harrisburg.

Despite the fact that Mac was only getting a few hours' sleep each night, the busy week had oddly energized him. He knew he had Holly to thank. Monday was the best day he'd had since he'd come home. Maybe returning to Bear Meadows wasn't such a bad idea, after all.

Wanting to touch base with each of the

other business owners, Mac had decided to save Holly for last. After he made sure she wasn't missing anything, he had a question for her.

He crossed the street and opened the door to Hair Today at the end of the little strip mall.

"Hey, Mac, looking for a haircut?" Megan threw him a smile as she worked on a pretty young woman in the chair.

"Any shorter and I'd be bald." Mac ran a hand over his closely shorn hair and grinned. "I was wondering if you've noticed anything missing the last few weeks."

"Funny you should ask." She lifted a strand of honey-colored hair and cut off an inch. "I'm missing three cans of mousse. I'm sure because I'm a stickler for inventory."

Being at the end of the tiny strip mall, Megan had plenty of windows, but they were all still intact. If someone had entered Megan's salon after closing, they had found another way. "Just so you know, we're keeping a close eye on this end of town. Let me know if you notice anything suspicious." When Megan nodded, Mac left the store.

Standing outside the hair salon, he stared across the street. Did Tom Johnson have a security plan in place? In all likelihood, he did. But being new to the force, Mac wanted to check.

Making a mental note to meet with Tom before the end of the following week, Mac headed toward the coffee shop.

"Daddy."

Mac flew backward as a tiny dynamo wrapped herself around his legs. He looked into his mother's smiling face. "What are you doing here? I didn't expect you until late tonight."

Erma settled into a nearby rocker. "We left yesterday, came halfway and did some sightseeing."

"I went swimming in a pool in the motel, Daddy."

Mac lifted her into his arms. Although tall for a five-year-old, she weighed hardly more than a feather. "Hi, Riley." He pulled at the tiny arms wrapped around his neck. Her fist clutched one corner of a blanket as the rest trailed to the floor. "You're choking me, kid." The tightness around his neck matched the tightness in his chest. He'd figured he had hours to prepare himself for this moment. He'd been wrong.

Riley let go of Mac's neck, leaned her head

against his chest and stuck her thumb in her mouth.

Mac looked at his mother in surprise. "When did she start that?"

Erma rocked gently and sighed. "Liz said she started right after the holidays."

Mac frowned. He had moved back to Bear Meadows in early fall and spent a week with his former in-laws at Christmas. He didn't need a psychology degree to figure out why his daughter had started sucking her thumb again. "Right after I left."

Erma patted Mac on the shoulder. "Well, now that she's with her dad I'm sure she'll stop soon enough. Come on, Riley. Let's get you home and settled into your bedroom. Okay?"

Mac peeled his daughter from his chest and set her on the porch. "Go with Grandma, Riley."

"Can we have pizza for dinner tonight, Daddy?" Leaning against his legs, his daughter peered up at him with light blue eyes identical to her mother's.

He fought a stab of pain in his chest. "Ask Grandma."

She turned her gaze to the older woman. "Can we, Grandma?"

"Of course. What time will you be home, John?"

He rubbed at his breastbone. "I don't know. You two go ahead and eat without me."

The rocker paused and his mother raised an eyebrow. "We should celebrate Riley's first night home. Surely you can make it to dinner."

Mac took a deep breath. "Sure, Mom. I'll get the pizza and be home by six."

Erma smiled and reached out a hand to her granddaughter. "Wonderful. Let's go, honey."

In just six months the girl had seemed to grow a foot. He hadn't realized how quickly children changed. One minute a toddler and then the next, a little girl, a tiny replica of her mother. He sighed and headed for the coffee shop.

CHAPTER EIGHT

HOLLY MADE AN iced latte and settled onto the stool at the end of the counter. She needed something to help her process the revelation that Mac's daughter was no longer hundreds of miles away but right here in town. Maybe a shot of caffeine would do the trick.

A child. Mac's child. *Is she old enough to eat a hot dog in a bun?* Valerie and Chris, Rose and the just-arrived Carolyn clustered around the chairs discussing the latest news.

"The new librarian started last week. Have you been to the new building, Mom?" Carolyn confined her curly hair with a massive clip.

Settling onto the arm of the chair where Chris sat reading a magazine, Rose shook her head. "My travels have been between the house and the coffee shop, plus Holly's books are keeping me entertained. Is she nice?"

"Seems to be. I took Freddy to story hour. She decorated the children's area with cat posters and stuffed animals and then read Dr. Seuss's *The Cat in the Hat*. The kids loved it."

"Is she married?"

"Single. I think she's a couple years younger than I am."

Holly leaned back and sighed. They all seemed so content, so comfortable with their lives and the paths they traveled. She, on the other hand, wondered if she had missed an exit somewhere. Or perhaps, to make the analogy more appropriate, if she had taken an exit when she should have stayed on the highway.

Sure, she knew Mac was a widower. She knew he was a father. A father from a distance. Until now. The news left a decidedly bitter taste in her mouth, as if she had swallowed day-old coffee. But then, Mac McAndrews's personal life was none of her business. She was in the coffee business. She sipped and swirled the rich blend around her mouth.

When the door opened she wasn't surprised to see Mac silhouetted against the lowered sun. He probably wanted to tell the Hoffmans his daughter was in town. Visiting. Holly squinted. The man walking toward her looked different. Older. Of course. He was a father. As if a veil had dropped from her eyes, she saw the two of them as they were. Adults. With responsibilities. Big responsibilities.

Gathering their belongings, the teenagers, quiet for a change, eyed Mac and sauntered past him.

"Hey, Mac, what's new?" Chris carried his daughter to the now-empty alcove, where his wife sat with a children's book in her hand. The afternoon sunlight shone brightly through the corner window.

Mac threw his old friend a smile before returning his gaze to Holly. "Hi. I wanted to talk to you, if you have a minute."

Holly willed a coolness over her body as she hooked her feet on the rungs of the stool. One kiss didn't mean anything. One kiss wasn't a commitment. "You've been busy this week."

"Last week of school, lots going on." Mac lowered his voice. "Nice seeing you away from the store last weekend. I was wondering if maybe you wanted to go out sometime, grab dinner, a movie." He smiled, but when Holly didn't answer, the smile faded.

Ba-bump. Holly took a deep breath. "You know, Mac, I've been thinking—"

"What are you two whispering about over here?" Carrying the empty cups left by the teens, Chris reached between Holly and Mac to set the dishes on the counter. He looked from one to the other. "Did I interrupt something?"

Holly caught Mac's eye just before he replied. Though they had never spoken the words, somehow she knew neither of them wanted her family involved.

"I was telling Holly I've decided to do a stakeout of the strip mall tonight."

Holly straightened on hearing this new information. "You are?" At Mac's widened eyes she said, "Yes, you are."

Chris leaned on the wall next to Holly and crossed his arms. "No kidding? Things are that bad?" He nudged Holly with his shoulder. "Were you robbed?"

"Not exactly. We've all been missing things."

"All of you? The only things you mentioned to me was your coffee cups and you said people just forget to bring them back."

"Right, I know," she said. "A couple mornings we had fewer cookies than I thought we did. But then, Sonny has a key. He's always hungry."

"You don't do inventory?" Chris furrowed his brow.

Hearing the words out loud, Holly couldn't believe it either, and she was grateful her father wasn't anywhere around. "Well, no, not yet. I haven't had time." She raised her voice to reach Carolyn and Rose, still discussing the library. "Did you two divide up the tips this week?"

"I didn't." Playing peekaboo with her granddaughter, Rose smiled.

"Me, neither." Carolyn shrugged.

Chris narrowed his eyes. "You should take inventory."

"I know, I know," Holly said, holding up both hands. "So when are you doing this stakeout?"

"Tonight."

"What time?"

Mac shrugged. "Sometime after everyone closes."

"Sue closes at four," she said. "And Cheri closes at five. Megan has an eight o'clock appointment tonight. Pierre is often in his shop till midnight."

"Okay, thanks for the information." Mac started to move away.

"So I'll meet you across the street in the

vacant lot at midnight." Her words brought him to an immediate halt.

Looking over his shoulder, he squinted, as if uncertain he'd heard correctly. "What? No, you won't."

"You obviously don't know this area like I do." Holly slid off her stool.

"Of course I do."

Passing behind the espresso maker, Holly stood next to the cash register and leaned on the counter. "What time is the trash pickup out back?"

Mac's chest rose and fell as he took a deep breath. He didn't answer.

Sending Mac a bright smile, Holly nodded. "Just as I thought. Midnight. Vacant lot."

"Listen, Holly, this is my job—" The hopeful face Mac was wearing when he'd first walked into the shop had disappeared, replaced by the professional one.

"And this is my livelihood, Mac McAndrews. If someone wants to ruin it they go through me." Holly took a deep breath. She was expecting more of an argument when the bell over the door jingled.

"Chief McAndrews, I've been looking for you all over town. I might have known I'd find you here."

Turning toward the newcomer, Mac gave her a professional smile. "Did you buy a Harley, Mayor?"

"Pshaw." The woman waved a hand, a bright yellow half helmet dangling from her fingers. "They're gas hogs. I got a motor scooter—" she pointed at a bright yellow motorized vehicle parked out front "—that gets sixty miles to the gallon." She stared at the machine, a pleased smile on her face when her expression changed and she remembered her mission. "Anyway, Chief, I do need to talk to you. Holly, may I have a coffee? I brought my thermos."

"Sure." Grateful for the interruption, Holly reached for the battered silver container.

"I'll take one, too. To go." Mac's voice carried an undercurrent of displeasure.

Grabbing a take-out cup from the stack, Holly filled it and the thermos, then set them both on the counter.

The mayor handed Holly a five-dollar bill, but her gaze was glued to the take-out cup. "Where's your travel mug, Chief?" Her hand hovering in the air for her change, the shorter woman frowned. "You should set an example."

Reaching for his cup, Mac chewed one

corner of his lower lip. "I don't have one, Mayor."

Hiding a smile, Holly handed the mayor her change. "You get more for your money when you bring your own container, Mac." She did a double take at his surly expression. "Just a thought."

Taking the coffee, the mayor linked her arm through Mac's. He narrowed his eyes. "We'll talk." Then Mac grabbed his cup as the mayor pulled him toward the door.

Holly suppressed a shiver as the bell over the door sounded their exit. *Sure, we will. Tonight.*

"Look at that vacant lot, Chief. The disarray reflects badly on the town." She set her rocker moving with a sneakered foot.

Mac's earlier good mood had disappeared like rain on hot pavement. Riley showing up when she did had thrown him completely off balance. Holly hadn't had time to give him an answer before Chris appeared. Her family did get in the way sometimes. Years ago Holly had been in the way. She and her friends had always tagged along with Chris and his friends. When had it changed?

He gritted his teeth. "I know, Mayor, but I

don't know what you want me to do about it. I'm more concerned with preventing crime."

"Can't you arrest litterbugs?" The mayor leaned forward, as if to get a better look at the vacant lot. A slight breeze scattered the bits of paper and blew them into the street.

"I suppose, but to tell you the truth, I haven't seen one litterbug."

They sat in silence as they studied the lot.

Mailbag slung over his shoulder, Bill paused at the door to the hair salon. Skinny legs protruded from khaki shorts. "Nice scooter, Mayor." He touched a finger to his hat and disappeared into the store.

The mayor was still eyeing the vacant lot, but she had a smile on her face that hadn't been there a minute ago. Why had Bill ignored him? He was sitting right there. "Are you and—"

"What about those kids who hang out in the evening?" The mayor rested her cup on the flat arm of the rocker.

Mac shook his head. He, too, had noticed the teens spending time in the lot at dusk, but they hadn't done anything illegal. Truth be told, they didn't have anywhere else to get together. "They have to hang out somewhere. What are they supposed to do?"

"They can go to the amusement park and leave their trash in the bins."

"The park costs money and requires wheels to get there. Not everybody has a car." Mac tapped his toe, anxious to get back to Holly and find out what she'd meant by *you know, Mac, I've been thinking.* "Why don't we put a trash can in the lot?"

The mayor rolled her eyes. "We have a trash can right here. Well, try to think up a solution, Mac. I could use some help with this." With a sigh the mayor stood and screwed the lid on her thermos. Then she descended the steps and placed the thermos in the little basket on the back of her scooter. Setting the helmet on her head she buckled it under her chin. "Don't forget to buy a travel mug." With a wave of her fingers, she motored down the street.

"Chief McAndrews." Pierre Lefonte stood at the door to his shop and beckoned.

Mac followed the Frenchman into his store. Electronic gadgets and parts lined the walls and computers covered a counter toward the back. "How's business, Pierre?"

Pierre gestured toward a stool, went behind the counter and sat on another stool. He stroked his chin, which always had just a day's growth of dark beard. "Unbelievable. When my wife suggested I open this shop, I didn't think we'd last six months, and it has already been a year."

"How is Jessie?"

"She's doing well. Busy, though. Economics is not an easy subject but she's in her last year. I don't know what will happen when she receives her doctorate. If she gets a job in another state…" He raised one dark, bushy eyebrow and waved a hand.

"In the meantime you're meeting a need in this town."

"I'm meeting somebody's need. Last night I closed late and didn't take my deposit to the bank. When I came in this morning I was missing a hundred dollars." He punched a button on the computer screen and a drawer popped open.

"How much was in the drawer?" Mac asked.

"A little over three hundred dollars, but still… We have bills to pay."

"Do you have any employees who might have borrowed the money?"

"So far, no, although I could use some help."

"That's odd. Why take just a hundred dollars?" Mac took in the clutter and apparent disorganization behind the counter. He chose his next words carefully. "Are you sure you're missing money? Why didn't you call me this morning, Pierre? I would've dusted for fingerprints."

Pierre ran a hand through his dark hair and shrugged. "Jessie said she needed some cash. I thought she stopped in on her way to school. We didn't talk until this afternoon. You know how it is, Chief. We're like two ships passing in the night. This is married life these days, no?"

Mac leaned one arm on the counter and stared out the window at the vacant lot across the street. He had finally adapted to Anne's loss, especially after he moved home and everything he saw didn't remind him of his wife. But sometimes, a person would say those things only married people identify with, and pain would stab him right in the middle of the chest, worse than any heartburn. He breathed deeply and focused his thoughts on the minor thefts occurring in the little strip mall. Sue and her change and now Pierre and his missing hundred dollars. The bank robbery, which he hoped had nothing to do with this, was a whole other story.

Mac ran his hand over his short hair and straightened. "I'll keep an eye out, but if this happens again, call us right away. In the meantime I'll have Officer Williams drive by on his patrol during the night."

"Thank you, Chief." Pierre came around the counter and patted Mac on the shoulder.

"Tell your wife I said hello."

Mac stepped onto the porch and shut the door behind him. After the air-conditioned store, the June heat hit him like a sledgehammer. He took off his hat and fanned his face. Across the street the vacant lot looked worse than it had in the spring. Paper cups and napkins littered the dirt and weeds grew in patches. He settled his hat on the back of his head and walked to his patrol car. Mayor Gold and her beautification program would just have to wait. So would Holly.

His mother and his little girl were expecting him home for pizza. And he was late.

CHAPTER NINE

"STOP OR I'LL SHOOT." Holly jerked her hands out of her jeans pockets and pointed her fingers at the full-length mirror on the back of her closet door. At eleven thirty Saturday evening, Holly could easily have been mistaken for a cat burglar. Black jeans, black T-shirt, black sneakers, black hair. What else did you wear to a stakeout? She tiptoed down the stairs of the big Victorian and slipped out the front door. No sense alarming her parents. Her father would tell her she had no business being on a stakeout, to leave everything to Mac. But she had no intention of leaving anything to Mac.

Carrying two travel mugs, she stepped into the shadow of the bank. Across the street all five stores were dark except for a single light burning in each. Nothing moved. At a rustle behind her she turned quickly to see the brown-striped cat slink past.

She stayed close to the wall, her shoulder scraping the rough brick, as she tried to avoid being seen. Coming to the edge of the vacant lot, she barely saw the front bumper of Mac's SUV. She scurried around the back of the vehicle, opened the door and eased onto the front passenger seat. The dome light didn't turn on, leaving the interior of the car pitch-black. "I brought you a coffee." She handed the travel mug across the console and waited till she felt Mac's fingers slide across her hand.

His voice came out of the darkness. "That wasn't necessary."

"Maybe not for you, but I won't be able to stay awake otherwise."

"All the more reason you should be home in bed."

Searching for a comfortable spot on the hard vinyl seat, Holly didn't respond. At least here, in the darkened patrol car, her family wouldn't be able to interrupt. Sipping coffee, she wondered how best to explain things. The muffled sound of a barking dog came through Mac's partially open window. "Looks pretty quiet over there."

His voice equally low, Mac responded. "No way of knowing what time the burglaries happen. Could be just before dawn."

Glancing out the side window, Holly rested her cheek on the seat back. On the far side of the vacant lot a tangled mass of brambles almost covered a wooden fence. She and her neighbors had hoped to revitalize this end of town. If the burglaries continued, the strip mall across the street would look just like the vacant lot and the old library building: empty. "We should talk about—"

"Your family treats you differently now."

Holly took a moment to process Mac's comment. When his words sank in, her stomach stirred uneasily. "What are you talking about?"

Mac, one hand still resting on the steering wheel, didn't take his eyes off the building across the street. "You used to walk into the room and, no matter what they were doing, your family would focus on you."

"You're crazy." Holly shifted in her seat. She sipped from her travel mug. "You've been to one family picnic in ten years and suddenly you're psychoanalyzing everybody? That's some training you got in the police academy."

When Mac turned to face her she looked away. "I didn't mean to touch a nerve, it's just…" He did another finger exercise on the steering wheel. "When you were a kid, your family circulated around you."

"Oh, come on…"

"If Chris had a choice between hanging out with the guys and watching one of your volleyball games, he and your whole family went to your game."

Holly met Mac's gaze in the dim light inside the car. She just barely saw the spark in his eyes. "That's why you were there. You wanted to hang out with Chris."

"Something like that." Mac shrugged. "Maybe that's why your family is treating you differently. Everybody protected you like the princess in the castle and now you come home and you're a warrior."

Holly scanned the vacant lot again, more to avoid Mac's look than to catch approaching burglars. Things hadn't felt right since she came home at Christmas, but she thought she was just being paranoid. The fact Mac recognized a change in the family dynamics was disquieting. She decided to turn the tables on him. "Why didn't you tell me your daughter was coming to live with you?"

The immediate answer was just a heavy sigh.

"I DIDN'T THINK about it." Mac laid his hand over the top of the steering wheel and flexed his fingers.

"You didn't think about your daughter?" Holly's voice carried a note of incredulity.

"Of course I thought about her." Mac tightened his fingers around the wheel, then sighed. "I just didn't want to talk about her." Mac couldn't blame Holly. Even he would admit it was strange for him to barely mention his daughter in all the times they had talked. How could Holly understand that if he didn't talk about Riley, then he didn't have to think about the past, and his part in his wife's death? "Her grandparents were raising her. In North Carolina."

"I see."

Mac leaned forward, straining to see what had caused a shadow on the boardwalk near The Cookie Jar. He caught a glimpse of a long tail disappearing underneath the porch. Settling back into his seat, he raised the coffee to his lips. A dog barked, this time closer.

"You know the kiss was a mistake."

"Which one?" He sipped his coffee and felt rather than saw Holly's face jerk in his direction. Bringing up memories of their teen years was risky.

Her voice was soft. "The last one."

So that's what she'd meant by *you know, Mac, I've been thinking.* "Because now I have a daughter?" His left knee cramped and he shifted so he could stretch his leg.

This time Holly sighed. "Look, Mac, we're not kids anymore. Seeing your daughter made me realize we've both changed. We have responsibilities."

"You don't want to have dinner?"

"Come on, Mac, get real. You were at the picnic. I'm a danger to children. And you have one. Case closed."

Holly was facing forward, so Mac couldn't read her expression. He could have sworn that her sister-in-law's remark about not having children had hit a nerve. Yet he'd never expected her to agree with the family's opinion of her maternal skills. "You don't want to have a family of your own?"

Holly sighed. "I met your daughter, Mac. We didn't exactly hit it off. I'm just not one of those women."

"What women?" Was it the sudden appearance of his daughter, or had Holly never forgiven him for the fiasco in gym class?

"You know, the kind who scrunch up their

faces when they see a baby and start talking in a falsetto."

"But—"

"Look at the cat."

Mac's gaze jerked back to the storefront across the street. The brown tabby had re-appeared on the porch and now paced back and forth directly in front of The Cookie Jar's door. "What's he doing?"

Holly leaned forward to get a better look. "I swear he's looking right at us."

"Well, if anyone plans to rob the place tonight they'll give up once they see me. You stay here till I give the all clear." He eased open his door and exited the car. Behind him he heard Holly's door open. He should have saved his breath.

Crossing the quiet street, he scanned the little strip mall. Nothing moved. Even the cat had stopped prowling and now sat at the top of the steps. Glancing over his shoulder, Mac frowned at Holly, who held up a set of keys.

"Let's check out The Cookie Jar." She started past him.

Mac grabbed the keys from her hand and held out his arm to stop her. "Stay behind me." He slipped the key into the door.

Before he knew what was happening Holly

was kneeling on the floor next to a prostrate Sue. "Suzanna, talk to me."

Dressed in a loose nightgown, the older woman moaned.

Mac knelt on Sue's other side. He rested two fingers on the side of her throat. "Her pulse is strong. Mrs. Hunter, can you tell us what happened?" He helped her to sit up and supported her with an arm behind her back. One tear ran down the side of her face. "Brad wants a divorce, Holly. I thought he was just having a fling, but he doesn't want to be married anymore. What do I do now?" Her words slurred.

The cat slipped through the open door, rubbed against Mac's leg and disappeared behind the counter. "What did you take, Mrs. Hunter?" Mac sneezed.

"Sleeping pills. Brad came just when I was closing and told me they're moving to Colorado." Tears leaked through tightly shut eyes.

Mac shot Holly a look, wondering if they'd have to take her to the emergency room.

"How many pills did you take, Sue?" Holly's low voice carried a touch of panic.

Sue groaned and attempted to rise before falling back to the floor. "Two."

"Two sleeping pills knock you out like

this?" Mac met Holly's incredulous gaze and smiled. Together they lifted the woman from the floor.

The baker gave him a droopy-eyed glare. "I'm sensitive."

THEY TOOK SUE back to the B and B and settled her in a second-floor bedroom—just beneath Holly's room. Early the next morning, Holly tiptoed past the door but Sue was already up, still wearing her nightgown. "I'm sorry I got you involved, Holly. Just take me back to the store before anyone else sees me in my nightclothes."

Seeing Sue back to the little storage room above the bakery that served as her temporary residence caused Holly to be late opening the shop. A steady stream of customers ensured she never caught up. By the end of the day she was exhausted. Retreating to her room as soon as she got home, she found a movie on the television. Only then did she realize Mac hadn't showed for their usual Saturday morning visit. Sunday was spent placing orders for supplies and, before she knew it, Monday rolled around.

Walking down the street in the early-morning mist, Holly was certain Mac wouldn't show. She wasn't sure if she felt relief or disappointment. Reaching into her pocket for the keys, she froze at the sight of a dark object at her feet, then smiled. A dead mouse. The brown tabby had given her another gift. Kitty had had a busy weekend.

Unlocking the back door, she found herself thinking about the stakeout and her declaration that anything beyond friendship was a mistake. Then she realized Mac hadn't exactly agreed. Turning Mac down had been harder than she'd anticipated, but if the kiss on the mountain had taught her anything, it was that she could easily fall for the adult Mac McAndrews. Nick had been a better match for her than Mac, and that relationship hadn't lasted. A relationship with Mac was destined for failure.

She unlocked the front door and sighed. In the early-morning light, the chrome appliances gleamed and the comfortable leather furniture beckoned. She ran her fingers along the shining countertop, pleased with the knowledge that in four short weeks, she had created a home away from home, a retreat, for the inhabitants of her little town.

She slipped her apron over her head and tied the strings in a bow. After making one pot of Wildflower Special Blend and one of Kenya, she set the timer for the peach tea to steep. Retrieving a bag of espresso beans from the back, she climbed up on the stool to refill the machines from the top. The pungent aroma of the freshly opened bag surrounded her and when the kitchen door swung open behind her she couldn't look away from the steady stream of coffee beans. "Good morning, Louise. I thought you weren't coming in until eight."

"She probably isn't but I have an early trip."

At the sound of Mac's voice Holly's hand jerked and espresso beans flew over the counter and onto the floor. She righted the bag and the cascade of beans finally stopped. Behind her she heard coffee pouring into Mac's cup. Holly let out the breath she didn't know she was holding and wrapped her arms around the espresso maker. Her legs were no longer able to support her. She pressed her palm against her pounding heart and breathed deeply. "What are you doing here?"

The lid snapped onto a take-out cup. "I'm getting my morning coffee." Mac rounded the counter and strode to the door, where he looked out at the street as if expecting someone.

Only then did Holly notice the tiny form curled up in a corner of the couch. "You brought your daughter?"

"Mom went to an early exercise class. She told me she'd meet me here and take Riley home."

Clutching her blanket to her chest, Riley stretched out on the couch. "Grandma went to spam class."

Holly laughed. "You mean spin class."

"That's what I said." Riley turned her face toward the back of the couch in a huff.

Standing on the stool, the bag of beans in her hands, Holly stared at Mac over the espresso maker. "What did I say?"

He shrugged. "I guess she doesn't like being made fun of."

"Sorry."

The girl's only response was an angry wiggle.

Something was off here... Holly stared at the small form on the couch. "You brought her out in her pajamas?"

Mac frowned, then shook his head. "I thought she got dressed."

Holly swept the loose beans off the top of the machine, muttering, "Kind of obvious. Even I noticed."

"I thought you weren't one of those women."

Holly's head jerked up. "Even I can tell the difference between play clothes and pajamas."

Cup in hand, Mac stood waiting at the door. "You were right about the—" he glanced at the tiny body on the couch "—thing. We have different…goals."

Holly's hands stilled. *Here we go.* She finished adding beans to the machine and replaced the lids. "We do."

No response.

Chris blew through the door, almost knocking Mac over in his haste. "We're off to Philly. Just need some caffeine for the road, sis." His vacation jeans had been replaced by khaki pants and a navy blue shirt. Her brother stopped short and peered at the floor. "What are these beans doing all over the place?"

Ignoring her brother's question, Holly smiled at him. "The usual?" She spied Valerie following her husband at a more sedate pace. Harley lay sprawled over her shoulder. "Hi, Val."

Val mouthed a *good morning* and settled into a chair.

Chris smoothed his hand over his gelled

hair. "Can you make us a skinny vanilla latte and a skinny amaretto to go?"

"Of course." Holly climbed down from the stool and pulled nonfat milk from the refrigerator below the counter.

Dressed in a pair of black yoga pants and a gray Penn State T-shirt, Mac's mother rushed into the door. "I got here as soon as I could, son."

Mac glanced at his watch. "I'm late, Mom."

Wiping the back of her hand across her forehead, Erma propped her hands on her hips. "I was afraid something like this would come up. Why don't you hire a sitter, John?"

"We talked about this." He reached for the door just as Wendy Valentine entered.

"Chief McAndrews." Wendy paused in her beeline for the counter. "I've been hoping I'd run into you."

Frothing milk at the counter, Holly saw Mac give the young woman a slow smile.

And so it begins.

"Daddy, wait." Riley rolled off the couch and ran to her father. "Can I have a hug?"

Shooting Wendy a grin, he gave his daughter a bear hug. Then he pulled a card out of his shirt pocket. "Give me a call." With that he was gone. Shoulders drooping, his daughter returned to the couch.

Poor kid. Holly's heart went out to the little girl pulled away from the only home she'd ever known and tossed from one caregiver to the other like a hot potato. All the more reason for Mac to find someone who knew how to raise a child properly, someone who understood the mysteries of hot dog preparation.

Their first meeting after she'd rejected him had gone better than she'd expected. Maybe even better than she wanted, she thought, remembering Wendy's pretty, flushed face. The least he could have done was appear disappointed.

She took another deep breath and straightened. She could do this. She could treat Mac McAndrews as an acquaintance, a family friend. She smiled, relieved to have the dreaded encounter behind her. Oh yes, she could do this. Just another day at The Wildflower. She went out onto the front porch to gather leftover cups and found the brown cat licking the dried foam from a mug. "Ah, you should have said something. You're a cappuccino drinker."

The cat lifted his head, opened his mouth and meowed.

Holly patted his head. "I'll take that as a yes."

CHAPTER TEN

THIS YEAR'S FOURTH OF JULY picnic was being held at the B and B because the meadow behind the house gave the best view of the fireworks set off at the amusement park. Having worked late on her books, Holly arrived home just in time to see the twins run screaming into the neighbor's yard. "What's going on?" Holly walked up to her father, who stood at the grill turning hot dogs and flipping hamburgers.

Eyes twinkling, he gave her a grin. "The girls talked Sonny into getting a puppy for their birthday."

"Daisy had her puppies. Oh, I have to go look." Her dad chuckled as he moved the meat around the hot surface. "What's so funny?"

"Sonny thinks he'll get away with one dog for two girls." He laughed so hard his belly shook.

Reflecting on the fact that she'd just seen

her father laugh for the first time since her shop opened, Holly followed her nieces through a hole in the hedge. Maybe he had finally accepted her decision. Daisy wandered over. Nudging her knee, the dog left a wet noseprint on her shorts. "Hi, girl, congratulations." She rubbed the black Lab's floppy ears.

Rachel and Rosalyn knelt on the back patio, huddled around a basket. Holly peeked over their shoulders. On a pillow, eight black puppies crawled and mewed.

"What do you think, girls?" Fran Collier sat on the back steps.

Rachel pointed to a chubby black puppy crawling toward her. "Is this puppy a boy or a girl?"

Fran inspected the pink-speckled belly. "This one's a little girl."

Rachel cradled the whimpering pup in her arms. Long black ears trailed over her elbow. "I want this one."

"I want to pick. Who said you get to pick?" Rosalyn pushed out her lips in a pout.

Rachel closed her eyes, giggling as the puppy nuzzled her neck. "He said we have to feed her, walk her and play with her."

Holly sat cross-legged on the patio and

leaned against the porch wall. "Maybe you can talk your dad into two puppies." She blamed her father for putting the idea in her head.

Rosalyn's face brightened. "Think so, Aunt Holly?"

Holly reached for a tiny pup crawling away from the others and handed him to her niece, whose frown was instantly replaced with a smile. "Are they all spoken for?"

Fran ran a hand through short, dark hair. "Not yet. We're keeping one and giving the others away, but everybody wants dogs with papers these days. Daisy was scheduled to be fixed when I found out."

One of the pups crawled away from his sisters. Holly picked him up and settled him in her lap. "This one has a brown nose. Any brown male dogs in the neighborhood?"

"Not that we know of. It's a mystery, believe me."

"This is the only one with brown—" Holly ran the long, silky ears through her fingers "—and these ears practically drag on the ground."

"The others are all black like Daisy," Rosalyn said.

Holly looked up just as Mac appeared in the break in the hedge. Her heart sped up just a little and she wondered how long it would take until she could treat Mac as just a family friend. She gave him a tentative smile.

Riley pushed past him. "Puppies." Her squeal could have shattered glass. She sank down next to the twins. "Can I have one, Daddy?"

Mac knelt beside his daughter and studied the pups. "I don't think so, Riley."

"Please." Riley picked up the smallest pup and held it, legs dangling, against her cheek. "Please, Daddy."

Mac rubbed a hand over his face. He cupped his daughter's chin and gazed at her sternly. "You know we can't. You might be going back to Grandma Liz's house when school starts and then what would happen to a dog?"

Riley tilted her head. "He could come with me."

Mac shook his head. "No way."

Riley was close to tears as she returned the squirming pup to the basket. She ran back through the hole in the hedge without saying a word.

Holly patted the brown-nosed creature in her lap. "Back to the basket, little fella. Sorry." She pulled on the long, silky ears and set him on the pillow. A shrill whistle rent the air. "That's Dad. The burgers must be ready. Let's go, girls." Holly followed her nieces toward the hedge. She looked back. "Are you coming over, Fran?"

Replacing the fence around the basket of puppies, Fran looked over her shoulder and nodded. "As soon as Mel changes out of his golfing clothes, we'll be right over. By the way, I have some paperbacks for your bookstore."

"Thanks." With a wave, Holly pushed through the hole in the hedge to find the family already crowded around the picnic table, where the food was set buffet-style. The grandchildren and Riley were already eating in the gazebo.

Holly carried her plate to the patio table. "You don't want me on kid-table duty. Look what happened last time. I think you're up at bat, Sonny."

Sonny sat on the stone wall surrounding the patio, half a hamburger in his hand. "I'll pay you," he mumbled around the other half of the burger.

Holly laughed. She set her chair rocking and picked up a glass of wine. "You don't have enough money, bro."

"Sonny, go." Carolyn pointed to the backyard, where the sound of children screaming carried from the gazebo. "They're too far away to be left alone and three of those children are yours. Holly's not a babysitter."

Sonny stuffed the other half of his hamburger into his mouth and quickly filled a plate from the array of dishes on the picnic table. "What's going on back here?" His roar carried on the summer air, accompanied by the squeals of the children.

Holly caught Carolyn's eye as she smiled and picked up a bottle of wine, pouring herself a glass. "Who is he kidding? He loves it." Another roar came from the direction of the gazebo accompanied by more squeals.

After putting away the food, the family wandered to the field behind the house to watch the fireworks. Giggling and wrestling, the children sprawled on a blanket. Behind them, the adults sat in lawn chairs. Holly spread a blanket off to one side. When she saw Mac watching the children, she pulled on his sleeve. "Want to join me? You can keep an eye on Riley from here."

"Are you too good to sit with the rest of us?" Sonny's voice boomed from the far side of the gathering.

Holly waved in the general direction of his voice. In the gathering darkness she could barely see him. "Chairs are for old people."

"Thanks a lot," her mother said.

"Sorry, Mom. Present company excluded, of course."

"Of course." Her mother threw a piece of hard candy at Holly and hit her on the foot.

Unwrapping the candy and popping it in her mouth, Holly leaned back on her elbows and stared at the horizon. A practice rocket exploded, showering the darkening sky with red, white and blue sparks. "So what's new?" The candy softened. Butterscotch. Her mother knew she liked butterscotch.

"I took your advice."

Focused on the sky, Holly didn't realize at first Mac had addressed the comment to her. Puzzled, she glanced over. "What advice?" She could just make out Mac's profile. He, too, was watching the horizon.

"I went out with Wendy Valentine."

Holly's stomach flipped. "I never said—" She tore her gaze from his face for a sudden, necessary inspection of her decades-old, orange flip-flops.

"You said we have different goals. I figured you realized my goal is to find a mother for my daughter."

"Oh." The candy had lost flavor.

"She's interesting. But she's just like you."

"She's nothing like me." Holly pictured the young professional in her mind. "For one thing, she dresses better than I do." Holly forced a smile.

"She's ambitious like you were. She wants to move to a bigger station. She's you ten years ago."

"What are you talking about?"

"Remember when you and Chris used to talk about all the places you wanted to visit?"

She nodded.

"That's where Wendy's at. She graduated college and took a job in her hometown. But she wants the big time." He threw her a sideways look, one corner of his mouth turned down. "Besides, she just wanted to interview me."

"Oh." Holly wasn't sure how to respond. So Wendy wanted to move on. Was she surprised? Not really. Was she glad? Maybe a little. She could've told Mac Wendy wasn't a good candidate.

"Then your mom told me the library hired a new director."

Holly bit her lip. "My mom?" *She went from pressuring me to date to finding dates for Mac?*

"Yes. One morning I came in for coffee and your mom told me about Eliza."

Holly bit down on the remaining piece of hard candy and heard a satisfying crunch. "You've been busy." Just over a month since the kiss in the meadow and he'd had dates with two different women?

"I didn't say I went out with her."

Not wanting to appear too interested in Mac's social life, Holly remained quiet. One rocket. Two rockets. "Why not?"

"I'm allergic to cats."

Carolyn had said the new library director was very pretty. Holly found it hard to believe the big, tough chief of police allowed a cat to get between him and his goal—a beautiful, smart mother for Riley. "You can't be around one little ole kitty for an hour or two?"

"Maybe one." Mac shot her a look. "Not twenty-three."

Holly laughed out loud. "The new librarian has twenty-three cats?" She laughed again, wondering why the news made her feel so absolutely giddy.

One of the twins walked over, followed by Riley.

Riley sat on her father's lap, her back toward Holly. She wasn't surprised. Their brief encounters had, thus far, been less than friendly.

Twisting her hands, the twin said, "Aunt Holly, can I ask you something?"

Holly reminded herself of the differences between the twins. Freckles. That was it. Rosalyn had more freckles than Rachel because she spent more time outdoors. "Sure, Rosalyn. What's up?"

"Daddy said you're a good rider. He said you used to take Twister to the fair."

"He did, huh?" Holly glanced at Sonny. "He's right. Why do you ask?"

Out of the corner of her eye she noticed Riley shift slightly in her father's lap. Instead of her back, Holly could see the child's profile. The ever-present quilt lay half in her lap and half on the ground.

"Do you have time to teach me to ride?"

"For lessons, Twister would be the best to learn on, but I haven't ridden the old boy in a long time, Rosalyn."

The girl's face fell. She turned to go back to the screaming children.

Remembering her own efforts to convince her parents to let her take riding lessons, Holly ran through her weekly schedule. "Rosalyn?"

Her face hopeful, the girl ran back to the blanket and knelt in front of Holly. "Yes?"

"Tell you what. Let me give the old boy a test ride first. I'll see what kind of shape he's in, how much he remembers, and then we'll talk. Okay?"

The girl's face lit up like the fireworks just starting over the horizon as she scampered back to the blanket and whispered in her twin's ear.

Riley jumped off Mac's lap and followed her new friend. She stopped in front of Freddy and showed him her stuffed dog.

"Freddy sure looks like his dad, doesn't he?" Mac said. "He'll probably play football like him, too."

"He'll be a big boy."

Holly inclined her head toward Riley, who was chasing Freddy around the blanket, her ponytail bouncing. The stuffed dog was dragging over the ground. "I hope that's no indication of how she'd carry a puppy around." Riley's giggle carried on the night air as she and Freddy walked their stuffed animals across the blankets.

Mac's expression darkened. "Riley doesn't need a puppy. She needs a mother. Someone waiting when she gets home from school, someone to braid her hair." He pressed his lips together.

"You're not exactly skilled at hair, are you?" Thinking of the girl's tangled mop the morning Mac brought her to the shop in her pajamas, Holly looked pointedly at Mac's short hair.

He grunted. "Funny."

"Riley takes after her mother, doesn't she?" When Mac didn't answer, Holly turned and studied his profile. "She's tall for her age, which she probably gets from you, but your hair is a darker blond."

She noticed a muscle in his jaw twitch. "Anne's mother said Riley looked just like Anne when she was a baby."

Lowering her voice, Holly touched his arm. "I shouldn't have brought it up."

Mac watched the kids, still hopping about, waiting for the fireworks set to music to begin. "I don't expect you to understand. You have this perfect family."

His skin was warm underneath her fingers,

but at his words she withdrew her hand. She wasn't sure what her family had to do with anything. "All the same, I'm sorry. I can't imagine—"

A few miles away the first rocket went off, sending a shower of white sparks cascading into the air. Timed to match the explosions, music drifted across the valley. Some of the rockets exploded with a flash and a loud boom. Mac jumped at the first concussion.

After the third boom Riley ran to her father and crawled into his lap, her stuffed dog clutched to her chest. Mac sat stiffly, one hand resting in the grass, the other wrapped loosely around the little girl.

Holly studied the quiet group, their faces reflecting the lights from the exploding fireworks. Her parents sat next to each other in folding chairs. Married almost forty years, they still held hands.

Sonny sat on the blanket, his long legs stretched out, leaning back against his wife's legs. Thomas and Beth were beside them—another couple who'd married young.

Holly and Chris had agreed their lives would be different. They'd both wanted to see the world, and she had followed her brother into the air force. Chris had gone on to earn a degree and become a pilot, while she had traveled the world. Now even Chris had married.

So where did that leave her? She glanced at Mac and Riley. How had he phrased it? *Someone waiting when she came home from school.*

She couldn't see herself waiting at home with a glass of milk and a plate of homemade cookies. No, things were progressing exactly as they should.

CHAPTER ELEVEN

THE NEXT MORNING Holly found a note on the kitchen counter. Beth had gone into labor, Thomas had taken her to the hospital and Rose went to the farm to stay with the children. She made a pot of coffee for the guests and set out some muffins before walking down the street. Not even seven o'clock and already the temperature was in the seventies. She unlocked the door and entered the quiet shop, turning on the air-conditioning on her way to the kitchen. As usual, Mac was her first customer.

By now he would walk into the store and help himself to the coffee. Usually he would perch on the stool at the end of the counter and the two would talk while Holly prepared for opening. This morning Mac took his cup over to the chairs, sat and stared out the window.

As Holly uncovered the plates in the display case, she glanced at Mac. He'd greeted her upon entering the store but had said nothing since. "Are you okay this morning? Hasn't the coffee kicked in yet?"

Mac gave her a half smile. "You didn't put decaf in the pot by mistake, did you?"

"I hope not." Holly shut the case and tossed the wrappers in the waste can.

When the bell over the door jingled, Holly was surprised to see the blonde woman, briefcase in hand. "You're up and about early."

Her lips curved in a gentle smile. "I have an early meeting. I enjoy your cappuccinos when I'm in town."

"Thank you."

Mac was staring at the woman with a look of almost shock on his face. Holly started when she remembered her own first impression of this woman. Rose had said she looked just like Mac's wife. Tall, willowy, with pale blond hair.

"Have a seat," Holly said, "and I'll bring your drink over when I'm finished."

She poured nonfat milk into a pitcher as the woman walked to her usual chair and smiled at Mac. He nodded and, when he thought she wasn't looking, peered at her over the rim of his cup.

Holly took the finished drink to her customer and set it on the table. "My name's Holly, by the way."

"I'm Katherine King."

"This is our chief of police, Mac McAndrews. If you'll excuse me, I have some tea to brew." She left then. She couldn't watch. The woman was perfect. Looked like Anne, thus Riley could easily pass for her daughter, and she was from the South. Mac liked Southern women.

The two conversed, and Mac seemed more alive than when he'd first come in. Holly started when he appeared at the counter with his empty cup.

"Have a good day, Holly." He gave her a half smile, then nodded at Ms. King. "Ma'am."

"You too, Mac." Holly leaned on the counter. Mac crossed the street to his patrol car. He said a few words to the bank president before driving away.

Something had changed in Mac and she had the feeling it had to do with their discussion of Riley's mother. Holly shook her head. If their talk was any indication, he was still having a hard time getting over the loss of his wife. Ms. King just might be the answer.

"Extra large double Americano, Holly." Ponytail swinging, Megan rushed through the door and slammed her Wildflower mug on the counter. "I've got three perms today."

The door hadn't closed behind Megan before Cheri rushed in. "Make that two." She slid her mug across the counter to Holly, who just managed to catch it before it landed on the floor. "Hey, did one of you open my boxes by mistake? The delivery guy left a shipment out back and when I got here this morning they were all open." She ran a hand through her curly hair.

"Of course not." The hairdresser grabbed biscotti from a jar on the counter and gave Cheri an appraising look. "Were they on the porch or in the alley?"

Cheri tossed her head, setting her silver hoop earrings swinging. "Right outside my front door."

"They were open when I arrived. I couldn't believe you were here so early." Holly set their drinks on the counter.

Cheri threw her head back and laughed out loud. "Guilty as charged. You know I'm a night owl."

"Chief McAndrews asked me if I was missing anything. I wonder if someone's supplementing their income at our expense."

Megan handed Holly a pocketful of change. "I'm barely making ends meet as it is."

"If you see our handsome police chief send him my way." Cheri smiled and wiggled her eyebrows.

"Isn't he a little young for you?" Holly kept her tone casual, but the idea Cheri was checking out Mac irritated her.

"Honey, once you're over thirty, age doesn't matter." She grabbed her cup and backed toward the door. "By the way, one of the boxes was full of polo shirts. You interested?"

Holly squinted. "Why would I be interested in polo shirts?"

"I thought you might want to have a consistent look for your staff." Cheri exchanged a look with Megan. "But no biggie… If you want them, stop over. If not, I'll just put them out for sale." The door clanged shut behind her.

Holly caught Megan's eye. "That woman makes coffee nervous."

After the initial morning flurry, business slowed. The same four teenagers came in around midafternoon and huddled in the alcove, the girls poring over fashion magazines. Skinny Smith stopped in for a bag of fair trade coffee beans and Holly got a delivery of tea bags.

Tom Johnson stopped over in the late afternoon. "How's business?"

Holly finished making iced tea and approached the bank president. "Business is good, Tom. Is this the first you've been in?" Although Holly had needed minimal loans thanks to her savings and the loan from her parents, she had worked with the bank on short-term advances for supplies. Tom didn't need to know with the onset of summer weather that business had slowed significantly. "Would you like an iced tea to go? It's on the house."

"Thanks, Holly. Yes, an iced tea for the road and my wife wanted me to pick up some of your special blend beans."

Holly pulled a bag from the shelf and prepared his drink. She nodded toward the alcove. "I think your son is here."

"Ethan?" Tom leaned away from the counter as he looked at the teens. "Kids that age don't want to be seen with their parents. But thanks for the heads-up. At least I know where he's hanging out these days."

Holly set the tea and beans on the counter. "They're quiet, I will say that. I hope your wife likes this blend. If not, tell her to come in and she can sample some different ones."

"Thanks, Holly, I will." Tom tipped his head. "And, by the way—" he lowered his voice "—you need a loan, my door's always open." As the bank president approached the door, a huge man filled the entrance.

Officer Williams practically blocked out the sun.

Holly nodded at the big man as he strolled up to the counter. "Hi, Moose, what can I get for you?"

"One coffee with cream and sugar, to go, please, ma'am." Holly grabbed a cup and stuck it under the coffee spout. As he waited, Moose's head was rotating like a searchlight, taking in everything and everyone.

"Your coffee's on the house."

Moose pulled a wallet out of his pocket. "No, thank you, ma'am. Chief said you would try to give me coffee but we're not allowed to take gifts." He laid the money by the register, picked up the cup and walked away.

The teens gathered their belongings and the girls waved goodbye to Holly as they left. She smiled and prepared to close.

Just as she turned off the lights, except the one over the counter, she received a text from her mother, begging her to bring coffee to the farm.

Holly grabbed a pound of breakfast roast and locked the door behind her. She walked home in the dusk, got in her car and drove out to the farm.

Her mother met her at the door.

"Any word?" Holly handed her mother the pound of coffee.

"Not yet. Should be anytime now." Rose kissed her on the cheek. "Thanks for bringing this out. I don't know how those two function without making coffee in the morning." She set the coffee on the counter next to the coffeemaker.

Holly smiled. "Do you need me to do anything for the people in the Sunflower room? I left muffins out for them this morning."

"They're pretty self-sufficient. They're visiting the Belleville auction tomorrow. They'll leave early."

Holly tilted her head toward the parking area. "Whose car?"

"Erma and her granddaughter came out to see the horses."

Holly stood at the kitchen door and stared up the lane, thinking of Riley and Mac at the fireworks. "I think I'll go and say hello. Want to come along?" She opened the fridge and grabbed some carrots.

"Sure." Her mother turned off the kitchen light and followed her out.

They walked up the lane and rounded the barn, where they found all five grandchildren plus Riley perched on the wooden fence rails. Erma stood protectively behind Riley.

Holly handed each child a long, orange carrot. When she came to Riley she paused. "Riley, do you know how to hold your hand when you feed the horses?"

"I remember. Grandpap taught me." She held her hand out flat to demonstrate, then offered the treat to the cream-colored gelding, whose lips gathered the carrot gingerly from Riley's outstretched palm.

Holly ran her fingers through the coffee-colored mane. "Whose pony is this anyway? He's gorgeous."

"He's mine, Holly," Riley said. "His name's Frosty."

Holly raised an eyebrow. "He is?" She realized this was the first time Riley had used her name. With a guilty start, she realized the same could be said for her. She had become accustomed to calling Mac's daughter *kid*. Maybe they had reached a compromise.

"Frosty is Riley's pony," Erma said. "Riley's mother had the mother to this horse. She bred her mare and kept the colt. He was intended to be Riley's."

"He's gorgeous." Shocked at the revelation, Holly studied the beautiful animal. From head to rump, his conformation was excellent, and if his demeanor at the rail was any indication, his attitude was good, too. "I gather she doesn't ride him. Does anybody?"

Erma shook her head. One hand smoothed over Riley's ever-present ponytail. "Anne never finished the training. Mac's so afraid of Riley having an accident he doesn't want to have the animal trained."

"What a waste." Holly moved up behind Riley, who stood on the second railing running her hand down the pony's face. "He seems gentle enough."

"Grandpap used to take me with him, but since we moved here I don't ride anymore."

"Do you remember riding with your mother?" Doing some quick mental calculations, Holly figured Riley would have been two when her mother died. *How could she remember?*

Riley's face lit up. "I remember bouncing and Mommy laughing."

"He's a nice pony, Riley."

"I wish I could ride him." She laid her cheek against the pony's muzzle. Frosty stood motionless as if he enjoyed the connection with his owner.

Holly shot a look at Erma, who raised an eyebrow in acknowledgment of Holly's own thoughts. "Maybe someday your dad will change his mind."

"Maybe." The little girl had withdrawn with the talk about her mother and the pony. Holly couldn't blame her. The topic was a lot for a child to think about.

"Did you ride Twister yet, Aunt Holly?" Rosalyn stood at her other side, her green eyes hopeful.

Holly placed an arm over the girl's shoulders. "Not yet. But I will. I promise."

An unfamiliar warmth spread through Holly at the thought of teaching her niece to ride, of sharing a love of horses. At the same time she wished she could make the same offer to Riley. But the business was her priority. She had expanded her hours, and since she still couldn't pay any staff, she was the only person available to run the place. She needed to be careful making promises she might not be able to keep.

WEDNESDAY MORNING MAC stopped by as usual. Sitting on the stool at the end of the counter, coffee in hand, Mac caught a whiff of Holly's scent as she whooshed by. "You know, you have this curious combination of coffee-and-vanilla scent. You should market that. It wakes a guy up in the morning."

With an uplifted eyebrow, Holly disappeared into the kitchen, only to reappear with two containers of milk. "Coffee, vanilla and just a drop of dish detergent. Yes, I'm sure the combination is extremely appealing."

Mac took the milk from her and leaned down to put them away in the lower refrigerator. "Just a thought. You could sell eau de coffeehouse on the side. Bring in more revenue."

Holly knelt by the pastry case and pushed open the sliding glass door. "If I thought that would work, I'd do it. I knew business would slow as the days got hotter, but I didn't expect this. I even added flavored Frosty Coffees to my menu."

"I'll have to try one." He held up his cup. "Not in the morning, though."

Holly tucked a piece of hair behind her ear. It was growing out, the curls brushing her cheeks. He pulled a bill from his wallet.

"Mac. You don't owe me anything."

"I appreciate the offer but I really prefer to pay." Besides, she needed the money.

"There's no gray area with you, is there? It's black or white, all-or-nothing." Holly lifted two covered plates from the case and set them on the counter.

"Now who's doing the psychoanalyzing?" He stuck his wallet back in his pocket. "Keep the change." He couldn't figure out how paying for his morning coffee said he had no gray area…whatever that meant.

"Speaking of Frosty Coffees, I ran into your mom and Riley at the farm yesterday."

Mac rubbed a hand over his face. Maybe he wasn't awake yet, but he couldn't make the connection between Holly's new coffee drink and his family. "Did your sister-in-law have her baby?"

Lifting the covering from a plate of peanut butter no bakes, Holly smiled. "She had a little girl, born five minutes before midnight. At least she only has two older brothers, instead of three, like me."

"You didn't turn out so bad."

"No, I guess not." Holly put the plates back in the case. "Anyway, I met Frosty. Why didn't you tell me you were boarding her horse at the farm? I could help her handle him."

A sudden chill gripped Mac. How could he explain to Holly, a woman who could ride anything, why he didn't want Riley on the horse? Across the street, petunias bloomed in riotous color at the base of the flagpole in the bank parking lot. "We're just boarding the horse because Riley refused to sell him. But the animal hasn't been fully trained, so please don't encourage her." He reached for his cup and stuck it under the coffee tap. Watching the rich liquid fill the cup, he felt Holly's eyes on him. He knew she would challenge him, but no way was he letting his five-almost-six-year-old daughter ride an untrained horse. Riding was dangerous enough. And seeing the horse always reminded him of Anne and his failure.

When Holly spoke, her voice was soft and persuasive. "Your mother told me Anne bred him for Riley. Why did you move the horse north if you had no intention of using him?"

"My in-laws insisted." Mac rubbed his forehead and fit the top on his cup.

"But they own a horse farm."

"Tell me about it. I don't understand their reasoning, but they said something about needing room for their breeding program. So they took care of moving the horse up here. I had nothing to do with it."

He met her eyes. "All water under the bridge, Holly. If Anne were still here she would have trained the horse, Riley would have taken lessons and someday ridden Frosty. But that's not happening."

Her voice followed him as he rounded the counter. "Well, I don't know if you remember, Mac, but I'm a pretty fair rider myself. I mean, I wasn't on the cover of any magazines, but I did win some ribbons."

"Holly." Mac smacked his cup on the counter with more force than he intended and was instantly sorry when Holly gasped and took a step back. "She's my little girl. Horses are dangerous. I well remember your skill with animals—" he grimaced "—at any sport, for that matter." He chose his next words carefully. "I also remember you rounding a barrel and flying six feet in the air and landing in the dirt. You didn't move. You should have seen your parents' faces." He gave her a half smile. "I've got to run."

"You should have seen her face light up when she talked about riding with Anne."

Mac froze halfway to the door. A picture

of Anne riding Black Coffee Morning holding two-year-old Riley in the saddle flashed into his mind. The two of them laughed with each bounce as the Welsh cob trotted around the arena. With his heart sinking, he turned and faced Holly. "What do you want me to say?"

Holly held up her hands, palms out. "Do you care if I ride him?"

She wouldn't give up until she got the answer she wanted. "No." He opened the door.

"No you don't care or no I can't ride him?"

Mac let the door slam shut behind him. Let her figure out what he meant. Standing on the porch staring at the vacant lot across the street, Mac wondered how Holly had forgotten their kiss on the mountain so quickly. And he didn't like that any more than he liked the idea of someone other than Anne training Riley's pony.

CHAPTER TWELVE

AFTER LUNCH CAROLYN strolled into the shop. "Busy?"

Sprawled in one of the easy chairs, Holly put down the Western she'd been reading. "Swamped. I'm so busy I let the customers help themselves. More efficient that way."

"Ha-ha. Very funny." Carolyn perched on the arm of the chair opposite and fixed Holly with a speculative look. "Rosalyn said she asked you about riding lessons."

Sighing, Holly dropped her feet to the floor. "She did. I just haven't had time to check out Twister. Since I extended our hours I'm here late every night. Sundays I've been setting up inventory and I'm definitely missing baked goods and bottled drinks and—"

Carolyn held up her hand. "I get the picture." She looked around the empty store. "Why don't you run out now?"

"Now? I can't close now."

"I didn't say close. I'll watch the place."

She picked up Holly's discarded book. "I can read Westerns as well as you, although I might look for a romance instead."

"What about the kids?" Holly fought the urge to jump to her feet and run out the door. Even she knew asking a working mother of three to watch the store while she went horseback riding wasn't fair.

"Scout camp, all three of them."

"What about Sonny?"

"Builder's conference in Harrisburg."

Excitement built in her chest. "You would do that for me?"

"Well, actually, my motives are a bit selfish. The sooner you ride Twister the sooner you start lessons with my daughter."

Holly reached over and patted her sister-in-law's knee. "Thank you, Carolyn. I've been here so much lately I dream espresso recipes."

"Of course, once school starts and I start teaching again I won't be able to help out here but I guess we'll cross that bridge when we get to it." Carolyn stood and wandered down the line of books. "Get along, there, little doggy."

With a laugh, Holly retrieved her purse from the kitchen and ran out the door. At the house, she grabbed a protein bar and water bottle and drove straight to the farm. The five horses crowded the fence when she pulled up to the horse barn.

Eyeing the cream-colored gelding, she scratched behind his ear. "Maybe next time, fella." Mac's answer hadn't been clear. In the meantime, she had her own horse to ride.

Throwing a halter on Twister, she led him down the concrete center aisle of the barn. Hooking him up to the cross ties, she curried and brushed him. Cleaning his hooves, she ran a hand over his legs, checking for unfamiliar bumps or swellings. Satisfied he had no issues, she threw on a blanket and saddle.

Holly led him out to the lane and stepped into the saddle. Leaning over and running her hand down the soft hairs of his neck, she allowed herself a minute to enjoy the feel of the horse beneath her. Once she was in the saddle, she wondered what had taken her so long.

"Come on, Twister, let's go for a walk." She settled into the rolling gait as they walked up the lane toward the pond. Twister's ears pricked forward and back, his head rotating as he looked around at the scenery. "Been a while, hasn't it, fella?"

Although the gelding was twenty-five, he was in good health. He dropped his head and they started up the slight incline toward the ridge.

Squirrels peered from around the trunks of leafy maples as they traversed the wide path. A grouse flushed out of a stand of rhododendron. Twister's ears perked but otherwise the sudden appearance didn't sway him. Holly patted his neck. "You're a good boy, Twister."

When they reached the field on the ridge, she put Twister through his paces. Walk, trot and canter. Back. Sidestep. The horse was as responsive as ever. Before starting back down the mountain, they rested a moment. The creek below could barely be seen for the lush growth of the forest. To the west the sun sat poised on the blue tops of the distant mountains.

Holly kicked her feet out of the stirrups and let her legs dangle, the reins looped around one finger. Sending out last rays of light and turning the sky glorious shades of orange and red, the sun disappeared below the horizon.

Picking up the reins, she nudged Twister's sides and he turned, already knowing without her asking that they were heading back down the hill. When they passed the spot where she and Mac had kissed, a curious tingling sensation swept through her body and for a moment she wondered if she had done the right thing, telling Mac the kiss was a mistake. Riding through the woods, she tried to allow the buzzing of the locusts to drown out the doubts crowding her brain. *You think too much. Just let it be.*

But she couldn't. And of course she was doing the right thing. Today was a perfect example. She couldn't even find time to ride her horse thanks to the long hours spent at the coffee shop. How on earth would she meet Mac's requirement of a wife?

Leaving the woods, she slowed the horse to a walk so he would cool. The workout hadn't been long, but Twister hadn't done more in the past few years than roll around in the pasture. The activity would be good for him, just as having a purpose—a reason to keep looking forward—was good for people.

ROSALYN'S FIRST LESSON was Sunday after church.

When Holly arrived at the farm, she parked near the lilac bushes. Grabbing the gift for the new arrival, she headed toward the house.

Rose stood at the table, cutting up what was left of a roast. "Dinner is still warm, Holly. Do you want me to fix you a plate?"

Holly shook her head. "I just finished a protein bar."

Rose sighed. "Protein bars aren't natural."

Holly ignored her mother's comment. "Where is everybody?"

"Thomas and the boys are taking a nap upstairs. Beth and the baby are on the porch."

Holly tiptoed through the quiet house, where she found the girls clustered around Beth, holding the baby on the swing. "Hi, everybody."

"Hi, Holly." Beth motioned to a spot on the swing. "Can you squeeze in here?"

Riley, her bright eyes fixed on the baby's tiny fingers, sat next to the twins and closest to the bundle in Beth's arms. "She's so little."

Holly squeezed Beth's shoulder, unable to speak for a moment. This niece she would know from birth. "She's beautiful, Beth. What's her name?"

"Josephine Rose." She set the swing rocking as the baby's nose wrinkled and the tiny fingers resting on the cheek stretched and then relaxed.

"That's a big name for a little girl, but

she'll grow into it." Easing onto the swing next to Rosalyn, Holly rested her hand on the baby's blanket. She stroked the baby's hand and marveled at the softness of the perfect skin. "I brought you something." She handed the bag to Beth.

"You shouldn't have. This is our third baby, Holly." Beth tossed her long braid over her shoulder.

"But your first girl."

Peeking into the bag, Beth giggled. "I should have known." She pulled out a stuffed horse. "I love it."

Holly tilted her head toward Riley and raised her brows. "Why...?"

Riley was still occupied with the baby, and Carolyn lowered her voice. "Erma is on a bus trip and her dad, I don't know, maybe working. She and the twins have been spending a lot of time together so I offered to have her spend the day with us."

"I don't have a gift," Riley said.

Beth laughed and gave her a tight squeeze. "That's okay, munchkin. We already have lots of baby things for Josephine."

Riley touched a finger to the baby's cheek where Holly's had been a moment before. "She's soft."

Holly put her hands on her niece's shoulders, torn between watching the baby sleep and visiting with the horses. "Are you ready for your first lesson, mademoiselle?"

Jumping from the swing, Rosalyn reached for Holly's hand. "Let's go."

"Can I go?" Riley looked from Carolyn to Holly.

"I don't know..." Carolyn said.

"Please."

"If you come with us, you have to listen when I tell you something. Okay?"

Riley's brows wrinkled for just a moment. "Okay." She reached for her quilt.

"Why don't you leave that, Riley? The barn's kind of dusty."

The little girl looked down at the delicately stitched material, as if unable to decide. Her eyes cleared. "Josephine can have my blanket."

Beth smiled. "We'll keep it until you come back from the barn."

"No, this is my gift to the baby."

Holly and Carolyn stared at each other in shock. Holly ran a hand over Riley's hair. "She'll love it, especially because it's from you."

Though she managed a smile, Riley's

lower lip trembled. Holly's heart went out to the little girl. "Let's go get Twister ready for our lesson."

Walking toward the barn, the two girls chattered about the upcoming lesson. Only after they had brushed and saddled Twister did Riley ask a question. "What should I do?"

Holly turned and faced Riley. "Rosalyn can lead Twister to the paddock. You take my hand." Her nieces and nephews had been around animals all their lives. Riley was another story. "You can sit on the bench and watch. Sometimes the best way to learn is by watching someone else. Okay?"

Riley nodded and slipped her hand into Holly's. If anyone had told her the day Riley was pulling books from the shelves that the girl would voluntarily hold her hand, Holly would have told them they were crazy. But here they were. She gave the little hand a squeeze and settled the girl on the bench before turning to her niece. "Are you ready, Rosalyn?"

Rosalyn stared up at the saddle. "He won't buck, will he?"

"No, and I'll be close by." Twister must look like a giant, she thought, though for a quarter horse he was small. The ponies were even smaller.

Rosalyn's indecision showed on her face. "You promise?"

"I promise."

Holly boosted the girl into the saddle and showed her how to hold the reins.

As was often the case with children, Rosalyn's initial caution dissipated minutes after she was on Twister's back. Holly's biggest problem soon became keeping Rosalyn and her mount at a walk. Whether it was her early exposure to riding, natural ability or just plain youth, Rosalyn quickly grasped the concepts involved in communicating with her horse.

As their lessons progressed, the girl became more and more competent. Thomas fenced off the flattest part of the pasture to use as a riding ring. Every Wednesday evening and Sunday afternoon Holly and Rosalyn saddled Twister. Sometimes Riley was along. Sometimes she wasn't. Holly thought it strange Riley was spending so much time with her brother's family. Twice so far, after Rosalyn left, she had saddled the Welsh cob and ridden him in the paddock. Riding different horses was like driving different cars, and she enjoyed riding both horses.

One Sunday afternoon in early August Holly stood in the middle of the ring while Rosalyn posted, easily moving her body off the saddle and back down in rhythm with the horse's trot. The glare of the lowering sun shining directly in her eyes, Holly pulled down her ball cap. The farm was quiet, the rest of the family having gone to Sonny's pool. Despite the temptation of a pool on a hot day, Riley had stayed. She had kept her promise to listen to Holly.

"She looks great," Mac said.

Holly started, then let out a breath. "How long have you been standing there?" She strolled over, glancing at Rosalyn and Twister rounding the far corner. "Tighten up on the reins a little."

Rosalyn's fingers twitched as she responded to Holly's instruction.

Holly propped an elbow on the top rail, keeping an eye on the girl and the horse. "We're just about finished."

"Daddy." Riley jumped up from the bench, ran to her father and slipped between the rails to wrap her arms around his leg.

A faint smile on his face, Mac pulled his

daughter's ponytail. "I thought you were at the pool with Freddy. I stopped by and they said you were here. Aren't you hot?"

Riley turned from her father to watch the horse trotting along the fence. "A little, but I won't ever learn to ride if I don't watch." Holly lifted her arm to catch Rosalyn's attention. "Walk Twister over to the gate. I'll be there in a minute." Holly squeezed through the rails and came up beside Mac, who had frowned at Riley's comment.

"Daddy, can I ride Twister?" Riley climbed up on the second rail so she could look her father in the eyes.

Mac dragged a hand over his face and tried to smile. "I don't know…"

Riley wore the same expression of wanting she'd had since Rosalyn's first lesson. The *me, too* look.

"Riley's been here for almost all of Rosalyn's lessons, Mac. What if I just lead her around?" She laid a hand on his arm. "Twister's the safest horse she could be on."

"I just didn't want her to…" With a sigh, he gave a short nod.

Dismounting, Rosalyn held the reins as Holly and Riley walked over to the horse.

Lifting the girl into the saddle, Holly adjusted the stirrups. "Ready, cowgirl?"

Her answer was a dazzling smile. Holly winked at her niece, who climbed to the top rail of the fence.

She started at a slow walk, occasionally looking back to gauge Riley's ability to move with the horse. She needn't have worried. Riley looked like she'd been born riding Western, and Holly couldn't help but smile. Dressed in a pink print long-sleeve shirt, blue jeans with daisies on the back pockets and a white riding helmet, she was the picture of happiness.

After a while Holly was having so much fun she forgot Mac was even there. Riley's laughter trailed after them as they walked and trotted around the ring. Finally, Holly propped her hands on her knees as she caught her breath. Wiping a bead of sweat from her brow, she threw Mac a triumphant smile. "Look at your daughter, McAndrews. She's a natural."

Mac shook his head. "I'm not surprised. It's just—"

Holly tried to slow her breathing as she waited for the rest of his sentence. "It's just what?"

Mac stared across the ring. "She looks so much like her mother…" He brought his fist to his chest.

Holly's heart sank. She'd wanted to give father and daughter something to smile about, enjoy together, but she'd hurt him, forced him to once again remember he was a widower.

"I think you've worn Holly out, Riley." With his composure regained, Mac climbed through the fence and reached up to take the girl off the horse.

"One more time, Daddy, please."

Mac shook his head. "Look at Holly, Riley. She's not used to exercise anymore." He sent a wink toward Holly and she couldn't help but grin. "Tell Holly thank you."

Riley put her arms around Mac's neck, her eyes on Twister. "Thank you, Holly. Bye, Twister."

"Do you want help putting him away?"

Holly straightened. "No, Rosalyn will help. You two go on."

Father and daughter disappeared around a corner of the barn. Holly undid the cinch and set the saddle on the top rail to air. Underneath the blanket, patches of sweat had appeared. "That little girl gave us a workout, didn't she, old fella?"

High above, a red-tailed hawk screeched. Squinting into the sun, she spotted its pale belly as it soared overhead, on the hunt for an unsuspecting victim.

As she led the horse around the ring the sweat dried on both of them, and Holly knew one thing: as sure as the leaves change in the fall, Riley would want to ride again.

CHAPTER THIRTEEN

NEITHER SONNY NOR Carolyn was surprised when Rosalyn asked if she could enter the walk/trot class at the county fair. They agreed it would be good experience. Mac was another story. When Riley begged to go with her new friend, Mac resisted, until his mother informed him she had signed up for a three-day bus trip to New Orleans.

Carolyn and Louise agreed to take turns watching the coffee shop during the week while Holly was at the fairgrounds. Holly borrowed Thomas's horse trailer and she, Rosalyn and Riley took Twister to the fairgrounds Sunday. At the last minute Mac offered to come along.

The oddly familiar scents of fried food, hay and farm animals lay over the ramshackle buildings used by the fair committee once a year. Holly could just make out the top of the Ferris wheel at the other end of the grounds, and memories of warm summer nights with family and friends, spending money on carnival rides and games of chance, swept through her mind. *Dad, I'm out of money. Can I have some more? Louise wants to ride the swings again.* And her father would roll his eyes at her mother as he pulled his wallet out of his jeans pocket.

"This stuff doesn't faze him a bit, does it?" Carrying a bale of hay, Mac followed Rosalyn as she led Twister into the horse barns.

Smiling at her memories, Holly looked around the barn, doubting she would see anybody from her youth but looking just the same. "This is old hat for this horse. I think he might be enjoying the attention." Twister's ears pricked as Rosalyn led him into the end stall of the outside aisle. She slipped off his halter and closed the stall door.

"Holly Hoffman, is that you?"

Holly turned as she heard her name and saw a familiar-looking red-haired woman heading her way. "Tiffany?"

Dressed in jeans and a T-shirt, the woman nodded at Holly. "Don't tell me, this is your horse. Twister, isn't it?" She moved closer to the stall. "He looks great. Are you using him for your girls?" She smiled down at Riley, who leaned against Mac's legs.

Her cheeks burned at the understandable conclusion the woman had reached. "My niece Rosalyn is riding Twister. This is Riley. She's Mac's daughter and Mac is…a friend of the family."

"Oh." The woman sized up Mac and stuck out her hand. "Tiffany Clark is my married name even though I'm recently divorced. You remember Rich. Well, the rat cheated on me so I kicked him out." She looked over her shoulder at a redheaded girl standing in front of a stall halfway down the aisle. "That's my daughter, Amy. She's in the walk/trot class on Thursday." She looked down at Rosalyn with a critical eye. "You, too?"

Rosalyn grabbed Holly's hand and nodded.

"Yes, that's the one she's in," Holly said.

The woman put her hands on her hips and took another look at Twister. "Seems like we have a second generation competition going. I hope this old boy's up to it. Good luck. And give me a call sometime."

When Tiffany had strolled back to her daughter, Holly said, "How do women do that?" She suddenly remembered why they'd never become close… Tiffany was a poor loser. She would be friendly and helpful at the beginning of the week and by the time the competitions were over, if Holly had won, which she usually did, Tiffany would ignore her.

"Do what?" Mac asked, leaning against the stall.

"Throw their husbands out. Her husband probably has a hundred pounds on her." Her impish grin told Mac she was joking.

"Why do you ask? Are you looking to throw someone out?" He bumped her shoulder with his.

"Not at the moment."

"I've gotten involved in a few of those types of cases. Not fun, not fun at all." Mac continued to watch Tiffany and her daughter as they decorated their stall. "She seems like a nice lady."

Holly frowned. "Are you kidding? She's a—" Before the word left her mouth she noticed Riley staring at her. "Anyway, I think the 'call me' was for you, cowboy."

Mac grinned. "Yeah, probably. I have that effect on women."

Rosalyn tugged Holly's hand. "Did you used to decorate Twister's stall?"

"I did," Holly said, smiling. "In fact, I brought along Twister's sign. My dad made it one year especially for fair week." Holly slipped a long wooden sign out of a bag and hooked it to the front of the stall. Her father had smoothed and varnished the wood, and her mother had painted Twister's name, as well as colorful miniature tornadoes. Holly caught Mac studying the sign, doubt on his face.

"Twister's barrel racing days are behind him, Mac. He's perfectly happy trotting around the ring."

Mac ran a hand down his nose. "Will he be all right here?"

Holly glanced at the gray horse in the next stall and read the sign with her name. "As long as Good Golly Miss Molly is next door he'll be fine. Twister makes friends easily, especially with the ladies." She kissed his nose. "Don't ya, fella?"

"You kiss your horse?"

"Of course, Riley. He's my best friend."

"Can I kiss him?" Leaning against the gate, Riley stood on her tiptoes.

When Mac nodded, Holly held the girl up until she could reach the horse's nose.

Riley leaned forward and planted a kiss on the gelding's white strip. "I did it!" She turned to Holly with a smile.

"Now he's your best buddy, too." She ran a hand down the horse's nose.

MONDAY EVENING HOLLY closed the store early since the town was practically deserted. Mac was working, so Holly picked up Riley and Rosalyn and drove to the fairgrounds, where they practiced in the ring while everyone else was at dinner. When the ring filled with other riders, they returned Twister to his stall and went in search of dinner.

Holding Riley's hand, Holly stood at the end of a long line of food booths. The sizzle and smell of hot sausage permeated the air, competing with the sweet smell of monkey bread. "What do you think, ladies? What shall we have for dinner?"

Riley stared up at the signs in awe. She took a deep breath. "French fries?"

"Just French fries?" A curly fry stand sat next to the monkey bread vendor. "I don't know if that constitutes a dinner, honey." Riley didn't say anything. She just stared up at Holly. "French fries it is," Holly said and was rewarded with the familiar gap-toothed smile.

Tuesday evening Mac came along and they ended up at the Boy Scout booth eating meat loaf, mashed potatoes and green peas. Rosalyn, her sister and their mother went to see a popular boy band in the grandstand. Their raucous music could be heard all over the fairgrounds. Sitting at a picnic table, Holly nudged Riley in the side. "Don't tell Daddy what we had for dinner last night," she whispered.

Riley giggled, her eyes sparkling as she stuck a chunk of meat loaf in her mouth.

Sitting across from them, Mac narrowed his eyes. "All right, you two, what are you whispering about?"

Holly waved a fork in the air. "Having a private conversation here—you just eat your meat loaf."

Mac shook his head. "You two are wearing me out. Are we doing this tomorrow, too?"

"We don't have to. The fair lasts Sunday through Saturday, but most people with animals come every day. I was thinking about giving Twister a bath tomorrow afternoon."

Riley's gaze jerked from Holly to her father. "Can I help?"

Mac shrugged. "It's up to Holly whether—"

"Sure, why not?" She elbowed Riley's shoulder. "Just a heads-up. You might get a little wet. And dirty. And—"

"Hello, Chief McAndrews."

Mac's eyebrows bunched as he shook the woman's hand. "Ma'am. Have we met?"

Her laugh was like church bells, soft and musical. "You wouldn't remember. I was getting my hair cut at Hair Today. You came in to ask Megan if she was missing anything."

Mac's eyes lit in recognition. "Right. Now I remember."

"I'm Laura Norton. I'm the new first-grade teacher at the elementary school."

Holly studied the slim young woman standing at the end of the picnic table. Wavy, honey-blond hair ended in a gentle curve at her shoulders. Dressed in a pair of khakis and a fitted coral shirt, the woman was a breath of fresh air in a sea of blue jeans and T-shirts. One hand rested on the handle of a stroller, where a wide-eyed toddler sprawled.

"Will your daughter be in first grade this year?" Laura asked.

Mac's gaze darted from the schoolteacher to Riley and back again. "Well, we haven't decided yet if she's going back to her grandparents in North Carolina."

Laura leaned down and gave Riley a smile. "If you stay, I hope you're in my class."

Riley smiled shyly.

Laura tugged the sleeve of Mac's T-shirt. "You look different out of uniform. Friendlier." Her laugh drifted over the chatter of the nearby patrons. "This is my nephew," she said. "My sister-in-law just had a baby. I'm giving her a little break."

"I'm sure she appreciates the help." Holly didn't miss the admiring glance the young woman threw Mac's way. Mac had been the object of much interest in the barns, where women dominated the population.

"I don't mind. I miss the kids in the summer. I'll be glad when school starts. Nice meeting you." With a nod to Holly and a smile for Mac and Riley, the teacher moved on.

"I like her. Can I go to school here, Daddy?" Riley forked a chunk of meat loaf into her mouth.

"She's nice," Holly said. "Perfect, in fact." Exactly the type of woman Mac was looking for. Her appetite gone, she pushed away her plate. Watching Mac with another woman might be harder than she'd thought.

THURSDAY MORNING, TWISTER stood freshly bathed in the open area between the barn and the ring, his bay coat and black mane and tail gleaming in the morning sun. Holly stroked his neck as she and Sonny waited for Rosalyn to put on her boots. "You'd never know you're twenty-five, old boy. You take care of this girl, do you hear me?"

Twister's ears flicked back and forth. Holly laid her cheek on the soft hair of his neck and breathed in the familiar scent of horseflesh and leather. The saddle, the same one Holly had used as a young rider, glistened.

"I'm ready, Aunt Holly." Rosalyn stood next to the stirrup. Her thick chestnut hair was tied at her neck with a blue ribbon. A narrow leather belt engraved with daisy designs surrounded her small waist.

"Rosalyn, you look great." Holly's heart melted at the pleased grin on her niece's face. "You'll do amazing. Remember, Twister knows what he's doing. Trust him. Don't get nervous." She sat back on her heels and studied the girl's face.

"I'm not nervous, Aunt Holly." Rosalyn strapped her helmet under her chin. "Dad says riding's in my blood."

Holly caught Sonny's eye. "I reckon he's right about that, little one." She stood. "Let's get you on this horse."

Rosalyn put her boot in her father's joined

hands and he hefted her into the saddle. She barely touched the seat before she picked up the reins. Shoulders back, hands relaxed, she faced the announcer's stand.

Holly grabbed Sonny's arm and backed away. "We'll be along the fence." They walked to one side of the entrance. Fritz, Rose, Carolyn and her children, and Riley sat halfway up the bleachers set on the back side of the ring. Behind the bleachers a small stream flowed and on the other side a patch of woods provided shade for half the ring.

Rosalyn nodded at them, and then returned her gaze to the ring, where the judges handed out ribbons for the previous class. To polite applause and a few whistles, the students exited through the open gate.

Twister and Rosalyn were third into the ring. As each horse and rider entered, the judge announced their names. Rosalyn sat straight in the saddle, her elbows tight to her side, and looked ahead. The class of nine circled the ring, alternately walking and trotting as the announcer directed.

Holly leaned on the fence. "What do you think, brother?"

"Is it just me or is she the best rider in the group?"

Holly smiled. "It might just be you...but she is good." Fifteen minutes later they were proved right when Rosalyn and Twister got a red ribbon for second place.

Holly elbowed Sonny in the ribs. "Not bad for four weeks of training." She caught sight of Tiffany and her daughter as they accepted a ribbon for fourth place. "Tiffany tries too hard. That's too much horse for a little girl."

They spent the rest of the day at the fair. The family wandered around the displays of canned goods, flowers and vegetables set up in the many buildings. Mac found them midafternoon just as Riley had lost interest in the displays. She wanted to go on the rides and Mac bought a long string of red tickets. Folding the tickets in a neat pile, he murmured, "I should arrest these guys for robbery. The prices are outrageous."

Holly pushed him through the gate to the merry-go-round. "Riley's having a good time."

Mac turned halfway through the gate. "Hey, I'm not riding."

Riley grabbed his belt and pulled. "Come on, Daddy, you can ride with me."

Mac made a face before handing the scruffy-looking guy at the gate a handful of tickets. He followed Riley to the carousel, lifted her up on a horse and swung a leg over one nearby. Rosalyn climbed on a black horse and waved at her aunt.

Holly moved along the makeshift fence, watching the three as the carousel picked up speed. Riley was talking a mile a minute and the broad smile on Mac's face showed how much, despite his protest, he was enjoying the ride with his daughter. She thought back to the night of the fireworks, of Mac's stiffness when Riley had climbed onto his lap. Little by little, he was changing, softening.

Holly thought of Tiffany's assumption they were a family and for the first time, she entertained the possibility. Riley was easy to love. She was an inquisitive, active, loving little girl. Mac was easy to love, too. No trace of the taunting boy from gym class remained.

The carousel slowed and came to a stop. Mac lifted Riley off the horse. Feet moving before they touched the ground, Riley ran up to Holly.

"Can we go to the swings next?" Without waiting for an answer, Riley took off, with Rosalyn close behind.

Mac jogged after her, talking over his

shoulder. "This one's yours, Holly. I don't do swings."

Dressed in jeans and a casual shirt, Mac looked like any other father on an outing with his child. His hair was longer now, the blond streaks becoming more noticeable thanks to the summer sun. Holly followed them to the next ride and, after getting rid of more tickets, lifted Riley into a swing, hooked the chain across the front and settled into the outside swing next to her. Rosalyn insisted on getting herself into a swing.

A man approached Mac at the fence and they shook hands. Mac waved to get Holly's attention and he said something she didn't catch.

Hands grasping the chains of the swing, Holly leaned forward. "What?"

He pointed to Riley. "Keep an eye on her. I'll be back." He turned and followed the other man down the midway until he disappeared into the crowd.

Not until they had gained height did she take her eyes off Riley. In the ring, a halter class was underway. The smell of popcorn hung in the air and her grumbling stomach reminded her they had skipped lunch. The swings were losing altitude when she spotted a familiar hulking form in front of one of the games of chance. Moose Williams, a toy rifle dwarfed by his big hands, took aim at a line of moving ducks. She was about to look away when she saw a flash of blond hair standing just behind him. Moose had a girlfriend?

When the swings came to a stop she slipped out of her chair and helped Riley and Rosalyn get down. Both girls raced for the exit. Holly hurried behind. "Wait for me, girls."

They disappeared into the crowd. Holly's heart pounded as she ran after them. When she saw Rosalyn's curly ponytail and a mop of blond hair next to her, she breathed a sigh of relief. She wove through the throng and walked up to the stand. "I know you're double digits, kid, but don't run off next time. I thought I lost you two." She looked down at the little blonde girl next to Rosalyn. Only the child wasn't Riley. "Where's Riley?"

"She was right behind me," Rosalyn said. "She wanted to see the jewelry."

Holly's heart jumped into her throat. She spun around, looking for Riley's blond ponytail. Pushing through the crowd, she ran straight into Mac.

He gripped her shoulders. "What's wrong?"

"I can't find Riley." Once again she had failed.

Mac's hands dropped as he started looking in each direction. He raised his hand and pointed. "There."

Tapping Rosalyn on the shoulder to let her know it was time to go, Holly followed Mac through the crowd to a building. A goldfish Ping-Pong game was set up in the entrance. Riley stood pressed against the wire enclosure, watching entranced as white plastic balls bounced from one small fishbowl to the next.

Mac stood behind his daughter, taking slow, deliberate breaths when Holly and Rosalyn arrived.

The child hadn't gone far, but Holly had lost her. How could Mac ever forgive her?

CHAPTER FOURTEEN

FRIDAY MORNING MAC found Holly with her legs flung over the arm of one of her comfortable chairs, reading a paperback. "No customers this morning?" He went behind the counter and poured a cup of coffee before settling into the chair across from her.

Holly turned a page. "Everyone's either at the fair or getting ready to go to the fair."

"Are you going out to take care of Twister later?"

"Nope. Thomas and his gang are going this afternoon and he and the boys will check on Twister."

"They're taking a newborn to the fair?"

Mac finally got a reaction from Holly. She lowered her legs to the floor and set her book facedown on the table. "Yes. Mac…"

Mac held up his hand. "Forget about it. Water under the bridge."

Holly's eyes widened. "For goodness' sake, Mac, I lost your daughter. I feel awful. I'm such a failure with children it's a wonder my family lets me around their kids. That was the longest two minutes of my life."

She was right, of course. He knew better than anyone the risk of child abductions at an event like a county fair. He shook his head. All the more reason to find the right person to become a mother for his daughter. At the same time, he understood Holly's despair. The same thing could easily have happened to him.

Holly's shop was in perfect order. All the tables were wiped clean, the books and magazines were on their shelves and the pastry case was full. He sipped his coffee, his thoughts returning to the afternoon when he, Riley, Rosalyn and Holly had gone on all the rides Riley was tall enough for. He had always thought fun was a fishing trip with the guys, but he had to admit, he'd enjoyed himself more than he'd thought possible. After her initial coldness, Riley seemed to have accepted Holly's presence in their lives.

Holly's book was still facedown on her lap. The cover showed a cowboy on a horse. "You're reading a Western novel?"

"Louis L'Amour. His books are classics. I've never taken the time to read them before." She flipped the book over and turned another page.

"I wanted to thank you again for letting Riley tag along with you and Rosalyn." He caught a brief flash of green eyes as Holly glanced up and then back at her book.

"I enjoyed it. Twister did, too." She rested the closed book on her stomach as she stared at the ceiling. "That's something else I haven't taken the time for lately—riding." She sighed. "I've been home six months and not once did I take Twister for a ride. The girls reminded me how special horses are, you know?" She tipped her head, a question in her eyes. "What was the mare's name? Frosty's dam, I mean."

The sudden change of subject took Mac by surprise. He took a deep breath and exhaled completely before answering. "Black Coffee Morning."

"You're kidding."

"Nope."

Holly waited, as if hoping he'd continue the story. When Mac remained silent, she prompted him. "How did the horse get its name?"

Mac drummed his fingers on the arm of the chair. "Anne's father liked cream and sugar in his coffee, but when the mares were getting ready to foal, he wouldn't have time to fix his coffee the way he liked. So he used to say 'this is going to be a black coffee morning.'"

"What a great name," Holly said. "So what's Frosty's paper name?"

"Frosty Morning."

She glanced down at her paperback. "I like those names. I'm surprised she gelded Frosty."

Mac nodded. "I know. But he was the mare's fifth foal. Anne bred her right after Riley was born and intended…" He closed his eyes and let out a breath.

"You know, Mac, not using a beautiful animal like Frosty for his intended purpose is like…like not letting the public visit the Sistine Chapel. Beauty, and talent, should be appreciated."

"You're riding him. Isn't that enough?" Mac stared into the depths of his cup. His intention that morning was to warn Holly his daughter was becoming too attached, but now he wondered if it wasn't the other way around. "Holly—"

"Good morning, you two. Lovely day." Mayor Gold strode into the room, battered thermos in hand. "Don't get up, Holly, I'll just help myself and give you—" she dug into her pants pocket and dropped coins onto the counter "—the right change."

Mac grinned at Holly. "Pretty soon you won't even need to come in."

"They still need me for the espresso drinks." She rose and replaced her book on the shelf. "Thanks, Mayor."

Holly walked to the cash register and rang up the coffee. At twenty-eight, she was the woman the girl had promised to be...strong, independent, fearless. He had made the right decision that long-ago day. Holly ran a hand through her dark hair. "Are you letting your hair grow, Holly?"

She frowned and ran a hand through her hair again. "I was thinking about it. Why?"

Mac shrugged. "No reason. It looks nice."

"Thanks. I'll be in the kitchen if anyone needs anything."

The door swung closed and the only sound in the coffee shop was the crinkle of the mayor turning the pages of the newspaper. "Did you hear about the copper stolen from the construction site up on the mountain?"

"I did."

"Any leads?" She turned another page.

"Not so far."

She sighed. "People get desperate sometimes."

"Doesn't make it right, Mayor."

"I know." She folded the paper and poured coffee from the thermos into the lid, shaped like a cup. "Did you know I used to be married?"

Mac shook his head, wondering where she was going with the sudden change of subject. "No."

The mayor sipped her coffee and settled back in her chair. "Leon and I were married twenty-two years." She looked at Mac over the rim of her cup. "I'll bet you're surprised to hear that, aren't you? Someone like me being married."

"Not at all, Mayor."

"He died of cancer." She swirled the coffee in her cup. "I was devastated, still pretty young, just in my forties. I didn't think I could ever find anyone like him so I didn't bother looking. I've spent the last twenty years alone."

Mac didn't know quite what to make of the mayor's unexpected revelations. So far their encounters had been about recycling and the vacant lot. But he and the mayor had far more in common than he'd realized.

"I was right, you know. I wouldn't have found anyone like Leon. What I wish I'd known then is that I could've found someone else to love. I thought loving someone else meant I didn't love him as much, and that's just not true, you know?"

"My father died of cancer." As soon as the words were out of his mouth he wished he could take them back.

She focused on her coffee, somehow knowing Mac didn't want eye contact. "How old were you?"

Leaning forward and resting his arms on his thighs, Mac said, "Fifteen. We moved here a couple months after he passed away." At a loud crash from the kitchen, Mac jerked his head up. But the swinging door remained closed. He thought of meeting Chris, then the rest of the Hoffman family, and finally Holly, the apple of her father's eye.

Deb upended the cup, then reached for a napkin. "You never get over losing someone you love. You can move forward, but you never forget." Wiping the last of the coffee from the thermos lid, she strolled over to the door. "Look at those roses. Why, they're just a riot of blooms."

Mac joined her in the doorway. On one side of the vacant lot was the town library, and its boundary was marked with a wooden fence covered by old-fashioned pink tea roses. "Lots of thorns, too."

Deb elbowed him in the side. "The sweetest fragrance comes with a few thorns." She opened the door and walked out onto the porch. "They've grown next to the library ever since I can remember. We have to do something with the lot, Mac, money or no money." She set her thermos in the basket of her scooter and buckled on her helmet. "We'll think of something one of these days. Take care, Chief." She motored down the street.

Mac opened the door of his SUV. Across the street a cherry-red pickup idled in front of the bank, Ethan Johnson behind the wheel. Tom stood in the street talking to his son. Mac shook his head, unable to imagine being the father of a teenager. He envied the boy in the truck, then in a flash of insight wondered if he had envied Holly the year following his father's death.

The apple of her daddy's eye.

HOLLY BROUGHT TWISTER home Saturday afternoon. The rain started just as Holly unloaded him. She hooked him to the cross ties in the barn to undo his tail, braided for the fair. His reddish-brown hair was slick with water.

Hearing the door slide open, Holly turned, expecting Rosalyn.

Instead, Riley stood in the doorway. "Do you want some help?" She wore a bright green rain slicker.

"Hi, Riley. Is your grandmother with you?"

Taking a tiny step into the barn, the girl shook her head. "Rosalyn's mom picked me up because Grandma wanted to go grocery shopping."

Holly picked through the tool caddy for the water scraper. "And where is your buddy? I thought you two girls were joined at the hip."

Riley finally smiled. "She fell asleep on the couch when we were watching a movie."

"I see." The faint smile disappeared, and Holly knew one sure way to bring it back. "I was hoping someone would show up. I mean, look at the size of this guy. I could be here all day drying him off."

Riley's face lit with excitement. "I can help you."

"Are you sure? I mean, if you want to go

back inside I guess I can dry him myself even though it will probably take all day." Holly let loose a sigh.

Riley skipped closer and laid a hand on Twister's nose. "What should we do first?"

"We better dry him off some." Holly picked up a scraper and sluiced some water from the horse's broad back.

"Can I do that?" Unsnapping her raincoat, she hung the coat on a hook, then stood next to Holly.

Holly looked around the barn, wondering about the best way for Riley to reach the horse's back. She finally picked her up and settled her on her hip. "When your horse is wet, use a scraper to get the majority of the water off, then you can use a towel." She demonstrated once before Riley reached for the scraper and placed one hand on the horse's withers as she scraped with the other.

The little girl's face was a mask of concentration, her lips pressed tightly together. Her weight was negligible and it struck Holly what Anne must have looked like, small and fine boned. She took the scraper from Riley's hand and handed her a towel. "Try this now."

When the horse was as dry as they could get him with the one towel, Holly showed

Riley how to pick up the horse's foot and clean out debris, but didn't allow her to try. She handed the girl a comb and set her at the rump, working on Twister's tail while she combed the mane. The rain drummed on the metal roof of the building and the scent of hay hung heavy over the barn. Whoever would have thought she'd end up babysitting Mac's daughter? At least here, on her family's farm, Riley was safe.

Holly stood back and surveyed her horse, dozing as they worked on him, one foot propped on the hoof edge as he relaxed. "He looks good, Riley."

Riley stepped back, still holding on to the horse's black tail, the hairs feathering out from her hands. "I should brush Frosty, too." Her brow furrowed. "Even though Daddy said I can't ride him, I should take care of him. Right?"

Holly debated answering. She wasn't sure how Mac would handle Riley working with her horse. She also didn't know how the gelding handled since she hadn't actually ridden him yet. Although now she knew Mac didn't mind. "I'll tell you what, Riley. Let me work with Frosty first. Okay?"

At Riley's agreement they grabbed a blue

halter and headed out to the pasture. They approached the gelding easily and Holly led the horse into the barn. Tying him to the stall bars with a quick-release knot, she nodded at Riley. "You sit on those hay bales while I get to know your horse."

Riley climbed on the stack of bales and sat cross-legged at the top. "Frosty's five years old, same as me."

Holly ran both hands across the withers of the cream-colored gelding and along his back. "He is? Do you know when his birthday is?"

Riley was silent for a moment. "How do we know when his birthday is?"

Holly ran a hand down the horse's leg. "From his papers. Your dad must have his papers."

"You mean like newspapers?"

Holly laughed. "No, papers are the horse's birth certificate. They tell you who the mother and father were."

"You mean like my birth certificate has my mommy's name and my daddy's name?"

"Yes, just like that."

After running her hands over the gelding's legs and getting no reaction, Holly rubbed both ears. Frosty dipped his nose and stared at her. Holly studied the beautiful animal, taking in the blue eyes, pink skin and coffee-colored markings on the mane and tail. "Did your family own Frosty's mother?"

"Yes. Frosty's mommy is black. She lives with Grandma and Grandpap Drake."

So this was no accidental mating. Anne had known exactly what she was doing when she bred his parents. Holly felt newfound respect for the woman she would never meet.

She wiped the excess rain from the animal and then toweled him dry. Working first on the mane, she smoothed the tangles and brushed out the thick, dark-tipped hair. He stood as Twister had earlier, one hind foot tipped on its edge, eyes half-closed, as if he was at a spa. This animal was perfect for a young girl. Holly shook her head as she curried and brushed. The hard part would be convincing Riley's father. But now the fair was over, she looked forward to having the time to work with Riley's horse. She could hardly wait. After all, Sunday afternoons were open.

She stood back. "What do you think, Riley?"

Riley eased down from the hay bales and approached Frosty's nose, running one small hand down the length. "He looks beautiful." She sighed.

Holly pulled on the end of the lead rope and it slipped free of the bars. Sliding off the halter, she patted the gelding on the rump. "Go back to your friends, fella."

Riley followed the horse to the end of the barn and stood looking out at the pasture. Turning, she tilted her head. "It stopped raining, Holly. Can we go for a walk?"

Holly closed the big doors. "Sure. But you better put on your raincoat in case it starts again." They left through the front of the barn and walked down the lane.

Although the rain had stopped, the air was humid. Dark clouds hung over the ridge tops. They walked down the lane in silence.

Riley hung her head as she kicked at stones with her boots.

"You're awfully quiet."

Riley stopped in the middle of the lane and stared up at Holly. The little girl's face was as serious as a little girl could get and this time, Holly wondered if she was seeing Anne in Riley's expressive, light blue eyes. "Frosty's a good horse, isn't he?"

Crouching so she was on the same level as Riley, Holly nodded. "Without training him,

I can't be sure, but from what I've seen today, he seems to be a good horse."

"Mommy wanted me to ride him, right?"

Avoiding the intense look in Riley's eyes, Holly looked down the lane, which was rarely used since Thomas had installed a macadam drive on the other side of the house. The ruts contained traces of gravel, but the center was one long strip of grass and weeds. Unchanged since she was a girl, the little stream still ran alongside only to drain into Old Woman's Run and later into Little Bear Creek. Holly dropped a knee to the wet grass and rested her hands on Riley's shoulders. "That was her plan, Riley, but sometimes things change and it's nobody's fault."

Riley hung her head and scuffed her toe in the wet grass. "I guess."

Holly stood and took the girl's hand in hers. "I have something to show you."

Rarely mowed, weeds grew high along the lane. The stretch of jewelweed—growing in the damp soil since Holly was a girl—was still in the same spot. Tubular stalks with blade-like leaves and slipper-shaped speckled orange flowers leaned into the lane and over the trickling stream.

Holding the girl's small hand in hers, Holly

led Riley to the edge of the road and knelt. Pulling Riley close, she cupped the delicate orange flower in her palm. "This is called jewelweed. My grandmother used to call it touch-me-not."

Riley touched the blossom with a tiny, tentative stroke and gave a faint smile. "It's pretty." She bent to see the flower from the bottom. "It has spots all over."

Holly looked through the mass of green until she found what she was looking for. Reaching into the weeds, she pulled the stem toward her until a translucent green pod hung in front of them. "This is where the seeds are stored. When it pops, the seeds spring out over the ground and then next year, the plant grows again."

Riley nodded and frowned as if unsure where she was going with her lesson.

"My grandma showed me this, and now I'm showing you. It's our secret." Holly searched through the greenery for a plump seedpod. The touch-me-not flower always reminded her of her connection to her grandmother, gone almost fifteen years. If Mac married and Holly no longer saw Riley, they would still have this connection, maybe not through blood, like she and her grandmother, but through memories. Touch-me-not memories.

Holly took the little girl's hand. "Take your thumb and your forefinger—" she folded Riley's other three fingers against her palm and, Riley's hand in hers, reached out "—and give the seedpod a little pinch—"

Riley laughed as the outer layers of the plant curled up and the seeds bounced off her palm. "That tickles, Holly."

Holly laughed. "I know."

Riley, still on her knees, straightened and leaned into the greenery, searching for another pod. "How's this one, Holly?"

"Find a fat one, where you can almost see the seeds inside. There's a good one."

At Riley's pinch, another burst of seeds went flying. Holly wrapped her arms around the little girl, and Riley's laughter echoed in the warm summer rain.

CHAPTER FIFTEEN

IF HEARTS COULD BREAK, Mac's would have been in tiny pieces at his feet where he stood watching his daughter laughing with Holly.

He had planned on fishing at the lake with friends but the more he thought about it, the more he wanted to be with his family. Thinking he would surprise them and take them out to lunch after church, he arrived home to find both Riley and his mother gone. Standing in the quiet kitchen, he came to the realization something was wrong. Any father who didn't know where his five-year-old was had a problem. Three phone calls later, he tracked his daughter to the Hoffman farm. Finding the horse barn empty, he headed down the abandoned lane.

He'd been about to call out when he saw Holly kneeling beside Riley, lifting her chin with one finger. Whatever they had been discussing, he hadn't wanted to interrupt.

Mac tried not to think about his feelings

for Holly. He tried not to think about what, besides the coffee, drew him to The Wildflower every morning. He had convinced himself two old friends could spend time together.

But when he saw Holly holding his daughter, Anne's daughter, in her arms, he realized he couldn't kid himself anymore. Holly was talking to Riley as any mother would, and Riley was holding her as any little girl would, seeking comfort from a mother. But Holly was nothing like Anne.

By the time he reached them, Riley was laughing at the exploding seedpods. "This looks familiar."

Holly's eyes glistened. "You remember?"

Mac knelt, keeping Riley between them. "Sure, I remember." He reached out and lifted a particularly fat pod from the greenery. "Look at this one, Riley."

Riley leaned over and carefully eased her fingers around the pod. She squealed with delight at the explosion.

Mac smiled, remembering Riley as a toddler, screeching in delight at the antics of her grandparents' two golden retrievers. Watching the two of them, Holly and Riley, search through the greenery for fat seedpods, he re-

alized he hadn't heard his daughter's unin-
hibited laughter in a long time.

Until now. Until Holly.

HOLLY COULDN'T BRING herself to look at Mac
when he showed up, two days later, early on a
rainy Monday. She busied herself behind the
counter, filling the plates in the pastry case
and topping off the espresso beans. The third
time she exited the kitchen, a stack of plates
in her hands, Mac stood next to the cash register, one hand on each counter, blocking her
way.

"Are you talking or what?"

Holly pushed his arm with her shoulder
but she might as well be pushing an oak tree.
Mac wasn't moving.

She set the plates on the counter next to
the coffeepots. "I'm just distracted. The fair
is over so I figured I might be busy today."
She picked up the stack of plates and waited
for Mac to move.

"I'm not buyin' what you're sellin'." Mac
pressed his lips together and maintained his
immovable stance. "Why aren't you talking
to me today?"

Holly set the plates down again and sat on
the stool that had become Mac's usual spot.

Staring at his tanned face and bright blue eyes only took her back to the Mac she knew at seventeen and now, the Mac she knew at thirty. Both of them were dangerous. So here she was. "The touch-me-nots made me think about…"

The awareness in Mac's eyes told her he knew exactly what she was talking about. His voice was soft. "That was a long time ago, Holly. We were kids."

"When you saw Riley and me on the lane, you looked upset."

Mac turned away then, dropping his hands from the counters. "Yeah, I was a bit surprised to see the two of you like that, so close, I mean. I guess I hadn't realized—"

"—that we've become attached?" The churning in her stomach that only Mac could create was starting. He didn't want her around his daughter.

"You two didn't hit it off at first." He turned to face her. "She shouldn't be getting attached to you, she should be—"

Holly held up a hand. Mac had been about to say Riley should get attached to a new mother, not a family friend who happened to share a love of horses. "How's your dating going, Mac? Have you found anyone who meets your standards?" *Why is he so set on having someone home when the kid gets out of school? Of having someone who knows how to braid hair? I braid Twister's tail. Doesn't that count?*

Mac grabbed his cup and headed for the door. "I need some time to think, Holly. I'll see you around." He slammed the door so hard the bell fell to the floor.

You and me both, buddy.

Holly didn't bother to grab the bell, and it was still there when Louise came at eight.

"What's the bell doing in the middle of the floor?" Dragging a stool over to the door, Louise replaced the bell on its hanger, then brushed her hands together as if satisfied with a job well done.

Holly chuckled. Shaking herself out of her reverie, she focused on Louise, whose short blond curls looked suddenly familiar in the bright light of the café. "Were you at the fair on Thursday?"

Louise shrugged and took her purse into the kitchen. Catching the backswing of the door, she flew past Holly. "Maybe. Who wants to know?"

Before Holly could quiz her a short, muscular, dark-haired man backed into the shop with a large tray in his hands. "Which one of you is Holly?"

Holly jumped off the stool. "I am. What can I do for you?"

"I'm Matt McClain. My wife, Dottie, is helping Sue with the baking. She said you'd probably need some raisin-filled cookies first thing this morning."

"I do," Holly said. She lifted the edge of the towel covering the tray and the sweet aroma of just-out-of-the-oven cookies filled the room. "Matt, they smell fantastic. Just set them on the counter. Should I pay you?"

Matt set the tray on the counter and wiped his hands on his jeans. "No, ma'am, just pay Sue, as usual. We appreciate the work, especially since the factory shut down." He waved a hand in the air. "Nothing much a forty-year-old electronics technician is good for except electronics and delivering cookies." With a wry grin he turned to go.

"Matt, I think your son comes in here, with the Johnson boy?"

"He does? Yeah, those two have been friends since grade school. Once kids get their driver's licenses it's hard to keep track of them, you know." With his hand on the doorknob, he turned back. "He's not causing you any trouble, is he?"

"Not at all. Is he in sports at the high school?"

"He's a wrestler and a senior this year. We're hoping for a scholarship." He held up crossed fingers.

"I thought so. Well, good luck, and thank your wife for the cookies. Nice meeting you." The bell over the door rang once and he was gone.

Holly turned. "As I was saying, Weaz—"

The door jerked opened and the bell clattered to the floor, rolling to a stop at her feet.

Once again, the sun was blocked as a huge shape filled the doorway. "Goodness, I'm sorry, ma'am. Did I do that?" Moose Williams stared down at the bell resting at Holly's feet.

"You wouldn't be the first man to knock this bell off its perch." She held out the ringer. "No harm done, though. Could you hang it back up?"

"Yes, ma'am." He hooked the bell easily over the hanger, took off his hat and, holding it in front of him, glanced at Louise. "Good morning, ma'am." Two bright red spots appeared on his chubby cheeks. "I thought I'd come in for a coffee this morning."

Holly stood in the middle of the room, her eyes darting from the officer to her friend, who kept looking over her shoulder at the man as she filled a disposable cup. Suddenly a light went on in her head. Louise and Moose were at the fair together. *Talk about keeping secrets from your friend...*

Louise slipped a raisin-filled cookie from under the towel and dropped it into a treat bag. Pushing the coffee and cookie across the counter, she took the five-dollar bill from Moose with a smile. "I had fun last week, Rob."

The big man's eyes were glued to her face. "Even getting caught in the rain?"

Louise batted her blue eyes at the bashful man in front of her. "Especially getting caught in the rain."

Moose blushed. "The fair's over. What else would you like to do?"

Louise placed the change in the officer's hand, holding on to his fingers a split second longer than necessary. "Well, the amusement park is serving a spaghetti dinner on Wednesday. Why don't we check it out and then walk around the park?"

Moose pulled his hand away in slow motion and stuffed his change in his pocket.

"I'd like that. Can I pick you up at six?" He backed toward the door.

"Watch the—"

Moose backed into the display table, and two bags of coffee beans bounced onto the floor.

"I'm sorry, ma'am." His face fell.

Holly picked up the bags. "No problem, Moose. They're not breakable, and call me Holly." She replaced the beans as Moose, with a last look and a smile for Louise, backed out the door.

"Louise—"

Elbows on the counter and chin propped in her hands, Louise stared out the window as the officer crossed the wet street and climbed into the police truck. "Hmm?"

"His name is Rob?"

"Robert." She slowly straightened. "What? You think you're the only one who likes a man in uniform?"

"My goodness, Weaz, the man makes two of you, no, probably three of you."

Louise waggled a forefinger in the air. "Don't worry, Holly, I've got him wrapped around my little—" she stared at her hand before dropping the second digit and waving her pinkie "—finger."

"And he's younger than you. Mac said he just got out of the academy. There's probably a law against you cradle-robbing the poor guy."

Louise sashayed to the window and turned, hands on hips, head tilted. "He's over twenty-one and well versed in the law. And who are you to talk? You spent all last week with the handsome chief of police, so why begrudge me a little fun, hmm? At least I'm not analyzing things to death. You're not open to possibilities. Once your mind is made up there's no changing it."

"You don't understand." Holly settled onto the stool, Mac's last words uppermost in her mind.

Louise grabbed a bar towel and wiped an already clean counter. "Take ice cream, for instance."

Holly rubbed her eyes with her thumb and forefinger, waiting for her friend to make her point.

"I had a roommate once who said we could microwave ice cream. I told her she was crazy because who would think of microwaving ice cream." She squinted and shrugged her shoulders. "Ice cream melts, right? So one night we're digging into this half gallon of butter pecan and it's hard as a rock. So she sticks the carton in the microwave and I about had a heart attack."

Leaning against the wall, Holly hooked her feet on the rungs of the stool. "Get to the point, Weaz."

Louise held up her hands, palms out. "That is my point. I had never considered microwaving ice cream because I thought it would melt. But my roommate did it for about fifteen seconds and it was perfect dipping consistency, soft and creamy." She licked her lips. "You need to be open to new possibilities, Holly, things you may never even have considered in the past."

"Like you and Moose."

"Like me and Rob." Louise took her time folding the towel. "I've been a widow for almost three years, Holly, and away from nursing just as long. You think I'm not afraid to start living again?" She laid the towel next to the cash register and pressed her hands to her cheeks. "I'm scared to death, but I've got my whole life ahead of me."

Holly nodded. So what if Louise and Moose Williams dated? They were certainly an odd couple, but Holly was no expert in the realm of romance.

Did her friend's ice cream analogy apply to her? Had she closed her mind to the possibility of a relationship with Mac because he had a child?

THE RAIN CONTINUED until late Tuesday night. Wednesday morning Holly walked to work through a dense fog. Cooled by the thunderstorm, the air felt damp and fresh.

Katherine King showed up around eight, this time wearing a pale blue linen shift with matching jacket. Pearl studs graced her ears. Even though Holly knew she wasn't Mac's wife, the sight of her always brought Anne to mind. The woman requested her usual nonfat cappuccino, extra hot, and settled into one of the plush chairs, her laptop on a corner of the table.

Wednesdays were typically slow. With everything caught up, Holly wandered around the shop, wiping already clean tables and rearranging her cup display. The bell over the door jangled and Wendy Valentine walked in carrying her ever-present briefcase. "Hi, Wendy."

"Hi, Holly." Wendy approached Katherine and shook her hand. "Ms. King, nice to see you again." She glanced over her shoulder and said, "Could I have a nonfat vanilla latte?"

"Sure." Holly nodded, surprised Wendy knew the visitor. This threw a whole new slant on things. So much for Louise's speculation she was a country and western singer looking for a getaway home in the foothills of the Alleghenies. She made Wendy's drink and carried it over to the table. Katherine smiled at her. "Wendy tells me you just opened this spring."

Holly smiled and smoothed the front of her apron. In an attempt to hide the milk splash, she flattened her hand over her middle. She couldn't imagine these two women ever needing to cover a splotch. "Yes, we opened in May. I was in the air force for ten years and decided to return home and try something different."

Katherine nodded. "Well, you've done a lovely job. The coffee is great and the atmosphere is welcoming, which is what most people look for in a coffee shop. About the only difference between your place and the bigger cities is your uniform, or lack of one, I should say." She had a knowing glint in her eye. "I suspect that might have something to do with the ten years in the military."

Holly grinned, surprised at the woman's astuteness. She was beautiful *and* smart. "I guess that's a hang-up of mine."

"No matter." The woman sipped her cappuccino. "Your espresso creations speak for themselves."

"She's right." Wendy pulled a sheaf of paper from her briefcase and handed it to Katherine. "Ms. King is a recruiter, Holly. She searches for on-air talent for television affiliates all over the United States." Wendy pursed her lips. "You probably think I'm too young, don't you?"

Holly crossed her arms. "I was eighteen when I left home, Wendy. I don't think you're too young at all, in fact, the sooner the better."

"I agree completely." Katherine nodded as her gaze traveled from Wendy's taupe pumps to her shiny black hair. "You're at the perfect age to make a big move, although you've been rather limited in your exposure here." She tapped a gold pen against her lips. "No entanglements to distract you, right, Wendy?"

Wendy laughed nervously. "I don't think so."

"Because that's what it takes in this business. No men, no kids, not even a pet. Especially a dog. Your entire focus should be on your career." She tilted her head at Holly. "You're a businesswoman, Ms. Hoffman. Don't you agree?"

Katherine wore an expensive watch on her left wrist and a pearl ring on her right hand. No wedding band. "Focus. Definitely. I'll leave you two to your business. Let me know if you need anything."

The woman was certainly gracious, the picture of Southern manners. Holly looked down at her T-shirt. She had the black one on today, which clashed with the brown-and-yellow apron. Maybe her stubbornness was getting in the way of her business savvy. Maybe she should visit Cheri and see if she still had those polo shirts. Heading toward the kitchen to unload the dishwasher, she saw Pierre pass the window. She veered back to the counter.

"Holly, bonjour. How is business today?"

"Wednesday is my slow day, Pierre. But that's okay for a change. Would you like a cup of coffee?"

Pierre swung a lock of dark hair out of his eyes as he made a face. "American coffee? Surely, you jest."

Holly propped her hands on her hips.

"Don't knock my coffee until you've tried it, Frenchman."

Pierre held up his hands, palms forward. "I'm sure your coffee is good, but today I must have a double shot of espresso. I have so much work I will be here until midnight. My wife no longer knows what I look like."

Holly laughed as she reached for a demitasse cup and saucer. She drew the double shot and set the steaming brew in front of her neighbor. "I don't know if this will get you to midnight. You may have to come back."

Pierre closed his eyes and breathed in the vapors rising from the cup. "Ahh, I needed this. I can almost pretend I am at a sidewalk café in Paris." His eyes flew open. "I will bring you a collection of French songs. The illusion will be complete."

"When was the last time you were home, Pierre? Are your parents in France?" Holly leaned on the counter, wondering how he'd married an American and ended up in central Pennsylvania.

Pierre slurped from the small cup. "Jessie and I visited my family last summer. They live just across the border from Italy." He sipped again. "However, Jessie got an offer from a firm in Washington, DC. As soon as she completes her doctorate, we will be moving, so no going home this year. And if I leave, I have to close the store. I don't know what to do."

"You can't close your business. People rely on you. Why don't you hire someone to help?" Holly glanced out the window. The fog had finally burned off and the summer sun shone on the red-and-white petunias in the bank parking lot. As usual, traffic was light.

Pierre upended his cup and his gaze flicked to the espresso machine. He held out the cup and saucer. "I don't know who to ask. Who else can fix computers?"

Holly set the cup on the tray and drew another double shot. "Matt McClain just got laid off from the electronics factory. His wife's been doing some baking for Sue, but they've got four kids. Maybe he could help."

Pierre took the cup and saucer and started toward the door. "I will talk to Sue. Thank you for the suggestion." He lifted the demitasse cup in the air as he backed out the door. "And I will return this later. Au revoir, mon amie."

Holly waved before heading toward the kitchen. She pulled open the dishwasher.

Clouds of steam rose and she leaned against the freezer, waiting for the dishes to cool. Pulling out a rack of coffee mugs, she shoved through the kitchen door.

Rose came in, a big smile on her face. Outside, Erma was settling Riley onto the bench just under the window and wagging a finger under her nose.

"What's going on?"

Rose shook her head. "I'm sworn to secrecy, but I can keep an eye on things while you find out about Riley's surprise." She pointed at Holly's apron. "You might want to leave that in here."

Holly hung her apron on the hook and passed Rose and Erma as they headed toward the coffee. She pushed through the door and froze. "I don't believe it."

Riley's face was split with a wide grin. "I got a puppy, Holly." She held a pink camouflage leash hooked to a matching collar, which circled the neck of a chubby black puppy.

Holly eased onto the bench and put an arm around Riley. "I thought you weren't allowed to have a dog."

"Daddy said since I'm living up here now he figured we could get a dog."

"You're staying here?"

Riley nodded. "We signed up for first grade. My teacher is Miss Norton." She set the squirming dog on the bench between them.

Holly's heart fell. At one point she would have expected Mac to mention his decision, but ever since the encounter with the touch-me-not he'd been distant. She shouldn't be surprised. Mac didn't want Holly forming a close relationship with his daughter. Holly wasn't mom material. Maybe Riley hadn't gotten a new puppy just because she was staying in Bear Meadows. Maybe Mac had found a suitable mother. She pushed the troubling thought to the back of her mind. "What's her name?"

"Miss Molly."

"That's a good name." Holly ran a finger across the dog's shiny, soft fur. "How did you decide on her name?"

"Remember, Good Golly Miss Molly was the name of Twister's friend at the fair. I figured that was a good name for a dog, too."

"You're absolutely right."

Rose and Erma came out onto the porch with their coffees. Rose patted Holly on the shoulder. "I hope you don't mind, dear, but

I have a houseful for dinner tonight. I need to go home to get things started. And Erma was wondering if Riley could stay here with you for an hour."

Holly raised her eyebrows. "No, I don't mind. I don't expect to be busy. What about the puppy?"

"I'll take Miss Molly home and put her in the crate. You be good, Riley." Erma gave Holly a speculative look. "By the way, how did you persuade Riley to give up her quilt?"

Holly shrugged. "It was her idea."

Erma nodded. "If you say so." She reached for the puppy's leash. "Come along, Miss Molly." Erma and Rose walked down the boardwalk, the puppy trotting alongside.

Babysitting again, Holly thought. *Mac won't be happy.*

CHAPTER SIXTEEN

HOLLY SETTLED RILEY on the couch with an activity book and a box of crayons.

Washing her hands, she put on her apron and finished setting the clean mugs on top of the espresso machine. Passing through the kitchen, she noticed a missed phone call from Carolyn.

"What's up, sis?"

"Freddy came down with the flu, Mom's got a full house and Sonny's on a job. Will you be terribly upset if I don't come in today? I don't know what else to do."

Holly glanced through the small window in the kitchen door. Wendy and Katherine had left hours ago. Mac would pick up Riley within the hour. "Today's Wednesday. I shouldn't be busy. You take care of little Freddy."

"Thanks, honey. I'll talk to you later."

Holly put down the phone and wandered back into the store. She couldn't call Louise.

Her best friend was spending the afternoon getting ready for her big date with Officer Williams.

A white van pulled into a parking space right in front of The Wildflower. Immediately all four doors opened. "Uh-oh." A man and woman got out of the front and unloaded the rest of the vehicle. By the time they entered the shop, the family was comprised of two parents, two grandparents, two teenagers and a toddler. The faces of the parents were tense and for a minute, Holly felt sorry for them. "What can I do for you folks?"

After staring at the menu board, the mother shifted the baby to her other hip and wrinkled her brow. "Do you serve meals here?"

Although Holly knew she served nothing but drinks and pastries she had the strangest urge to double check her menu board. Four adults had stared at it for five minutes and the woman had *still* asked if she served meals. Holly nodded toward the pastry case. "The only food available is in the case. If you're looking for a meal there's a fast-food place about two miles down the road."

The husband's eyes lit up and he ran a hand over his smooth pate. "Why don't we do that, just this once? We're on vacation, after all."

The woman turned cold eyes on her husband. "I told you we are not feeding the children fast food. I won't be responsible for any clogged arteries they have at sixty."

Holly didn't want to remind her it was possible she wouldn't be around to see the clogged arteries at sixty but she bit her tongue as the four adults debated their options. The two teenagers disappeared into the alcove and Holly heard a pile of magazines slide off the shelf and onto the floor. "If you're looking for a more substantial meal, you'll find restaurants just off the interstate about twenty miles in either direction."

She looked at the toddler, who stared back with a frown on her chubby face. When Holly gave her a smile, the girl broke into a loud wail.

The mother jerked her head around, and she beamed the cold stare at Holly that just minutes before had been boring into her husband's skull. "What did you do?"

Holly's mouth dropped open. The blood rushed to her cheeks. "What did I—" Out of the corner of her eye she saw Riley pick up her coloring book and crayons and move to a table in the corner. She couldn't blame the girl for wanting to move farther from the stressed-out mother. She would've joined her if she could.

The grandmother handed a plastic lidded cup to Holly with an apologetic smile. "Could you put some whole milk in this, please?" She elbowed her husband. "Jack, get the twins back in the car. I'll get some cookies to hold everybody."

"Mother—" The wife's eyes flew wide in shock. "What about the sugar content?"

The grandfather, a tall man with fine gray hair, finally spoke up. "Ah, it won't kill 'em. You two load the kids back in the car and we'll be right out."

By the time the parents had shepherded their children back into the van, the grandparents had bought a dozen raisin-filled cookies, a dozen sugar cookies, six bottles of apple juice and two cups of coffee.

The grandmother perused the book shelves. "Are these books for sale?"

Holly rang up the food. "All the paperbacks are a dollar."

"Then charge me for two, please. I'm sure I'll find something." She pulled a book off the shelf and flipped it over to read the back cover.

"Kids these days." The man winked at

Holly as he paid for the food and drinks and the two books.

"They think they know everything and we don't know anything." His wife laughed as she approached the counter with her books. "But give them eight uninterrupted hours with their own children and they're pulling their hair out." She froze in front of the pastry case. Her eyes lit up. "Are those chocolate gobs?"

Holly leaned back to see where the woman was pointing. "We call them whoopie pies. You must be from Pittsburgh."

"Just north of the city." The man jerked his head toward the case. "Give us two of those gobs…and put them in a plain brown wrapper." He winked at his wife. "We'll have them with coffee tonight."

Holly smiled at the friendly couple as she handed them the full bag of supplies. "Where are you folks headed?"

"We're on our way to Gettysburg." The husband raised one bushy eyebrow. "We're having an educational vacation this year, a last hurrah before school starts."

"I just hope the motel has a hot tub." The wife threaded her arm through her husband's and waved goodbye as they returned to their family.

The van backed out of its spot and continued east. Holly dropped her head to the counter. "I'm ready to close. I'm exhausted."

The words were no sooner out of her mouth than she heard a thump and then a muffled cry from the direction of the alcove. She glanced at the corner table. Empty. "Riley?"

Her heart jumped into her throat as she raced around the counter.

Riley lay on the floor, her arm clutched to her middle. "My arm hurts."

Holly dropped to her knees. "What happened?"

"I was looking for a book to read. I couldn't reach." Tears started flowing. "I want my Daddy."

"I'm here, honey."

Holly hadn't heard Mac come in. His face was stern as he knelt and reached for Riley's injured arm. "Let me look, Riley."

"I don't know what happened. I had an irate customer and I saw Riley move to the back table. I thought she was coloring."

Mac nodded. "Yeah, well, that's why you need to keep your eyes on kids all the time, Holly." He picked up his daughter. "We better get this arm checked out at the emergency room."

"Do you want me to come?"

Ethan Johnson and Adam McClain came in with Crystal and Shelly.

"You have a business to run. I'll take care of my daughter." And with that he was gone.

Ethan approached the counter with his usual swagger. "How about four iced mochas, Miz H?"

Holly took a deep breath, her thoughts still on Riley's injury. "Four iced mochas, coming right up, Mr. Johnson." The teens congregated around the couch while Holly readied the ingredients for the drinks. Only the middle of the afternoon and she felt like pushing the teens off the couch and flopping down for a twelve-hour nap. She set the drinks on the end of the counter. "Four iced mochas."

The teens collected their drinks and disappeared to the alcove. Holly was wondering what condition the magazines were in when Hawkeye and Skinny Smith showed up for their monthly order of beans. "Hello, gentlemen."

The twins dipped their chins in unison. "Miss Hoffman."

"Could you make us two Spanish macchiatos, Holly? I read about them recently and they sounded delicious." Skinny leaned forward, one bushy white eyebrow raised in challenge. "Do you think you can make a Spanish macchiato?"

"Of course, Skinny. Have a seat while I get them ready for you." Holly gritted her teeth as she pushed through the kitchen door, wondering where her mother had put the sweetened condensed milk. Of all days...

BY THE HUNDREDTH time she'd wiped the counters, mopped the floor and cleaned the pots, Holly was exhausted. And she hadn't heard a word from Mac. She prayed Riley wasn't hurt badly.

After flipping the sign to Closed, she locked the door. The sun had set. The sky was the color of an old bruise. She tossed her apron on the counter, turned off all the lights and sank onto the couch. Slipping off her sneakers, she sighed. Her back was killing her, a steady pulsing that intensified as she lay down. She couldn't walk the three blocks to the house. She would just lie here for five minutes, just five minutes, maybe ten.

The last thing she saw was the square of light from the streetlamps shining through the windows onto the freshly mopped floor. Her eyelids slammed shut.

Holly was riding Twister at the fair. She trotted him around the barrels, her saddle creaking. The crowd looked bored, but for some reason she didn't want to go faster. Suddenly they started to applaud—another rider had entered the ring. *Wait a minute*, she thought. *I'm not finished. You're not supposed to come in the ring until I'm finished.* "You're too slow," someone shouted.

Using an English saddle, the other rider rode a magnificent black horse. She wore black riding pants with black boots up to her knees. Her white blouse sparkled and her black top hat set off pale blond hair tied in a French chignon. The rider was Ms. King. Somehow she was Mac's wife, too.

Twister continued to trot around the barrels. Her Western saddle squeaked loudly with each bounce, but the crowd had ceased to pay attention. All eyes were fixed on the black horse and pale rider as they cantered along the rail. When the pair was at the opposite end of the ring, a magnificent white stallion galloped through the gate. Dressed in white-tie and tails, Mac looked unbelievably handsome as he rode past Holly and Twister toward the woman on the black horse.

"Mac." Her lips couldn't form his name.

Suddenly night fell and a spotlight shone on the beautiful couple as they galloped around the ring to thunderous applause.

Left in the dark, Holly looked down at her jeans and dusty boots and her black T-shirt. Twister plodded around the barrels and the saddle continued to squeak.

"Be quiet." The judge in the box glared as she rounded the third barrel.

"I can't." The words formed but nothing came out.

"Shh."

Holly opened her eyes. She lay on the couch, her head wedged between the back cushion and the arm. The square of light from the streetlamp flickered as a shadow passed by. *What was that?* she thought. *Rats? No way, please don't let it be rats. Cappuccino cat must be sleeping on the job.* She pushed herself up from the couch, propping herself on the arm for support.

"Somebody's on the couch." The voice rang out clear as a bell. A shadowy form stood behind the counter at the cash register.

"Hey, who's back there?" Her brain still

felt foggy from sleep as Holly struggled to sit up.

"Let's get out of here." An unfamiliar male voice came from the door.

The person behind the cash register rounded the end of the counter and raced for the door. Holly shot off the couch. She reached out and caught the tail of the runner's shirt. He jerked away and she pitched forward, slamming her head into a table. The thief tore through the door. The last thing Holly saw before she blacked out was two dark shadows racing past the window, leaving the door wide-open.

CHAPTER SEVENTEEN

"HOLLY, WAKE UP." Mac patted Holly's pale cheeks. Ever since Pierre's call, Mac's heart had been pounding like a kettledrum. He should've done more about these petty thefts. It was only a matter of time until someone got hurt.

Her eyelids fluttered. "Mac?" She struggled to lift herself from the floor.

Mac wrapped an arm around her and helped her to her feet. "Feel okay?" He struggled to retain his professional demeanor, but the sight of Holly stretched out on the floor had sent fear like a dagger into his heart.

His arm tight around her waist, Mac walked Holly to the couch. Easing her onto the cushions, he sat beside her. "Do you remember what happened?"

Holly closed her eyes and rubbed her forehead. "I was having a dream, a weird dream." She rested her head on the back of the couch. "A customer was riding a horse, but then the customer was—" Opening her eyes, she looked at Mac.

"It doesn't matter, Holly. What did you see when you woke up?"

"I heard squeaking and I thought the noise came from my saddle. It was so loud, but I condition my saddles…at least I used to."

"The window back here is open," Moose called out from the alcove. "This is how they got in." The window squeaked, followed by a slam as Moose closed and locked it.

Pierre sat on the coffee table in front of Holly. "Thank goodness I was working late. I did not hear anything until they ran outside and down the porch. I saw two of them go around the side of the building." He squeezed her hand. "How are you feeling, mon amie?"

Holly leaned her head against Mac's shoulder and closed her eyes. "I have a pounding headache."

Mac wanted to do nothing more than wrap his arms around her, and he was just about to when Sonny burst through the door. "What the hell happened here?" When he caught sight of Holly he crossed the room in three short strides. Rounding the coffee table, he sat on the couch next to Holly and gathered her into his arms. "Oh, my goodness, is she dead? My baby sister is dead."

Holly's muffled voice sounded from the folds of his Pittsburgh Steelers sweatshirt. "I can't breathe."

"She can't breathe! Who knows CPR?"

Pierre glanced at Mac and raised his eyebrows.

"She's not dead, Sonny." Mac peeled the man's huge hands from his sister's head. "But she was unconscious a little bit. You need to stop bouncing her around."

Sonny eased away and looked down at Holly's face.

She took a deep breath and said, "You're not getting my share of the inheritance yet."

Sonny scowled. "That's not funny, Holly. What happened here?"

Holly managed a bleak smile. "Nothing."

"Are you kidding?" Mac said. "You were unconscious when Pierre found you."

"I don't think so. I was—um—shaken up. I've taken worse falls barrel racing." She rubbed her temples with both hands.

"Yeah, well, you're no spring chicken. After a while your body stops bouncing back like it used to."

Holly scowled. "What's with you and spring chickens, bro?"

Mac smoothed the hair from her forehead. "You have a headache? I better get you to the emergency room."

"But—"

Mac laid his hand on her cheek. "Better safe than sorry. The good news is it's the middle of the night. They should take us right in."

With her eyes only half open, Holly stared at him a moment as if deciding whether she wanted to argue the point. Apparently she didn't have the energy because she sighed. "Okay, Chief McAndrews, you win. But what about—" She pointed toward the counter.

Mac followed her gaze to the counter. The cash register drawer hung open as did the door to the pastry case. A basket of biscotti had been knocked all over the floor. He caught Moose's eye. "Dust for fingerprints before anybody else shows up."

"Why on Earth would they come to a coffee shop?" Holly mumbled.

Sonny tapped her knee. "Why were you here so late anyway?"

"I was exhausted." Holly threw her brother a faint smile. "I was busy today."

"And I wasn't around to help." Louise

walked over from the doorway and perched on the coffee table. "I'm sorry, honey."

"What are you doing here?" Holly's eyes widened.

Louise glanced up at Moose, who was staring at her with narrowed eyes. "I heard about the break-in." She patted Holly's hand. "Don't worry. Moose and I will take care of things here. Mac's right. You should get checked out at the emergency room."

"Listen to your friend, Holly. After all, she is a nurse." Mac propped his hands on his knees and levered himself off the couch.

"Good idea, although I know from experience she has a hard head," Sonny said, swiping at his eyes.

"Ha-ha." Holly elbowed her brother in the ribs.

Mac couldn't help but notice the look of affection passing between brother and sister, but then, he'd known the family for years. They were tight. "Let's go, Hard Head Hoffman." He lifted Holly from the couch and wrapped his arm around her waist. He had no intention of leaving her side.

HOLLY LAY ON a stretcher in the emergency room cubicle, a white curtain drawn around the bed for privacy. Her memory of the events of the evening was still fuzzy. The dream and the robbery were all one in her brain. "How did you hear about the break-in?"

Mac stood by the bed, his face drawn and circles under his eyes. "Pierre called 911 and Moose was on patrol. I forgot to tell you Pierre had been missing some money, too, and I told him we'd keep a watch on the place."

"That's right. I remember now. Pierre said he had so much work his wife would forget what he looked like." Holly ran her hand over the smooth sheet covering her middle.

Mac reached for her hand. "You said you were busy today?"

"Oh, man, I was inundated. First Wendy Valentine met with Ms. King. You know, she's a nice woman. Then our moms and Riley came over. Hey, she talked you into getting a puppy."

Mac's somber face finally creased in a smile. "She wore me down."

Holly sat straight up. "She was hurt. Oh, I forgot. Mac, is Riley okay?"

"She's fine. Not even a sprain." Pushing her back against the pillow, his face sobered. "Are you okay? Are you dizzy or anything?"

"My head hurts a little." She reached up and touched his face. "You look exhausted."

"Who else came in today?"

Holly closed her eyes against the bright fluorescent lights. "A family on their way to Gettysburg." Thinking of the helpful grandparents, she murmured, "I hope the hotel had a hot tub."

"Holly?" Mac patted her hand.

"They had a set of twins about thirteen or fourteen who went back in the alcove. Maybe they opened the window."

"Maybe, but I doubt the family came back to rob the place, although you never know. I've heard of parents who teach their children to steal."

"Terrible." Holly shook her head, and then winced at the shot of pain in her right temple. "The usual bunch of teenagers came in and they all ordered complicated drinks and, speaking of complicated drinks, the Smith twins came in for their monthly supply of coffee beans and ordered—" she placed a hand on her forehead as she struggled to remember "—something with sweetened condensed milk. Oh, I can't remember."

"Having memory problems, are we?" The doctor strolled into the cubicle, reviewing her chart. "Holly, what are you doing wrestling with hoodlums in the middle of the night?"

Holly smiled. "Believe me, that wasn't my intention."

"Twice in one day, Chief?"

"Not on purpose," Mac said, resting his hand on her arm. "Which reminds me, you said you were busy yesterday, but why were you still there at midnight?"

"That's what I was telling you. I was so busy with customers I didn't get cleaned up until late. I was so exhausted I sat down on the couch for five minutes to rest. The next thing I knew I saw shadows and heard people talking."

Peering into Holly's eyes, the doctor said, "Mac, do you know how long she was unconscious?"

"No. She had come to by the time I arrived."

"Vital sighs appear to be normal. Do you know what day this is, Holly?" Holly squinted as a beam of light shone into her eye.

"Well, when I went to work this morning, it was Wednesday, so if it's after midnight, it must be Thursday."

The doctor straightened and glanced at

Mac. "I don't think it's necessary, but I could order a CAT scan."

"I don't want—"

"CAT scan? She needs a CAT scan?" Rose rushed into the room, followed by Fritz. Holly's heart sank as she saw the exhaustion on her parents' faces.

"I'm fine, Mom. I don't need a CAT scan. Edna the librarian might need a CAT scan, but I don't."

Mac smiled. "Her name's Eliza."

"Who's Eliza?" Her father pressed his lips in a firm line and waited for an answer.

Her mother smoothed the hair from her forehead and rested her hand on Holly's cheek. "Oh, honey, I'm so glad you're okay."

"A little bump on the head, no big deal. I'll be up and about in no time."

"Twenty-four hours," the doctor muttered, scribbling madly on the chart.

"What's that, Doctor?" Mac stepped back and reached for the doctor's sleeve as he started to leave.

"The nurse will give you all the instructions, but she needs to have someone nearby for twenty-four hours to keep an eye on her, watch for signs of confusion, dizziness. With those provisions, I'm releasing her." He nodded briskly and pointed his pen at Holly. "No more wrestling with hoodlums, young woman."

Her father rounded the bed and stood next to Mac. "She was safer in the military."

"Oh, Dad, don't start."

"You are pale," Rose said.

"Why don't I leave you three alone while I follow up with Moose?" Mac wiggled Holly's foot under the sheet. "I'll be back."

Rose trailed after him. "I'll call your brothers."

Fritz settled into the chair by the bed. "How do you feel?"

"I am so ready to get out of here."

Her father glanced at the clock on the wall. "Shouldn't be much longer. How's your head?"

"Like Sonny said, I have the Hoffman hard head. I'm fine, Dad."

Fritz drummed his fingers on his leg, first crossing his right leg over his left, and then switching back.

"Something bothering you, Dad?"

Shaking his head, her father leaned forward and rested his elbow on his knees. He stared at the linoleum floor. "Out of all my children, you've given me the majority of my gray hairs."

The familiar irritation stirred in her gut. "Why? Because I'm a girl?"

He shot her a sideways look. "No. Your brothers made sure you could take care of yourself."

"What choice did I have?" Memories of summer softball games and fishing in the creek flooded her mind. Her youthful philosophy had been anything her brothers could do, she could do better.

"Because of all our children, you're the one who has taken the most risks. Joining the military, flying into war zones…"

"For a week—that's nothing. Lots of guys do multiple tours."

"I know, but still, we worried. We were never quite sure where you were or what you were doing."

Holly lay back on the stiff pillow and stared up at the fluorescent light over her bed. She tried to hold back the nagging question but failed. "Then why were you so against my coming home and starting the business?"

Her father cleared his throat and glanced at the door, as if hoping for a reprieve. "I had mixed feelings, for sure." His fingers drummed on the bars of the bed. "You have to understand, I've farmed all my life, up until I retired and Thomas took over. Farming is not an easy life."

Her father rubbed a hand over his five o'clock shadow, the stubble white against his gray-tinged skin. "You lost me. What do farming and running a coffee shop have to do with each other?"

"Because you are solely responsible for the success of the operation. If you fail, you can lose everything. I had four kids to feed." He gave her a wan smile. "I envied your steady paycheck, your opportunities. In fact, you shocked me, giving all that up. Why did you?"

"No place else was home. I wanted some roots." She laid her hand on her father's fingers, still gripping the railing. "I missed the seasons…the first snow, the first crocus in the spring, the humidity in the summer…"

"Yes, nothing quite like making hay on a hot, humid August day. Good way to lose five pounds." Still holding her hand, he leaned back in his chair. "We don't have many museums around here."

Holly shrugged. "Been there, done that…"

Her father squeezed her hand. He blinked

several times, his green eyes watery. "I wanted to know you were okay."

"What are you—" A lump formed in Holly's throat and she swallowed. Her voice came out raspy. "What are you talking about, Dad?"

"When you broke off your engagement with Nick, I figured well, she's not interested in marriage. At least she'll have a pension to fall back on. Then when you said you were leaving the air force…" He pursed his lips. "I thought, no family, no security… What will become of my little girl when I'm gone?"

"Oh, Dad." Holly pulled back her hand and rubbed her eyes. "I don't need a man to take care of me."

"I know. I'm talking about someone to share your life with, like your mother and me. We watch out for each other."

"Mom says you work too hard."

He chuckled. "That's just her way. She works hard, too."

Holly sighed. "Yes, helping me when she should be home puttering in the garden. You were right. I don't know anything about running a business. My sales are down. I won't be able to pay you back." Tears burned at the back of her eyelids.

"Do you think that's important to me?"

She sniffed. "You said you wanted to be paid back in a year."

Fritz sighed. "I was hoping making the payment plan more difficult would convince you to stay in the military."

"I can't pay you back yet."

"You've only been in business a few months. Now stop worrying." He squeezed her hand.

The rings holding the curtain on the metal bar jangled as Rose pulled the material aside. She came to the other side of the bed, her gaze moving from the monitors to Holly's face and back again. "Did the nurse come in yet?"

Holly smiled at her mother's look of concern. "Not yet."

Rose glanced up at Fritz. "The doctor did say she could go home, didn't he? You don't think—"

"Mom." Holly waited until she had her mother's attention. "Quit worrying. I'm fine."

"Why don't I see what's going on?" Her father patted her hand. "I'll be right back, honey."

"I still can't believe this happened in a quiet little town like Bear Meadows. What's this world coming to? I'm glad Mac brought you to the emergency room. You could've hit your head harder than we thought."

Yes, Mac can do no wrong. Her mother had always had a soft spot for the fatherless boy. "Well, that's what he does. He knows how to handle emergencies."

"He cares about you, Holly. He told me you could stay at his place if I was too busy with our guests. He's so thoughtful."

"Why would I stay at his house?" Would Mac really want her spending more time with Riley?

"Might be easier, is all." Rose smoothed Holly's hair back from her forehead.

Irritated, Holly brushed her hand away, and then picked at a loose thread on the smooth white sheet. "I'm not sure I need to stay at Mac's place. My room is pretty quiet, being on the third floor."

"True, but I still expect him to offer. You've been spending a lot of time together. He cares about you."

Holly was more surprised than her mother when her eyes filled with tears. The words came out before she could stop them. "He can't care, Mom. He needs a mother for

Riley. Everyone knows I don't have a maternal bone in my body."

"For goodness' sake, Holly, women aren't born maternal. Like any skill, practice makes perfect." She chuckled and raised one eyebrow. "Poor Sonny. When he was born I knew nothing. I was the youngest, too, remember. Sonny was my experimental baby."

"Which explains a lot." She shared a laugh with her mother.

"You want it all—a career and a family. So join the club, Holly. We all want it all." She pulled a tissue from the box on the stand and handed it to Holly. "All I know is, I saw the way Mac took care of you tonight and it wasn't because he's the chief of police." She peeked around the curtain at the sound of voices. "Be right back."

Holly took a breath and stared up at the tile ceiling. Wow. She should visit the ER more often. She hadn't had such a deep conversation with either of her parents in a while. And the revelations… Was being a parent wanting to see your child always safe, taken care of? She was dabbing at her eyes when her parents returned.

"The nurse is coming down the hall." Sitting in the chair next to the bed, Fritz sipped from the cup in his hand, then grimaced. "This coffee is strong."

"It's not strong, it's—" Holly caught her father's raised eyebrow. "On second thought, you're probably right." Returning his smile, she realized they hadn't laughed together in a long time.

She was holding the hands of both of her parents when the nurse walked in, followed closely by Mac. "I have some instructions for you, and then we can send you on your way."

"See, Mom," Holly said. "I'm fine."

The nurse, who looked to be in her mid-forties, reviewed a clipboard. "You should have someone with you for twenty-four hours. Watch for signs of confusion, dizziness, memory loss. Take acetaminophen for pain."

"I can go back to work, can't I?"

Pen poised over the clipboard, the nurse peered over her glasses. "What do you do?"

"I own the coffee shop downtown." Certain she would be cleared for work, Holly waited for the nurse's answer.

The nurse's face lit in recognition. "You're Louise's friend." She smiled. "I hope she comes back to work. We miss her. But being on duty when a loved one is brought in would get the best of any of us." She looked down at the chart as if just remembering her instructions. "The doctor says you should rest, Holly. In fact, you shouldn't be climbing stairs, either, in case you get dizzy."

Rose sighed. "Our house is full of parents moving their kids into Penn State for fall term. Where can we put her?"

Fritz put an arm around his wife. "She can take our room."

Holly glanced from one parent to the other. "Hey, you two," she lowered her voice and said, "I can make it to my room."

The nurse shot her a look. "I—"

"I'll take her to my place." Mac's voice was full of authority. "Everything's on one floor. The house is quiet with just my mother and Riley." He grinned. "Well, pretty quiet for a house with a five-year-old."

Holly's mother smiled. *Just as she had said.* Holly's protests fell on deaf ears. The other four all agreed Mac's suggestion was the best solution to the problem. Twenty minutes later Holly sat in the passenger seat of Mac's patrol SUV as the vehicle traveled the quiet, dark streets of Bear Meadows.

When they passed the strip mall, Holly sat up and peered at her shop, dark except for the light over the counter. Someone had placed a Closed sign in the window. She sank back onto the seat. "Do you have any clues yet?"

"No. The only thing we know so far is they must have come in through the open window in the alcove." He pulled into the driveway of his sprawling ranch house. A single light burned in the front window. "I called Mom. She said the guest room is all ready for you." He came around to help her out of the vehicle, and then with his arm around her waist led her toward the back door.

"Stop." Holly leaned her head back, staring into the night sky. Mac's house was located at the edge of town, so there were no streetlights on the road. The night sky glittered with stars. "I saw a shooting star."

Just as the words left her mouth, two more stars streaked across the sky. Even though she wasn't the woman Mac was looking for, she would savor this moment. Nights when she was alone, she would pull the snapshot out of her mind's photo album and relish the feel of his arms, the quiet of the night, the flash of the stars.

Someday Mac would find the woman who could step into Anne's English riding boots. But now, wrapped in the warmth of his arms, she leaned against him. Meteor after meteor shot across the sky and burned out entering the atmosphere.

Mac's voice was quiet. "We better get you inside."

Holly fixed her gaze on his face and for just an instant wondered what her life might have been if they had become a couple all those years ago, if the hurt had faded and they'd seen each other differently. She sighed. "Okay."

CHAPTER EIGHTEEN

"ARE YOU ASLEEP?" The whisper edged into her consciousness. Through closed lids, Holly noted the room was lighter. She slowly opened her eyes.

"You're awake." Riley's face, inches from hers, broke into a smile. One of her bottom teeth was missing. "Holly, look. I lost another tooth last night." She opened her mouth wide and then slammed it shut. "Why are you sleeping in our house? Is something wrong at your house?"

Mac strode into the room, dressed in jeans and a T-shirt. "Riley Anne, we told you not to wake Holly."

Riley eased onto the bed, sitting cross-legged and staring at Holly with a happy face. "I didn't wake her up. She waked up all by herself, didn't you, Holly?"

Holly couldn't help but laugh. When Riley took it upon herself to wriggle under the covers, she threw Mac an apologetic look. "I certainly did."

Mac perched at the foot of the bed, his face unreadable. "How do you feel this morning?"

Holly stretched and yawned. "I feel surprisingly good, considering. What time is it?"

"Eight o'clock. I thought I'd stick around and make sure you're okay, and go into the office later. Would you like a cup of coffee? Ours isn't as good as yours but it's better than nothing."

Holly leaned back on the pillow and glanced at Riley, who had cuddled next to her and now watched them both with bright eyes. "I don't suppose you'll let me go to work?"

"I'm afraid you're a captive here, ma'am."

"We can watch cartoons, Holly. Do you like *Dora the Explorer*?"

Holly wriggled her fingers into the cartoon horse embroidered on the girl's shirt until she giggled and disappeared under the covers. "I love *Dora the Explorer*."

"Are you hungry, Holly?" Erma came into the room carrying a tray. "Riley thought you might like some blueberry pancakes this morning. John, put that little table on the bed, will you?" She started to set the tray on the short-legged table when she paused. "You can't eat like that. John, prop her up a little, put a pillow behind her back."

"Wait a minute, you guys are going to way too much trouble for—" She stopped when Mac leaned in, put his hand behind her back and pulled her forward.

"You're wasting your breath," he whispered, his breath fanning her cheek. Shoving a pillow behind her, he eased her back until she was in an upright position. "How's that, Mom?"

"Much better." She set the tray in front of Holly.

A plate of steaming blueberry pancakes was surrounded by coffee, orange juice and a pink tea rose in a small vase. Overwhelmed at the attention, Holly blushed. "You guys are spoiling me. I might never go home." Riley shot a look at her father and he gave a quick shake of his head.

"Can I eat my pancakes with you?" Riley asked.

"Sure."

No sooner was the word out of her mouth than Riley shot out of the room. A minute later she returned at a slower pace, balancing a plate and a small glass of orange juice. Holly made room on the tray and, with a grin of satisfaction, Riley set her plate down next to Holly's and cuddled close. She stuck a bite in her mouth.

"These are great." Holly nodded at Erma, who stood by the bed watching them with a smile of satisfaction.

"The berries are fresh. I have a few bushes out back." She waved a hand in the air and backed out. "I'll be in the kitchen if you need anything."

Holly glanced at Mac. His fingers were tapping out a rhythm on his thigh, as if he wanted to be anywhere else but here. "Your mom seems happy this morning. If she likes having guests, maybe she should open a B and B, too."

Frowning, Mac shook his head. "She likes to travel too much. She just informed me she's going on a medical mission's trip in October. A month in South America."

Holly glanced at Riley, busy eating a syrup-dripping pancake. "What about…"

Mac shrugged.

Riley reached for her juice. "Are you staying in bed all day, Holly?" Her eyes grew wide when her father took a bite of her pancake. "Daddy, stop eating my pancake."

"I'm hungry." Holding Riley's fork, Mac took another bite.

Riley crossed her arms in indignation, and Holly nudged her shoulder. "I suppose we could share."

Riley rolled her eyes. "I suppose." And the three of them sat on the bed sharing blueberry pancakes.

Holly grinned as father and daughter pretended to fight over the fork. Watching the strong man she had known since childhood playing with his little girl, she felt happy for him. Apparently people could change.

Riley's fork dropped to the plate with a clatter. "Daddy, I forgot about Miss Molly." She jumped off the bed and ran from the room.

"Where's Miss Molly?" Holly finished the last of her pancake and reached for her cup.

"Let me get this out of your way." Mac took the tray and set it on the table in front of the window. Rescuing his coffee, he returned to the bed. "Miss Molly is being crate trained. Riley's supposed to take her outside first thing in the morning."

Holly chuckled. "I disrupted her routine, didn't I?"

Mac smiled, bringing the cup to his lips.

"You sure did." He was about to take another sip when he stopped and balanced the cup on his knee. "Last night, the nurse mentioned something about Louise being on duty when a loved one was brought in. She wasn't talking about Louise's husband, was she?"

Holly leaned back against the pillow and nodded. "Louise is a registered nurse. She was working the night shift in the emergency room when her husband was in a bad accident on the interstate. The roads were a sheet of ice. He didn't make it. She hardly left her house the first year. In fact, I was surprised when she offered to help me with the coffee shop."

Mac didn't answer, just continued to stare into the depths of his coffee cup. The screen door banged. Holly could hear Riley giving instructions to her dog, but after a moment, the words faded away.

She realized in that moment what she had to do. A shiver ran through her as she studied his mouth and remembered the long-ago kiss. Why remember a thirteen-year-old kiss and none of the kisses in the intervening years? Like the Italian guy she dated in Rome. One would think she'd have an album of remembered kisses from him, but the only thing she recalled was the great pasta dish they'd had on a side street on their way to the Colosseum. Or the pilot she dated briefly in Florida. Instead she remembered the stomach-turning, awesome ride in an F-15. And certainly Nick. The man had occupied four years of her life. *Nothin'*.

"You know, Mac, I've been thinking." Holly took a deep breath. Her decision as they sat laughing over pancakes had seemed simple. But now, the memory of that summer day still fresh in her mind…not so much. But doing the right thing doesn't always come easy. "Wendy wasn't right for you."

Mac shrugged, his mind obviously on something else. "No kidding. She's just getting started in life."

"And Ms. King, well, maybe she looks like Anne, but she isn't Anne."

Mac nodded, his gaze downcast. "I know."

Holly took another breath. "And Edna the cat lady, well, goes without saying, you two were not a match."

Mac lifted his gaze and met hers. "You mean Eliza." He smiled. "I sneezed for two days and I only visited her at the library."

"Getting back into the dating scene was an

important step for you." Holly's palms dampened as her heartbeat accelerated.

Mac's brows knit. "What are you getting at?"

"The perfect wife for you and the perfect mother for Riley is…Laura Norton, the new first-grade teacher."

Mac's hand jerked, spilling coffee on the flowered comforter. Holly grabbed a tissue and blotted at the stain. Maybe she should have eased into the topic of Mac's future wife a little more slowly.

FRIDAY MORNING MAC sat next to Holly on the couch in the coffee shop. *How could she not know how I feel?* To be fair, he hadn't been sure himself until he'd seen her stretched out on the floor of the coffee shop. They had spent the summer together getting to know each other again, yet yesterday morning she had practically married him off to a woman he'd met twice. After learning about Louise's tragedy, he realized he wasn't the only one to have experienced loss, that maybe it was time to stop wallowing in grief. Then he remembered Riley's accident in the coffee shop, and the scare at the fair, and realized his feelings didn't matter. Riley's welfare came first.

He looked around at the store owners who had gathered early to discuss the interrupted robbery. Mac hadn't wanted Holly to come, but his protests had fallen on deaf ears. At least Carolyn and Louise, insisting she rest, stood behind the counter, providing caffeine to the group who, at the moment, was all talking at once.

Mac held up his hands. "Wait a minute, everybody. One at a time."

Sue paced back and forth across the middle of the room, her face a mask of anger. "What are you doing to catch these culprits, Mac? It might not seem like much money to you but I can't afford one cent."

"Well—"

"You've known about this for months but have you done anything? No, you haven't, and here Holly is getting hurt—"

"Now, wait just a minute, Sue—" Mac found himself wishing Brad Hunter would come to his senses soon so Sue would stop attacking every male in sight. On the other hand, the woman had a point.

"Hey." Holly's shout stilled every voice in the room. "I've still got my parade-ground voice." She smiled, then grew serious. "I appreciate your concern but I'm fine. And by the way, they didn't touch the money in the cash register."

"You scared them off when you woke up," Sue said.

Sitting in one of the cushioned chairs sipping an espresso, Pierre waved his fingers in the air. "Maybe it's because they only want a few dollars, maybe somebody who is short of cash—"

"Well, don't look at me. I work for every dollar I make." Sue ran a hand through her short, bleached-blond hair, causing the strands to stick straight up.

"Oh, for goodness' sake, Sue, put a lid on it." Cheri leaned both elbows on the counter and fingered one of her big hoop earrings. "You act like you're the only one who works hard."

Mac propped his elbows on his knees and stared at the floor, obviously thinking. When he looked up he had come to a decision. "We'll keep up the patrols in the area and hope that we spot something. In the meantime, let us know if you see anything suspicious." He looked at Holly and wondered again how she could feel nothing when he was beginning to think they were meant for each other.

HOLLY POURED COFFEE into two extra-large take-out cups, fitted lids on both and set them by the cash register. She rinsed the coffee urns and set them upside down to drain. Mac and Moose had been doing surveillance on the mall each night since the break-in. Grabbing the cups, she hurried toward the door, shutting off the light on her way out.

Holly crossed the street and slipped around the corner of the hardware store. She could barely make out Mac's patrol car in the dark shadow cast by the three-story building. "I brought you coffee. Since you're going to be up all night I figured you could use the caffeine."

Mac accepted the cup and set it on the dash. "Thanks, Holly. I took a nap this afternoon but these stakeouts can drag." He noticed the cup in her hand. "Are you visiting?"

Holly sipped her coffee. "I'm joining you."

Mac sighed. "Again? Remember what happened last time?" He sat back, cup in hand, staring across the street at the five storefronts.

"I do. We found Sue on the floor."

The streetlight in front of the hardware store illuminated scattered paper cups and soda cans. She drummed her fingers on the console, the noise loud in the confines of the car.

Mac covered her hand with his, stilling her fingers. "Holly, this is serious. You could have been badly hurt. These thieves could be just some locals looking for quick money or they could be tied to the drug trade out of the city. We don't know who we're dealing with."

"I know," Holly muttered.

Just as on their first stakeout, the sound of a barking dog came through Mac's open window. The same deep voice shouted, "Be quiet."

Holly shifted her position. "Don't you get bored on stakeout?"

Mac glanced out the open window and then returned his gaze to The Wildflower. "We're trained to stay alert."

Holly leaned her head back on the seat and thought about the thefts taking place in the county since the beginning of summer. Petty thefts of baked goods were one thing, but robbing the local bank branch was something else. She kept her voice low as she turned to Mac. "Do you think we know them?"

Mac hesitated. "We might. Like you said, you think you know someone…" He gave Holly the ghost of a smile.

"Do you have any suspects in mind?"

"Well, actually, I can't figure out how the Smith brothers' finances have had such a turnaround in the past few months." He waved a finger in front of her face. "And don't you dare repeat what I just said."

"Those two have lived on that farm all their lives. They're locals." She batted away his waving finger. "Ms. King's not a local. She dresses like a big-city gal. Maybe she's a kleptomaniac."

"Are you jealous? It's that blonde-brunette rivalry, isn't it? I've heard the feud goes back centuries."

"Very funny." Holly took a deep breath. "Can I ask you something?"

Mac grunted.

Holly wasn't sure if the grunt was a yes or a no but she continued with the question she had wanted to ask since the first day he'd appeared in her coffee shop. "Why were you so mean to me?"

Mac had been still before but at her question she could feel the tenseness radiating from his body. "What are you talking about?"

Holly propped her elbow on her open window. The dog barked again, and again a deep voice told the dog to be quiet. Despite the fact they were parked in a vacant lot with its share of refuse, the night air carried the scent of roses. "Chris brought you to the family Christmas party. We had fun. Then school started and your gym class and mine were the same period and you turned into this—"

"Your family was so perfect," Mac said. "Everybody's happy, nothing ever goes wrong. After what I had been through—"

Holly stared at him in surprise. "We're not perfect."

"Sure, you are, even now. Everybody's happily married to their childhood sweetheart, well, except Chris, and his story reads like a romance novel."

"I'm not married to my childhood sweetheart." The words came out before she could stop them, but then, she had said them low enough she was pretty sure Mac didn't hear. "Did you know Sonny and Carolyn almost divorced?"

Mac narrowed his eyes. "You're making that up."

Holly shook her head. "When they found out she was pregnant with twins, Sonny wanted her to quit college and Carolyn refused. Then Dad took Sonny's side and Mom took Carolyn's side. It wasn't pretty. Carolyn moved in with her mother until Sonny came to his senses." She chuckled. "Trust me, we are not a perfect family. That's only one story of many." Then she remembered her original question. "But why were you so mean to me?"

"Well..." Mac drummed his fingers on the steering wheel. "I suppose it might have something to do with losing my father and you—" he turned and caught her gaze "—being the apple of your father's eye."

"Ha, not anymore." She tilted her head to the side. "Is that what you want, Mac? A perfect family? Did you have that with Anne?"

"For a while." Mac's response was almost inaudible.

Holly bit her lip. Why did she insist on putting herself through this torture? Mac was right. She should've stayed home. "Do you remember the time you, Chris and I went riding and your horse came back without you?" Eyes closed, Holly stretched her legs as far as she could in the confines of the SUV and pictured the paint mare trotting down the lane with the stirrups flapping at her side. She tried but couldn't hold back the chuckle. When she received no answer from the other seat, Holly opened her eyes.

Mac's lips turned down in a decisive frown. "To this day I think that horse dumped me on purpose."

Holly pictured the pretty paint mare and tried to remember whose horse Mac had borrowed. "Whose horse was she anyway?"

Mac's answer was a growl. "I borrowed Sonny's horse."

"Oh, right. You borrowed Pepper. Sonny finally sold her to a girl who needed a horse for team roping. She was fast."

"Tell me about it." Mac's voice was low.

"I don't think she liked men." A cat slunk past the patrol car.

"Excuse me?"

"How can you guys sit in one spot for so long?" Holly rearranged herself in the seat, trying in vain to find a comfortable spot. "Anyway, I was saying, I don't think Pepper liked men."

He leaned across the console, his eyebrows scrunched. "So why was she Sonny's horse?"

Holly shrugged. "She was so beautiful. When she was in the field with the rest of the herd you could pretend you were out West somewhere looking at a herd of mustangs." She sighed at the vivid memory.

"Did Sonny pick her?"

"I missed seeing Riley today," Holly said. "What did she do?"

Mac put a finger under her chin and turned her to face him. "Did Sonny pick the horse or did you?"

Holly grinned and wrapped her hand around his finger. "It was a long time ago and it's hard to remember…but I might've put my two cents' worth into the discussion."

Mac leaned back in his seat and chuckled. "Oh, man. Poor Sonny. So did he get another horse?"

"Nah, he got a motorcycle. Remember the red dirt bike he had? That's what he bought with the money from selling the horse." She shifted in her seat. "So…what did your daughter do today?"

"Mom took her to a movie, but not before making me promise to take her next time. Maybe you could come along."

If only… She gave him a smile. "You know who you should take?"

"Who?"

"Miss Norton." She was surprised at the effort it took to say the name, although it was easier than the first time, back in Mac's guest bedroom.

"Not this again." Mac rubbed at his eyes.

"She's the type you're looking for, right?"

"I don't know what I'm looking for and—"

"That's Mister Cee."

Mac's head jerked toward her. "What?"

"The shadow you just saw on the porch… that's the tabby cat. Remember? He's the one who told us Sue was in trouble. Like Lassie, only he's a cat."

Mac sighed.

"He likes cappuccinos. But coffee's not good for animals so I froth the milk and let it cool. We call him Mister Cee because Mister Cappuccino takes too long to say."

Holly drummed her fingers on the console. Once again Mac's hand silenced them.

"Read my lips. Stakeout."

The gleam in Mac's eyes told her he was losing his patience. "Okay. You won't hear another peep out of me." Holly zipped her lips with her thumb and forefinger. She sipped her coffee and stared straight ahead, thinking of Mac and his search for the perfect family.

Mac's low voice broke the silence. "You should go home and go to bed."

Holly shrugged. "Believe it or not, I'm not tired."

FIFTEEN MINUTES LATER Holly was slumped against the window, breathing rhythmically. She must have developed an immunity to caffeine. Mac eased the cup out of her fingers and placed it in the cup holder.

Holly always managed to get her own way—from putting Riley on Twister, to training Frosty. It was only a matter of time before she and Riley brought up Riley riding Frosty. He rubbed his chin. He had forgotten to shave that morning and his beard was rough against his fingers. Holly was smiling in her sleep. Probably thinking of the trick she'd played on her older brother with the man-hating horse.

He tore his gaze from her face and perused the buildings across the street.

As usual, one light remained on in each of the storefronts. So far, nothing had moved. He reached for his cup and saw something out of the corner of his eye.

He picked up the mike and keyed it. "I have movement."

Parked in the alley behind the stores, Moose picked up immediately. "Where?"

"The Cookie Jar." Mac eased out of the car and closed the door without waking Holly. He stayed in the shadows of the hardware store. Talking into the mike at his shoulder, he eased around the front of the building. "Are you in position?"

He heard a grunt and then a muffled "Yeah" from the other officer.

Mac stayed in the shadows until he was directly across from the bakery. He ran quietly across the street.

He pressed his back against the door, pushed it open and yelled, "Freeze." Mac flicked on the light switch.

The doors to the baked goods case stood open. Dark forms huddled on the floor. He held his gun in both hands and moved forward, careful to survey the rest of the store. "Williams?"

"I'm here." The big man appeared from the kitchen, also holding his gun in a two-handed grip. He could see the culprits from his standpoint. Mac couldn't so he was surprised when Moose lowered the gun a fraction and told them to stand.

Two frightened faces peered over the top of the pastry case. "Are you kidding me?" Mac said.

If Mac hadn't recognized the footsteps pounding behind him, he and his gun would have gone flying as Holly ran into the store and crashed into his back. As it was, he had to brace himself. Looking over Mac's shoulder, Holly repeated his words. "Are you kidding me?"

CHAPTER NINETEEN

ONE O'CLOCK IN the morning and the six adults sitting in The Wildflower looked exhausted. The two teenagers looked plain scared.

Standing, his back to the counter, Ethan Johnson spoke first. "This was all my idea. I thought sneaking into places without anybody knowing would be exciting, kind of like espionage."

Adam McClain poked him with his elbow. "We did it because I never had any money to go out. It's my fault. We just took a little bit so it wasn't really stealing." The teenager finally looked at his parents, who sat on the couch. Matt had his head in his hands. "We took change to play the games at the park."

Adam's mother, Dottie, looked furious, her normally pale complexion a bright red. "These people provided us with work, Adam. How could you do this to them? Not to mention, it's wrong. We taught you better than this. What kind of example are you setting for your brothers and sisters?"

Adam hung his head, mumbling, "I'm sorry. The whole idea was stupid."

Mac sighed. He had intended to take the boys to the police station, but Holly had convinced him to call the parents and talk to everyone in her shop. Now he wasn't so sure he'd done the right thing. Holly perched on the arm of his chair.

Ethan's parents, Tom and Laura Johnson, sat at a table nearby. "Do you know how much money you've taken altogether?" Tom asked.

Ethan met his father's stern gaze. "I don't think we took more than a couple hundred. We took the most from the computer store because he didn't have much food other than candy bars and stuff. Most of the time we just took cookies—we didn't think it would matter as much."

All four parents turned to Mac, who, rather than meet their eyes, looked at the floor. He was torn. The boys came from good families and their actions, rather than malicious, had been just plain stupid.

"You know I have to bring them in and I have to take a statement from Holly. She was hurt during the commission of a crime. We're talking assault. We're talking breaking and entering. We can't just sweep this under the rug."

Holly grimaced. "I know. But I'm okay and the cost of the food they took is minimal. Can't we call this fiasco something else, something less...serious?"

Mac sighed. "Maybe." He stood and walked over to the two young men. "You're free to go home with your parents, but I want to see all of you in my office at eleven o'clock. Understand?"

"Yes, sir." Both boys spoke in unison and each let out a huge sigh of relief. "Thank you, sir," Adam added.

Mac frowned. "Don't thank me yet. This isn't over."

SEVEN HOURS LATER The Wildflower was jammed. News traveled fast in the small town. After the initial influx—and after Holly had provided everybody with free coffee—the crowd had settled into every available seat.

"Turn off the camera, Wendy. This discussion is not for the evening news." Mac pointed at the weatherwoman and gave her his sternest look. What had he been thinking, asking the newshound out on a date?

She frowned and then nodded at her cameraman. He lowered the camera. "Okay, Mac, but I still want to report the story. I can do it in front of the shop." She glanced at Holly, standing quietly behind the counter. "You'll get some free publicity."

"Oh, great. Come to The Wildflower. You might get robbed while you're here but our coffee is worth it." She did a ta-da stance, throwing her hands out to the side and smiling brightly.

A chuckle ran through the assembled group.

"Wendy, stop frowning," Mac said. "You'll get wrinkles."

Immediately her face went blank.

"Do the story out front. Just make sure you stress the culprits have been apprehended and they are underage. You cannot, I repeat, cannot, identify them."

Holding her pen poised over a notebook, Wendy pursed her lips. "I know, Mac. I am a professional."

Mac caught Holly's raised eyebrows and wry grin. Glancing back at Wendy, now scribbling madly, he continued. "Okay, then.

I gather you all heard what happened last night and that's why you're here."

"I need my money, Chief." Pierre Lefonte perched on the windowsill. "Moving is not cheap."

"Charge them with assault," Sonny said. "I don't care if they are underage. Holly could have been badly hurt."

Holly held up a hand and waited until everyone was quiet. "The decision is mine, right? I mean as far as the assault charge."

Mac leaned against the door and crossed his arms. He had a feeling he knew where she was going. She didn't want to charge the teens with assault. "Holly, underage or not, these kids need to be held accountable."

The room burst into excited chatter as everyone ventured an opinion. Mac held Holly's gaze as she gave him a wordless shrug. Someone tugged on Mac's sleeve and he swiftly brought his hand to his arm, only to find himself grasping Mrs. Hershberger's hand.

She smiled, her gray eyes sparkling behind rimless glasses. "I have a thought, John."

Mrs. Hershberger was the only person, other than his mother, to call him John. When she did, Mac always felt as if he was back in high school. "Yes, ma'am." He raised a hand and the murmuring ceased.

The teacher clasped her hands together and cleared her throat. "I've taught most of you in school, and I don't believe anybody in this room hasn't been involved in some kind of mischief at one point or another."

The guilty looks shared by the group would have been funny if the subject wasn't so serious. "Do you have a suggestion?" Mac asked.

"Holly should decide whether or not to press charges for the assault," Mrs. Hershberger said. "We can't know how she felt."

Every eye in the room focused on Holly.

Holly sighed. "I don't want to press charges. A record could ruin them for life. There must be something else we can do to make sure they've learned a lesson."

Fritz leaned forward and propped his elbows on his knees. "Holly, those boys are the size of grown men and—"

Rose rested a hand on his arm. "Olivia is right. The decision is yours, Holly. I suspect if they're charged with—" she tilted her head and glanced at Mac "—perhaps trespassing or vandalism, the charge won't follow them into adulthood if they stay out of trouble."

Mac nodded. "Depends on the value of the property they stole."

"Regardless, they should reimburse us for our losses." Sue, her apron covered with flour, stood next to Pierre. "I mean, surely the son of the bank president can cough up the money."

Cheri ran a hand through brown hair with recently frosted tips. Big silver hoops swung from her ears. "Don't be too hard on Tom and Laura. I haven't raised a child myself, but I know from watching my sisters raise their kids it's close to impossible to control them once they get their driver's licenses—short of locking them in their rooms."

"So are you saying…" Sue pressed her lips together and took a deep breath. "We don't get our money back? Easy for you to say. You didn't lose any money."

Cheri held up both hands and opened her mouth to speak when the mayor spoke up.

"I've got an idea."

"I'll bet your idea has something to do with the town going vegan," Sonny chimed in.

At the ensuing laughter the mayor smiled and shook her head. "As tempting as that is, Sonny, I have an idea to benefit the entire town, but I don't want to say anything until I meet with the board."

Pierre threw his hands in the air and headed for the door.

"She's right. As involved as all of you are, it's not your place to decide what happens here. We'll meet with the magistrate. Let's all get back to work." Mac motioned for everyone to leave. The consignment shop owner was the last one out.

"Hey, Cheri." Holly waved as the woman passed in front of the window.

Cheri stuck her head through the door. "What?"

"Do you still have the polo shirts?"

Cheri raised her eyebrows. "Why, I believe I do. Why do you ask?"

Holly grinned. "I'll be over later to check them out."

"You got it, girlfriend. That hit on the head must have knocked some sense into you." Cheri smiled and disappeared.

She'd no sooner left than Skinny Smith, hat in hand, came up to the counter. "I heard you had some excitement, Miss Hoffman. How are you?"

Holly smiled at the older man. "I'm fine, Mr. Smith. Where's your brother?"

Skinny shook his head and looked at his feet. "He's feeling poorly. The doctor says he's got bronchitis. He wasn't up to traveling into town this morning."

"Too bad," Mac said. Of the two brothers, Skinny had seemed the frailer twin. One never knew.

Holly poised her fingers over the cash register. "What can I get for you today?"

"I'll take one pound of my usual. Brother's been drinking tea lately." He tapped his ball cap against his hand as he studied the shop's menu board.

Mac laid a hand on Holly's arm as she started toward the kitchen. "I'll see you later."

Holly flashed him a smile, the same smile he remembered from their teen years. Even then it had made his heart beat faster.

When he stepped onto the porch Wendy was ready to pounce on him.

"Come on, Chief, you've got to give me something. This story could be my big break."

Mac frowned at her and then held up a finger. "One minute."

Wendy nodded at the lanky, long-haired cameraman and waited until a red light came on. "What can you tell us about the couple arrested for the recent bank robberies in our area?" She tilted the microphone in his direction.

Mac shook his head. "People who admire that sort of lifestyle need to remember that eventually they'll get caught. Even Bonnie and Clyde were finally apprehended."

"What about the culprits in the copper theft?"

Mac glanced at the camera and then back at Wendy. "Sometimes people rationalize stealing, but if the property's not yours, it's theft. They will be prosecuted."

He answered a few more questions, and then, as the cameraman put his equipment back into the news van, Wendy touched his arm. "Could I clear up some background, Chief?"

"What background? I've told you everything I can."

"I mean about you." Wendy pulled her pad and pen from a large briefcase sitting on the porch. "You've been in this position less than a year. You served on the police force in Fayetteville, North Carolina, correct?"

Mac's brows bunched. Annoyance flared at Wendy's persistence. "What does my prior employment have to do with anything?"

She looked at a sheaf of papers. "You came back home after your wife was killed in an automobile accident, right? It says here she was driving during a freak snowstorm."

Mac clenched his fists and pressed his lips together tightly. If he had learned one thing about dealing with the press, it was to not say the first thing that popped into your head. "Wendy, all you need to know is I had four years of experience with the Fayetteville police force." He sliced the air with his hand. "That's it." Mac headed for his vehicle.

Wendy's words followed him across the street. "Chief, why did they ask you to leave?"

CHAPTER TWENTY

HE DROVE AROUND for an hour, not wanting to talk to anyone at the station, needing to be alone with his thoughts. Wendy's question had unearthed some long-buried memories. She was sharp. His answer would've provided her with a juicy news bite. Instead he had walked away.

When he found himself at the edge of town, he decided to pay a visit to the Smith brothers. Skinny hadn't been his usual jovial self when he'd picked up the coffee. Mac drove up the gravel drive and parked at the foot of the porch steps.

Skinny showed him into the living room where Hawkeye lay on the couch, his legs covered with an orange-and-brown-ripple afghan. When he moved to get up, Mac waved his hand. "Don't trouble yourself, Hawkeye." He took a seat in the chair.

Hawkeye worked on a piece of wood cupped in his hands.

Skinny perched in the chair opposite Mac and nodded toward his brother. "That's what makes our turkey calls so special, is Hawkeye's handwork. Look at the detail."

Mac peered at the wooden box in the man's hands and glanced back at Skinny. "Turkey calls?"

"Those boxes in the hallway are all full. Orders ready to be shipped." He chuckled. "Who woulda thought two old codgers like us would have a website?"

Mac swallowed. "You have a website?"

"How else could someone find Smith turkey calls out here in the middle of nowhere?" He peered at Mac. "How about I make us a fresh pot of French press? I picked up some cookies at the bakery, too. The Hunter woman isn't the friendliest but she's a fine baker."

Before Mac could respond, Skinny had disappeared down the hall. Mac had never really suspected the twins of foul play, yet at the same time he felt bad for assuming the two older men were no longer able to make a living. On the contrary.

A grandfather clock chimed the hour. Mac cleared his throat. "Maybe I should—"

"I hear you're courting the Hoffman girl."

Mac's head jerked up. The sentence had

to have come from Hawkeye because no one else was in the room. The man's head was still bent, his gaze focused on the piece of wood. "Excuse me?"

Hawkeye grunted. "Young people don't say courting anymore, do they?" Bright blue eyes peered at Mac for a second. "I should say, I hear you're dating the Hoffman girl." His voice was surprisingly well modulated, not at all what Mac would expect after hearing his twin brother's local twang.

"No," Mac said. "What gave you that idea?"

Although his gaze remained fixed on the call in his hands, the corners of Hawkeye's mouth twitched. "People talk."

Mac twirled his hat in his hands. "People gossip, you mean."

"You're a lucky man."

"How so?" As soon as the words were out of his mouth, Mac regretted his sarcasm. Maybe the old man wouldn't notice. Regardless, he didn't know Mac, or that he'd lost his wife and was raising a child on his own.

Hawkeye's brows lifted in surprise. "You've had the love of two women in your life. Most of us are lucky to have had one." His long fingers worked the point of the knife into the wood.

Mac pursed his lips and stared at the polished hardwood floor between his boots. How Hawkeye knew about Anne, Mac wasn't sure, but then this was a small town and yes, people talked.

"I had a girlfriend once," Hawkeye said, "dated her all through high school. Then Vietnam and the draft came along and I got an all-expenses paid tour of Southeast Asia." He grunted. "Betty wrote to me every week, sometimes two or three times a week. So I come back from 'Nam, skinny as a rail and mean as a snake, and find out she's gone to California with her cousin. They drove a Volkswagen van the whole way across the country—you know the kind, the ones with flowers painted all over them. She left a letter asking me to follow her." He held the box up to the light, blew off the wood shavings and inspected it before bringing it back to his lap.

Mac waited for Hawkeye to continue, but he'd become engrossed in his carving, his lips pressed tight with concentration. Curiosity getting the better of him, he asked the obvious question. "So did you go to California?"

Hawkeye looked up as if surprised to

see Mac still sitting in the chair. "Oh, sure. I hitchhiked out. Spent the summer at the vineyard where she was working. We had a time of it. Bought an old panhead Harley we would take out on Highway One. Good times."

"Did you get married?"

Hawkeye dropped the call onto his lap and pulled a blue handkerchief from under the blanket. He coughed into the hankie, returned the cloth to its hiding place and took a sip of water. "We tossed the idea around, and then I got a letter from home. Beginning of August and Skinny was sick. He's had a heart condition ever since he was born. The doctor didn't think he would make it. Anyway, that's why he didn't get drafted. So Skinny and my dad had acres of tomatoes planted that summer and no one to pick them. Planting all those tomatoes is probably what got Skinny sick in the first place. If I'd been here, well..."

Mac waited. When Hawkeye leaned back and shut his eyes, he couldn't stay quiet any longer. "Did you and Betty come home?"

Hawkeye didn't answer and with his head resting on the pillow and his eyes closed, Mac thought for a minute he had gone to sleep. But the voice that answered was quiet. "I came home. Betty stayed and married the oldest son of the vineyard owner." He paused. "I still get Christmas cards from her."

"Are you talking about Betty?" Skinny entered the room carrying a silver tray with the coffee carafe and three cups and saucers. "You dodged a bullet, brother. What kind of woman doesn't wait for her man?" He set the tray on the coffee table and filled the cups. "What do you think of my brother's talent, Chief?" Removing the box from his brother's hands, he handed Hawkeye a cup and saucer. Then he gave the box to Mac.

Mac studied the carving on the side. Recognition shot through him. "This is Buddy, your coonhound." He glanced at Hawkeye, who sat up drinking coffee.

"Yep."

"He usually does simple drawings, like a turkey feather, or a pinecone. They don't take as much time as something intricate like Buddy." Skinny beamed with pride. "Of course, the call itself is what sells it." He set down his cup and took the call out of Mac's hands. When he scraped the thin sliver of wood across the open end of the rectangular box, a high-pitched gobble emerged.

Skinny tilted his head, one ear to the box, and peered at the ceiling. He slid the piece across the edges of wood again and this time, Mac would have sworn a turkey was in the room. "Takes a little time, but it's not too hard once you get the hang of it." He handed the box to his brother, who dropped it in a dark blue felt bag with a red drawstring.

Hawkeye set the bag on the coffee table and picked up his cup. "I hear you caught some teenagers stealing in town. What will happen to them?"

Mac shrugged. "They've been released to their parents. A lot depends on how much money they took and whether Holly presses charges."

Skinny shook his head. "Darn shame. Kids don't have enough to keep themselves busy so they get into trouble. You ought to be able to harness their energy somehow. Now if we had them out here on the farm back when we were growing vegetables, they'd be too tired for monkeyshines, how about it, brother?"

"Yep."

Mac set down his empty cup. "I should get back to town." He touched Hawkeye's afghan-covered knee. "Hope you're feeling better soon."

Skinny picked up the tray. "I'll take this back to the kitchen while you say your good-byes." He left the room.

Hawkeye picked up the felt bag and held it out. "This is for you."

Mac dropped his hands to his side. "I can't accept, Hawkeye. It's your dog. You should keep it."

Hawkeye shook his head. "What would I do with it? Leave it to Skinny?" He chuckled. "Although he will probably outlive me. No, I want you to have it, maybe pass it down to your girl—" he raised his eyebrows "—or boy, if you have one."

Mac held out his hand and the old man laid the cloth bag in his palm. He waited until Mac met his gaze before saying, "Remember, you're a lucky man."

For a moment Mac didn't think he could force any words past the huge lump in his throat. He swallowed. "Thank you…what is your real name?"

Hawkeye smiled. "Joseph."

"Why do they call you Hawkeye?"

"A story for another day."

"Thank you, Joseph."

Joseph Smith lifted the afghan off his legs

and stood, thrusting out his hand. "You're welcome, John."

Mac waited until Hawkeye settled himself back on the couch and then left. Outside, Skinny leaned against his truck.

Mac looked around the immaculate front yard. A late-blooming shrub grew red roses at the foot of the steps. "Where's Buddy?"

Skinny looked off into the distance, as if remembering long-ago coon hunts. "His heart finally gave out. Went to sleep the other night and in the morning we found him stretched out at the foot of Hawkeye's bed. He always was more Hawkeye's dog than mine. My brother's takin' it pretty hard."

Mac tightened his hand around the turkey call. Hawkeye had created the drawing from memory. He held the bag out to Skinny. "Maybe I shouldn't have accepted this. He might want it when he's feeling better."

Skinny waved his hand away. "The turkey call was a gift, son. Life gives you a gift, you accept it graciously and move on. Kind of like Hawkeye comin' home all those years ago when I was sick. If it weren't for me, he'd probably still be in California with a couple of kids." He shrugged. "Water under the bridge." With a finger to his cap, Skinny walked back to the house.

"I HAVE A proposition for you." Holly rested her feet on the coffee table and hugged her mug to her chest. Her heart thumped against her pale yellow polo shirt.

"I'm not sure I can take any more excitement." Mac rubbed a hand over his face. "Last night they caught the couple who robbed the bank in Shadow Falls and the guys stealing copper up on the mountain. This has been a crazy week."

Holly had finished her inventory by the time Mac stopped by. After dropping Riley off at Sunday school, he had developed the habit of checking on Holly, alone at the store.

She'd been thinking about this for a week, ever since Mac had dealt with the irate storekeepers so patiently. "It's about to get crazier."

Mac narrowed his eyes. "What are you talking about?"

"Did you ever go out with Miss Norton?"

Mac shrugged. "Why do you ask?"

Holly sat up and dropped her feet to the floor with a bang. "Mac, your mother leaves for South America in a month and you have nothing arranged for your daughter. Unless you're taking a leave of absence?"

Mac frowned. "We're a two-man force. How can I take a leave of absence?"

"My point exactly." She sipped her coffee and said, "So did you ask her out?"

"No."

"Why not? She's perfect. Good with kids. I'm sure she can braid hair. What are you waiting for?"

Mac shrugged. "I talked to her when I took Riley to sign up for first grade. She started dating Tim at the hardware store."

Holly lowered her voice. "So you don't want to marry her?"

Mac rolled his eyes. "What? No. I barely know her."

"And Edna has too many cats." Holly smiled.

"Eliza." He returned her smile.

"Wendy wants to leave the area and Ms. King travels extensively."

"What are you getting at?"

Holly set her cup in the middle of the table and rested her palms on her knees. "That leaves me."

Mac didn't answer.

"You have smoke coming from your ears."

"I'm confused." Mac's voice was soft. "What exactly are you saying?"

Holly rubbed her hands on her jeans and looked at the floor. "I've decided to close the business. Carolyn starts teaching soon and Louise, well, this might force her to go back to nursing, where she belongs. It's a win-win. I'll borrow from the bank to pay off Dad. I can braid Twister's tail so I should be able to figure out how to braid a little girl's hair although Riley said she prefers pony-tails and—"

The rest of her rambling sentence was lost as Mac pulled her out of her chair and up against his rock-hard chest, the same chest she'd run into months ago. "Holly, are you saying…?"

"My mom said women aren't born mater-nal so I thought I'd get some books on parent-ing from the library. Whatever it takes." She wrapped her arms around his neck and came up on her tiptoes. She was mostly happy, a little sad maybe, but mostly happy. "We'd have to marry, though. I don't think it would be proper for me to live—"

Mac pressed his lips against hers and Holly melted into his arms. Their third kiss. Maybe

Mac didn't love her, maybe he would never get over the loss of his wife, but she had enough love for the both of them.

CHAPTER TWENTY-ONE

THE KISS WAS SWEET, passionate. Holly expected nothing less when Mac was involved. He pulled away and looked at her steadily. "Are you sure?"

Unable to speak, Holly nodded. She had said the words. No going back.

What had she just done? She fingered a gold cord hanging from Mac's shirt pocket. "What's this?"

Mac pulled out a blue felt bag and held it in the palm of his hand. "Hawkeye gave me a gift."

Holly upended the bag and slid a smooth wooden box into her hands. She studied the intricate carving. "Hawkeye did this?"

"That's another crazy thing. Those two have an internet business—the source of all the money for remodeling the homestead."

"Get out of town. An internet business?" Her breath caught in her throat as she studied the intricate carving. "It's gorgeous. Is this his dog?"

Mac nodded. "Black-and-tan coonhound. He just died. Poor guy. Hawkeye looked like he lost his best friend."

Placing the box in the middle of the table, Holly eased out of Mac's arms and sat, her legs suddenly weak as the magnitude of what she had done threatened to overwhelm her. She pushed the realization to the back of her mind. The offer had been made and accepted. Case closed. Time to move on. "My grandfather had a black-and-tan years ago. He loved that dog. Said he was the best dog he ever had."

"Skinny used the same words to describe Buddy."

"So their dog was a black-and-tan coonhound?"

Mac's brows bunched together. "I just said that. You're not getting headaches are you? Maybe we should go back to the doctor."

"No, silly, I'm thinking." Holly tapped her finger against her lips.

Mac grimaced. "Well, give me some warning next time. I was getting worried."

Holly laughed. "I was thinking about the Colliers' Lab, Daisy. All her pups looked like her except one. Did you see the one I was holding the night we had fireworks?"

"All the pups looked alike to me. They're black Labs."

"The one I was holding had a brown nose and brown paws. You don't think…"

Mac frowned. "From the Smith farm to town is pretty far…"

"Yeah, but when you're in love…" Holly tilted her head and batted her eyes.

They sat in silence, Holly calculating the distance—as the crow flies—the coonhound would've traveled. "My grandfather used to say his dog could cover a lot of miles when he was on a scent." She leaned forward, fixing Mac with an intense look. "I'll bet the Smiths' dog is the father of Daisy's puppies." When Mac didn't answer, she continued. "If Fran still has the male with the brown paws, I'll bet they'd love to have him."

Mac shook his head. "I don't know, Holly, a puppy…"

"…might be what the old guy needs to get back on his feet. Come on, Mac, let's see if Fran still has the dog. We'll pick up Riley, too." Holly reached for Mac's cup and carried the mugs over to the counter. Behind her Mac was muttering something about always getting her own way. She glanced over her shoulder ready to argue the point and saw Mac waiting at the door. Well, as long as she got her own way...

"Holly, are you sure?" Mac's blue eyes looked troubled.

Holly slipped her arms around his waist. "Mac, it's the perfect solution." She kissed him, then opened the door.

Across the street, Ethan Johnson and Adam McClain had just finished tilling the vacant lot—with the use of a rototiller on loan from the hardware store. Now, shirts discarded, they raked rocks and weeds out of the loosened soil.

"The lot will look beautiful in the spring." Holly leaned an elbow on Mac's shoulder as they watched the two boys work in the hot September sun.

"Restitution, probation and community service. They're lucky that's all they got." Mac grimaced. "The army straightened me out."

She ran a finger along the curve of his clean-shaven jaw. "Good thing you went."

"Thank your dad."

Holly dropped her hand to her side. "Did you just say the army was my dad's idea?"

Mac nodded. "I got in a bit of trouble. Your dad caught me."

"That explains the big dog thing." When Mac gave her a quizzical look, she quickly continued. "What did you do?"

"I smashed the taillights on Mrs. Hershberger's new car."

Holly gasped. "Why would you do that? She's a sweetheart."

"She caught me smoking cigarettes on school property and marched me into the principal's office. I got three weeks detention."

"You were angry. You lashed out. So where's my dad come in?"

"He was making a night deposit at the bank and saw me. The deal was I work at the farm for a month and pay Mrs. Hershberger for the damages, then go straight to boot camp."

"You kissed me the day before you left." All those years of keeping her distance and the day before he leaves town he surprises her with a first kiss.

He nodded. "The military taught me to control my emotions."

Holly wanted to say *too well*, but she bit her tongue.

"Mayor Gold did have a pretty good idea." Mac eased out from under Holly's elbow and slipped his arm around her waist. "Have they done their time with you yet?"

Holly chuckled. "Not yet. Next Wednesday they're coming here for boot camp, Hoffman-style. Who needs the army?"

"Adam might if he doesn't get the wrestling scholarship," Matt McClain said as he came out of the computer shop. He grimaced. "Man, it's hot out here. Wonder if those young men have learned anything yet?"

Across the street Adam caught the three watching them and waved.

"I'm thinking yes," Holly replied as she waved back. "I understand you're taking over the store for Pierre. Have they left yet?"

"Jessie has. Pierre is closing up the house and working with me this week. He's driving a moving van down next weekend." He shook his head. "I was shocked when he asked me to take over the store, what with everything that went on."

"Give people a chance and they'll do the right thing."

Holly slipped her arm through Mac's. "You're such an optimist, even if you do occasionally suspect your friends of criminal activity."

Mac covered her hand with his. "People will do the right thing, but sometimes they do the wrong thing, too." He tilted his head toward the boys across the street. "That's where reparations come in—sometimes people need a little reminder."

"I understand your brother is building raised beds for growing vegetables," Matt said.

Holly nodded. "Tom Johnson is buying two benches in honor of local veterans. The stone quarry is donating gravel for the paths and the hardware store is donating grass seed. The Garden Club is planting flower bulbs along the fence next to the library. The whole thing just snowballed."

"Would you believe Sue had those two boys and their girlfriends icing cakes the other day?" Matt laughed. "They don't have time to look for excitement anymore." He stuck out his hand to Holly. "We have you and Mac to thank for it."

Holly shook his hand but said, "No you don't, Matt. Everybody agreed this was the best route to take."

Mac glanced at his watch. "We better get

moving if we want to catch Riley in between Sunday school and church."

Thirty minutes later Mac, Holly and Riley sat on Fran Collier's back porch. The brown-and-black pup whimpered as it stood on Riley's lap and licked her face, causing Riley to giggle.

"Careful, Riley, Molly might get jealous." Mac smoothed a hand over his daughter's head. "I'm surprised this one's still here, Fran."

Fran sat in a rocker, Daisy by her side as the pup they were keeping chased a grasshopper across the porch. "Nobody is interested in a black Lab that doesn't look like a black Lab. I'd be thrilled if the Smiths want him."

"We'll give it a shot, but I can't guarantee it. This was Holly's idea."

"And a fine idea it is, Chief McAndrews," Holly said. "We won't be bringing this little fella back, Fran. He'll have a good home."

Mac stood and stretched. "Let's go find out. Riley, can you carry him?"

Riley pushed up from the porch and grabbed the squirming puppy around the middle. "I don't think so, Daddy. He's too wiggly."

Mac took the pup from his daughter and carried him, cradled in one arm, to his truck. Once Riley was belted into the backseat, he set the dog in her lap. "Hold tight, Riley."

After backing out of the Colliers' driveway, Mac headed for the Smith farm. The only sound in the truck was Riley's high-pitched singing and the pup's yips. They crossed the suspension bridge.

"What are you singing, Riley? The song sounds familiar." Holly looked over the seat and smiled at the sight of the little girl singing to the pup, nose to nose, as the puppy tried unsuccessfully to lick her chin.

"I'm singing a song I learned at Brownies." She giggled as a pink tongue swiped her cheek. "It's about making new friends but keeping old friends."

"I remember that song," Holly said.

"Molly and this puppy are like new friends. Is Holly an old friend or a new friend, Daddy?"

Holly caught Mac's eye as he said, "She's my old friend, Riley." He pulled onto the gravel drive of the Smith farm. "She's a very good old friend."

"Then you're supposed to keep her, Daddy. The song says keep your old friends."

"Okay, Riley, I'll keep her." Mac smiled as the gravel crunched beneath his tires.

Before Holly could respond, they spotted Skinny sitting on his porch steps. He rose as they parked and ambled down the steep stairs. "Got company with ya today, Chief?" He nodded toward Holly.

"I do, Skinny." Mac opened the back door of his truck and lifted Riley down, pup still grasped tightly in her hands. "We brought you something."

Riley looked up at the man in front of her and held out the puppy.

Skinny studied the wriggling animal—his brown nose, brown paws and long ears—and rubbed his chin with his fingers. "Well, I'll be…"

"He's not purebred, Skinny. Holly's neighbors have a black Lab who had a midnight visitor. We're not sure but we thought maybe Buddy…"

"…had one last hurrah?" Skinny chuckled. He bent down and said, "Is this your puppy, little girl?"

Riley shook her head. "I have his sister and Daddy says I can only have one dog at a time." She thrust the puppy into Skinny's arms. "This is your dog, if you want him."

Skinny ran a long, silky black ear through his fingers. "Well, I'll be…" he repeated softly. Riley leaned against his shoulder, stroking the dog's back. "I don't need a dog."

Holly sighed. She had been so sure the Smiths would be the perfect owners for the mixed-breed dog. "But—"

"But my brother does. You three come into the house with me." He stood and, carrying the dog, led them into the house. In the hallway, he stopped and gave the dog back to Riley. "You go on in and see Hawkeye. I'll fetch some lemonade. Too hot for coffee, Ms. Hoffman." With a broad wink, he disappeared down the hall.

Holly let Mac and Riley precede her into the living room, where Hawkeye lay on the couch, his legs covered with the brown-and-orange afghan. With a knife, he worked on a turkey call in his hands. "Chief, who's this?"

Mac waved Holly into a chair facing the couch. "You know Holly Hoffman, from The Wildflower."

Holly nodded, and wondered at the faint smile he threw in her direction. "I do. Nice to see you, Miss Hoffman."

"And this is my daughter, Riley."

Riley walked around the coffee table and

leaned on the couch, spilling the puppy into the old man's lap. "He's for you, if you want him."

Hawkeye handed the knife and box to Mac, and pushed himself higher on the couch. He dropped his feet to the floor and patted the couch. "He's for me, you say?" He ran a long, silky ear through his fingers and studied the dog. "Where'd he come from?"

Holly smiled as the puppy sniffed the man's hands. "My neighbor has a female black Lab who got herself in the family way. We think maybe your dog paid a visit. I know it's far but…"

Hawkeye nodded as he lifted a brown paw with his finger. "Doesn't surprise me. Hounds often travel for miles. It's almost impossible to pull them away when they're on a mission." He chuckled. "Well, I'll be…"

Riley leaned against his shoulder. "So will you keep him? Will you?" She took a breath. "What's his name? Do you have a name yet?"

With a gentle smile, Mac tugged the girl's ponytail. "Riley, enough with the questions."

Skinny appeared with a silver tray carrying an etched crystal pitcher full of lemonade, ice and sliced lemons. One mismatched glass had faded pictures of cartoon characters. He filled the glass half-full and set it in front of Riley. "This glass belonged to my little sister. She lives in Pittsburgh, used to teach music at Carnegie Mellon." He nodded toward Hawkeye. "So what do you think, brother?"

Hawkeye stroked the pup with one finger from the top of his domed head to his rump as he lay curled upon the man's lap. "I think Buddy the Second has found his way home."

After lemonade and raisin-filled cookies, Mac, Holly and Riley waved goodbye to the two men standing on the front porch. The pup nestled in Hawkeye's arms.

Mac slammed the truck door and studied the two farmers still waving from the porch. "I think the dog got Hawkeye off the couch, Holly." He waved and then started down the long gravel lane, turning left at the end. "Good idea."

"I think so, too," Holly said. "Seeing Hawkeye like that made me wonder…is it possible to let yourself fade away?"

When Mac didn't answer, she answered her own question. "I suppose it might be easy if you're alone." She bit her lip. "I'm glad we brought him the pup, Mac." She looked across the truck console and was rewarded with a smile.

"Me, too, Holly. They belong together."

Mac stopped the truck in the middle of the suspension bridge. "See any fish jumping, Riley?"

Snug in her booster seat, Riley stretched to see the smooth surface of the creek far below. "Nope." She settled back into her seat. "Now what, Daddy?"

Mac raised his eyebrows. "Honey, we're going home. Haven't you had enough excitement for one day?"

"Nope. I think I need some more excitement."

Mac shook his head. If he didn't know better, he would think Holly was rubbing off on his little girl. His suspicion was confirmed at Riley's next request.

"Can I go see my horse?"

Mac looked at Riley's hopeful face in the rearview mirror. He glanced across at Holly. "Do you mind?"

She shook her head. "I should check on Twister."

Mac shrugged. "Okay, I'll drop you two off at the farm, run into the office and then come back in an hour or so."

When they arrived, Twister seemed to be waiting for them, and Holly had the horse saddled in no time. Riley sat on the bench as Holly trotted Twister around the paddock.

Age slipped away from the old horse as he responded to Holly's touch, and Holly reflected on the importance of purpose in life, whether you were old or young, human or animal. Not unlike Hawkeye and Buddy the Second. "Do you want to ride?"

"What about Frosty? He wants some attention."

Holly followed Riley's line of sight and saw Frosty peeking over the arena fence, blue eyes watching Twister with interest.

Rounding the corner, Holly pulled Twister to a stop. Holly hadn't worn a watch since she left the military, but she knew it had to be getting close to the time Mac would be coming to pick them up. She was about to respond when she saw Riley cross the corner of the paddock and approach her horse. She reached up to rest her hand on the perlino's muzzle. The cream-colored horse and the small girl stood motionless in the bright afternoon sunlight. They looked like a painting, a frozen tableau. Behind them the green field stretched to the pine-covered hillside.

Hand still on the horse's nose, the little girl turned. "Rosalyn said you've been riding Frosty. Can I watch you?"

"Okay, you miniature diplomat, you win. Let's take care of Twister first."

Riley's gap-toothed smile was a thing of beauty and Holly wondered how Mac was ever able to say no to the little girl.

Working together, they unsaddled Twister, turned him out with the others and saddled Frosty.

The Welsh pony had been easy to handle and was a dream to ride. Holly cantered him around the edge of the ring and then cut through the middle, the horse effortlessly changing leads. Coming around the far corner, she traversed the center again. Holly caught sight of Riley as she rounded the far end, sitting quietly on the top rail of the fence. She had put on Rosalyn's white helmet. Holly's heart skipped a beat. "What do you think, Miss McAndrews? How do we look?" She skidded to a stop in front of the girl.

The look on Riley's face melted her heart. "You look wonderful, Holly." She caught a few strands of the coffee-colored mane in her hand and bit her lip. "I wish I could ride him."

Holly rested her hands on the saddle horn and realized she should have seen this coming. Of course Riley would want to ride Frosty. The gelding was her horse. He was a connection between Riley and her mother and anyone with a fraction of the horse sense Riley possessed would want to ride the animal. She tilted her head and studied the little girl, still trailing the mane through her fingers. "Your dad said he didn't want you riding Frosty…"

Riley nodded slowly.

"…but he didn't say you couldn't ride with me." At the gleam of excitement in the girl's eyes Holly felt a burst of pleasure. She inched back in the saddle and motioned to Riley. "Stand up."

Riley held on to the fence with one hand and stretched a leg over the saddle in front of Holly. Holly wrapped her arms around the warm little body and settled her in the saddle. A frisson of guilt tickled her spine—both because Anne was missing the child's first ride on Frosty and because somehow she knew Mac wouldn't have agreed with her rationale.

Riley leaned her head against Holly's chest and looked up.

"What are we waiting for?"

Holly smiled. "What are we waiting for, indeed?"

Riley's girlish laughter trailed after them as they transitioned from walk to trot to canter.

"Holly, Frosty's wonderful. He's so smooth and he seems happy, don't you think, Holly? Don't you think Frosty is happy because I'm riding him, Holly?"

Holly laughed and was about to say yes when she caught sight of Mac standing next to the fence. The look on his face was a mixture of surprise, regret and anger. When she met his eyes she knew no amount of rationalizing would persuade him she hadn't misled him.

Her proposition wasn't even twenty-four hours old. And she could tell the deal was off.

CHAPTER TWENTY-TWO

"HEY, MAN, WHAT'S HAPPENIN'?"

Mac tore his gaze away from Holly, taking a moment to process the fact that Chris Hoffman was home again. "Hey, Chris." Mac's response was less than enthusiastic.

"What's goin' on?" Chris propped one foot, still clad in his tasseled driving moccasins, on the bottom rail. He glanced at his sister, who was lifting Mac's daughter down from the horse. "Hey, Riley finally got on Frosty. That's great." He elbowed his friend in the biceps. When Mac didn't respond, he continued. "What's up with you? You look like you're ready to spit nails."

Finally fed up with Chris's probing, Mac barked out a reply. "I told Holly *my* child was not to ride that pony and she deliberately went against my wishes." He took a deep breath. "How dare she?" Fists clenched, he turned his back on the pair as they led the pony into the barn. The guilt was back, along with the fear.

When he got no response from Chris, he stole a glance at his friend and almost did a double take. The friendly skies professional pilot was gone, replaced by...

...Holly's brother. Chris had a belligerent tilt to his lips and both hands fisted at his side. His normally sparkling green eyes were cold as pond ice.

"What?"

Chris leaned into Mac's face until their chins were almost touching. "You're telling me my sister has spent the entire summer getting to know *your* daughter, spending time with *your* daughter, answering the million questions little girls have...and you really think she would do something that wasn't in that child's best interest?" Chris curled his lip and his voice came out in a soft growl. "I don't think so."

It occurred to Mac that Chris, too, had spent time in a war zone and deep inside his friend lived another man, the man who always came to the defense of his loved ones. "You don't understand." Mac put a hand on Chris's shoulder and the lip uncurled a fraction.

"Oh, I understand. You're still getting your

head together. Well, guess what? You're outta time. Step up to the plate, man. Quit letting other people pinch hit for you. You're a father. Act like one. Being a good father is more than just finding adequate childcare. You need to be there. You, not someone else."

"I can't care for a little girl. I couldn't even protect the women I loved. First Anne, and then Holly." Mac stared into the field where the horses stood, tails swinging, in the shade of an old apple tree. "Anne wanted so badly to train Frosty. That's all she talked about."

"As sure as I'm better-looking than you are, Anne is up in Heaven looking down here and saying, 'I didn't breed that foal special for my daughter just so he could lounge around in the field with his buddies. About time, you fool.'"

Mac choked out a laugh. "I'm not sure if there's any truth in your statement. Once you said you were better-lookin' you kind of lost me."

Chris rested his arms on the rail next to Mac and followed his gaze to the horses. "The fact Anne is gone is not Holly's fault, Mac."

Mac nodded. "I know." He spoke on an exhaled breath. "It's my fault."

Mac felt Chris's startled gaze but he couldn't look him in the eye. "Anne's death is my fault," he said again. "I was working the night of the accident. The snow was coming down like crazy and you know people down South don't know how to drive in the snow." He waved a hand in the air and gave a half laugh. "Up here everybody's got snow tires, and chains, and four-wheel drive." He wiped his hands over his face and started walking up the lane, not knowing if Chris followed him or not. The memories swept over him, leaving him chilled.

Chris came alongside. "So you were working. Was Anne working? Did she have to drive home in the snow?"

Mac chuckled. "That's just it. She didn't have to drive. She was home safe and sound with Riley and her parents."

"Why was she out driving?" They had reached the pond, and Chris crouched, looking through the scattered stones for a flat rock. Standing, he flipped the stone sideways across the pond.

"Four skips. Not bad for an old guy." Mac had trouble forming the words.

"Yep, I've still got it." Chris knelt again and dragged his finger through the stones.

His head bent, he asked again. "Why was she out driving?"

Mac sighed. He wished Chris would let the matter drop. "Typical husband-wife stuff. She'd been asking me for two days to pick up milk for Riley and I kept promising I would…but I didn't. Riley was two. Anne couldn't stand the idea of her baby not having milk." He was looking at the hay field across from the pond but in his mind he saw sleet and snow driving at the windshield of his SUV. "I had the all-wheel drive, her father had the truck—he was picking up feed for the mares—and she had the car, the rear-wheel drive car, the absolutely worthless-in-the-snow car."

"That doesn't make the accident your fault, Mac. Do you know how many times Val has asked me to pick something up and I've forgotten? I don't even want to tell you." He skipped another stone. "But what does that have to do with Holly?"

The ripples from Chris's stone spread out on the pond, overlapping. The pain in Mac's chest threatened to explode and he gripped a sharp rock in his hand until he felt it break the skin. "I love seeing Holly with Riley, but then I remember Anne was supposed…"

Chris's hand grasped his shoulder. "That must hurt, but listen, man. Stuff happens in life and there's not one damn thing you can do about it except pick yourself up and keep on going, one foot in front of the other." He took a deep breath. "One more thing, my friend."

Mac looked into the green eyes. The ice had melted. "There's more?"

"Love is a risk. When you open your heart, there's always the chance you could get hurt. That's why you push everybody away. I've watched you do it ever since your dad died. Your daughter just needs you to love her."

Mac turned away. The realization that Chris noticed his inability to connect with his daughter hit him like a sledgehammer. And Chris wasn't even in town most of the time. "Easy for you to say. Your wife's home, your mother was home. The perfect family has always come easy for you. Not so much for the rest of us."

"You are so dense." Chris propped his hands on his hips and shook his head. "Valerie works from home. She shows houses in the evenings. If I'm on a trip, she hires one of the neighbor girls to watch Harley. And what do you mean, Mom was home? She's a nurse."

Mac's anger reignited. He thought of his own mother working in the hospital gift shop during the day and taking nursing classes at night. "Later, maybe, after you left home. When we were in school your mother was always home. She went to all Holly's games. Who are you kidding?"

"She had enough seniority at the hospital she could choose her schedule. She worked swing shift, Mac. She just retired a couple years ago."

The air left Mac's lungs in a rush. "Who watched the kids?"

"If Dad wasn't around, Sonny was in charge. That was fun." Chris rolled his eyes. "Not. He used to pay us a quarter to do his chores."

Mac's knees buckled. He eased himself down on the ground. The ripples from Chris's stone disappeared against the far bank. "All this time I assumed your mother didn't work."

"Well you assumed wrong."

"So all these years…" Mac had always measured his version of the perfect family against the Hoffmans. But he'd only seen part of the picture, or maybe what he wanted to see. "They let me go, Chris."

"Who did?"

"Fayetteville. They were real nice about it—said I needed some time to pull myself together. I lucked out with Chief Stone."

"So you got a second chance, in more ways than one." Chris slapped a hand on Mac's shoulder. "So how can you ask Holly to give up her dream to meet your distorted sense of what a family should be?"

"I didn't ask." Mac shuddered. She had told her family already? He supposed he shouldn't be surprised. "She volunteered."

"Holly called a family meeting. She said she's closing the shop—borrowing from the bank to pay Dad and staying home for Riley. You should've seen the disappointment in my father's face."

"In Holly?"

"Heck, no. In you, big shot. I mean, what century are you living in?"

"I thought she would be okay with that."

"Man, dense doesn't begin to describe you."

"Hey, back off."

"One more thing."

"This makes two more things." Mac

crouched by the side of the pond, tossing stones into the water. High in the trees, locusts chirred then grew silent. In the field across the way a groundhog came out of his hole, eyes checking for predators. Finding none, the animal scampered across the field in search of a tasty morsel.

"What can I say? I'm on a roll." Chris bent at the waist and skipped a stone across the water, leaving five perfect circles in its wake.

"Lucky for me."

"My sister loves you—I have no idea why—but she does. I guess that's why she's willing to give up her dream. You better treat her well." He straightened and the professional pilot returned. "We should get back." He pointed to his shoes. "My driving moccasins are getting dusty."

HOLLY KNEW MAC was angry. She had seen the set of his jaw and the flash of his eyes. She also knew he wouldn't take out his anger on Riley. She would be the lucky recipient. No matter. She could take it.

When Chris and Mac appeared in the open doorway at the end of the barn, Holly was ready. "Hi, brother. Would you mind taking Riley to the house while I take care of

Frosty? I heard a rumor Thomas and the kids are making homemade ice cream."

"You betcha." Chris stuck out his hand. "Let's go see what's happening at the house, Miss McAndrews."

After a questioning look at her father and an answering nod, Riley took Chris's hand and the two disappeared down the lane.

Hooked to the cross ties, the perlino stood patiently as Holly ran a brush over the sweat marks on his belly. She discarded two opening salvos before finally deciding on the best approach. "I know Riley is your daughter, Mac, and I should have cleared the ride with you first." She took a deep breath to quell the butterflies in her stomach.

"I know."

"But she was so despondent I couldn't say no." The idea of never again riding with the little girl sent shivers down her spine.

"I know."

"The horse is such a dream to ride." She had to convince Mac to allow her to bring horse and child together.

"You know, encouraging me to date was very clever of you."

"I wanted to share the experience with…

Wait, what did you say?" Holly leaned an arm on the horse's back.

Mac came closer, with the same cowboy swagger she remembered from the beginning of summer, minus the accompanying jingle of spurs. "Do you love me, Holly?"

She resumed her brushing, choosing to ignore his question. A minute later, she turned and found him just a few feet away. She gasped and pressed a hand to her pounding heart. "You scared me, sneaking up like that."

"Answer the question. Do you love me?" Mac ran a hand down the perlino's nose.

Holly took a deep breath and exhaled slowly. "Love isn't relevant in our situation."

Mac took the brush out of her hand and set the tool on a nearby hay bale. "Chris said you loved me. Do you?"

Holly tried to pull her hands away, both now firmly in Mac's grasp. "What would he know? He's thirty thousand feet above the ground most of the time. He probably suffers from oxygen deprivation."

Mac chuckled. "Your brother is an astute observer of humanity. Don't tell him I said so. I'm tired of pretending, Holly. Why can't you admit you love me?"

Holly looked into Mac's blue eyes, looked for sincerity, for love. Those eyes seemed the same as they had that day when Mac had walked back into her life. Warm. Compassionate. *But love?* Love couldn't be identified as easily as compassion.

Holly jerked away from Mac's loosened grasp. She picked up the discarded brush, sank onto the hay bale and leaned back against Twister's stall. "I love you both. I said it. Are you happy?"

Mac unhooked the perlino and with a slap on the rump sent the horse through the open door into the paddock. He leaned against the stall opposite and crossed his arms and then his ankles. "Yes." He smiled the same slow smile she had seen him give Wendy.

But he still hadn't said anything about loving her. "You said that Riley needed a mother, someone like Anne, someone who could braid hair, would be there when she came home from school."

Mac jerked out of his relaxed pose and walked to the open paddock door.

Whenever she thought of becoming a family with Mac and Riley, her thoughts always returned to Anne—delicate, gentle, refined Anne. Holly stared at the hay-strewed concrete floor. She had to ask. "Are you having second thoughts?"

Mac strode across the space separating them. He knelt in front of her. "No, I'm not having second thoughts. And I don't want Riley's teacher, or the librarian or someone who looks like Riley's mother. I want you, Holly. I figured I needed someone who could be a good parent because I...I... I don't know how to care for her properly."

Holly's heart ached for Mac. All the love he had for his child he couldn't express and he still thought the girl needed someone else. "Do you love your daughter?"

Mac jerked back in shock. "Of course I love her."

"Then you'll figure it out, just like everybody else. You just need some practice. People aren't born knowing how to be a mom or a dad. At least that's what my mom said. She said Sonny was her experimental baby."

"That explains a lot." Mac gave her a small smile. "And then you find him a man-hating horse. I'm surprised the man is as successful as he is."

Holly laughed, then quickly sobered. "I asked you once why you were so hurtful to me after the family Christmas party."

Mac grimaced. "I told you I was—"

She pressed a hand to his cheek. "You were in pain. I understand now. And when you're in pain you lash out. Like with Mrs. Hershberger's car. Like now, seeing me with Riley and Frosty." She stopped, uncertain how Mac would react to her armchair psychology. He was a master at hiding his feelings behind a mask of toughness, but now, she could see the mask begin to slip.

Mac wrapped his arms around her waist. "You're right, Holly. Your brother helped me see I've been looking at things all wrong. And I can't ask you to give up the coffee shop. We'll figure something out."

"Mac." A kettledrum had replaced her heart. She had to ask. "What about me?"

Mac cupped her cheek in his palm. "What about you?" He smiled.

"Do we still have a deal?"

"Of course."

The kiss was perfect, as sweet as the first kiss. But he still hadn't said the words. Mac still hadn't told Holly he loved her. *Of course* would have to be enough.

CHAPTER TWENTY-THREE

THE BEAR MEADOWS CUBS had won the first Friday night football game of the season, and it seemed as if the whole town was celebrating.

Adam McClain came out from the kitchen, carrying a rack of clean coffee cups. "'Scuse me, Miss Hoffman." Adam set the tray on the counter and proceeded to place the cups on top of the espresso machine.

"I didn't even see you come in," Holly said. "What are you doing working?" She noticed the two black dashes of face paint underneath his eyes. "You just won your first game. You should be celebrating."

"Yes, ma'am, but I noticed you were low on cups." He pointed to the seating area, where Ethan wiped crumbs from the low tables. "We thought we should help out since you're so busy tonight."

"Okay, well, great. Carry on, then." A glimmer of satisfaction bloomed inside her chest as Holly glanced over at Louise, busy refilling a plate with no-bake cookies. "I see you're wearing your new shirt."

Louise raised an eyebrow. "About time you coughed up some money and got us decent shirts." She brushed a piece of lint off the sleeve of her pale yellow polo shirt. "This shade looks good with my hair, don't you think?"

"I need a nonfat vanilla latte, Holly, pronto. The game footage has to be at the station for the eleven o'clock news and I've been up since six." Wendy Valentine stood on the other side of the counter, dressed in a blue blazer with a plaid scarf looped around her neck. Her sleek black hair curved perfectly under her chin.

Holly reached for a cup and, writing the order code on a yellow sticky note, set the cup next to Carolyn, who stood at the espresso machine steaming milk.

She winked at Holly. "I saw her coming and already poured the milk."

Holly turned back to Wendy. "Are you doing sports now? I thought you did weather."

Wendy swiped her debit card, a pleased smile on her face. "I got an offer from a station in Atlanta. They suggested I try some other venues and my station manager agreed. I leave for Atlanta the first of the year, which is why Ms. King and I have been meeting here. She wanted to get to know me better."

"Good for you, Wendy. I'm not surprised." Carolyn set the latte on the counter. "Good luck to you."

"Oh, and—" Wendy blinked her long, black lashes "—if you see Mac, tell him I'm sorry. Sometimes I get carried away."

"Sorry for what?" She couldn't imagine why Wendy would be apologizing to Mac.

"He'll know." Wendy practically bounced to the door. "Thanks, ladies." With a backward wave she was gone.

"Two soy decaf lattes, Holly." Mayor Gold placed two Wildflower travel mugs on the counter and glanced at a tall, thin man by the door.

"Two? Coming right up, Mayor." Holly wrote the abbreviations on sticky notes and set the cups on the counter to the right. "Is Bill the mailman waiting for you?"

Deb nodded, smiling at the man in the knee-length shorts and Hawaiian-print shirt. "That's my Bill." She handed Holly a ten. "Turns out he's into composting. By the way,

I've been meaning to ask, what do you do with your coffee grounds?"

Holly handed over the change along with the travel mugs and frowned when she felt an instant surge of guilt. "I put them in the trash."

Deb's mouth dropped open and for a minute, Holly thought she was about to make one of her speeches. "Well, then, we need to talk. You give me your coffee grounds and we'll look into giving you a discount on your rent. But wait until after the weekend. Bill and I are going away." She wagged a finger in the air. "And tell that man of yours to start using one of your travel cups. He needs to set an example." She winked and handed one of the cups to her new friend.

The couple walked to the mayor's yellow motor scooter. The basket had been removed, apparently for Bill, because they both strapped on helmets and climbed onto the scooter, the mayor switching on the lights as they drove down the street.

Carolyn carried the milk containers to the sink and turned on the water. "Can you get some milk from the kitchen? I'm almost out."

"Sure." Holly shoved open the door into

the kitchen and ran right into her father. "Dad, what are you doing here?"

Leaning against the sink while her mother emptied the dishwasher, her father gave Holly a smile. "Big night for you."

Holly eased past her parents, her gaze flicking from one to the other. She had interrupted a discussion. Of what, she had no idea. "Yes, it is. I thought you didn't like crowds." She disappeared into the cooler and returned with two jugs of milk. Closing the door with a hip, she paused in front of her father. She couldn't have been more surprised at what came next than if a movie star had walked into the coffee shop.

Fritz wrapped his arms around her shoulders and kissed her on the cheek. "I'm proud of you, Holly. You've done a good job here."

Despite the milk containers in each hand, she wrapped her arms around her father. "Thanks, Dad. Your support means a lot."

Rose slammed shut the dishwasher door, a smile on her face. She wrapped her arms around Holly and her husband. "See. You two should talk more often."

Holly's face was against her father's shirt and her mother's hair was tickling her nose.

"Hey, can't breathe here. Carolyn is waiting for milk."

Laughing, her parents released her.

Her back against the door, Holly paused. "The travel cups and T-shirts are selling like hotcakes, Dad. Thanks for the suggestion."

Her father just nodded, a smile playing about the corners of his lips.

Holly pushed through the door, equal parts amused and thrilled at her parents' praise.

"Three vanilla lattes, Holly," Sue said. "And I'll have an order of cinnamon rolls ready for you first thing in the morning. Those Penn State fans start coming through town pretty early."

Depositing the milk in the refrigerator under the counter, Holly said, "Three lattes?"

Sue nodded in the direction of the two boys, still picking up after customers. "Since the fellas are busy, the girls figured we'd mix up some cookies. They feel guilty because they knew what the boys were up to all along. Shelly's even considering culinary school to be a pastry chef. She wants to work for me part-time." She shrugged. "Life sure is funny, isn't it?"

Holly chuckled as she prepared the three

lattes. Life was hilarious. Just when a person thinks she has the game figured out, the rules change.

Finally the only people left in the shop were Holly, Mac and Riley, who lay curled up on the couch. The Flowers Bed and Breakfast was full of Penn State football fans in town for tomorrow's game and Rose and Fritz had returned home to prepare tailgating snacks.

After cleaning out the pots and covering the pastries, Holly leaned on the counter. "Late night."

Mac leaned on the counter across from her, his eyes thoughtful as he watched his daughter sleep. "She's had a lot going on lately. She started first grade last week, had a birthday party and tonight she was beyond excited to sit with Thomas's kids at the football game."

"She likes coming here after school." Holly tilted her head toward a small desk near the window. "She settles in with a strawberry-banana smoothie and does her homework."

"Coming here after school makes her feel special. I'm glad this worked out, Holly."

She touched his arm. "Is your truck outside?"

"Parked across the street." He picked up Riley and rested her limp body on his shoulder.

Coming around the end of the counter, Holly gave him a smile. "Do you mind if we walk?"

Mac's brows bunched in puzzlement. "Why should we walk when we have a perfectly good vehicle right outside the door?"

Holly wrapped her arms around man and girl as she kissed him lightly on the lips. "A full moon is out and the smell of fall is in the air. We'll take Riley to your house, come back for the truck and go for a drive."

After making sure everything was off except the light over the counter, Holly locked the door behind her. "I love football weather." She breathed deeply and the scents of wood smoke, dry leaves and decaying vegetation filled her lungs. The smell would always remind her of Pennsylvania in the fall. Holly had found nothing to compare anywhere in the world. She put a hand on Mac's shoulder. "So, are we walking?"

Mac grinned at her over Riley's head. "Don't you always get your own way?" He started down the steps, his arms protectively around his daughter, who was still sleeping.

"I didn't get you." Holly bit her tongue.

She hadn't intended to say anything but the words slipped out. Despite their détente, despite their closeness, despite her resolution to let it go, Holly still couldn't understand why Mac had kissed her with such passion and then left town.

Mac turned at the base of the steps. "What are you talking about?"

Holly took a deep breath and plunged in. "Anne got you." She pressed her hands together to still the trembling. "She was the beautiful Southern belle, the equestrian. She knew genetics so she must have been smart, too, and…you had a child with her." Holly descended the steps slowly. When she reached the bottom she continued down the sidewalk. "She's the opposite of me."

"First of all, the two of you are surprisingly similar." Mac caught up and together they walked down the darkened street.

"I met Anne when I was stationed at Fort Bragg. They had this public relations thing where local families invited troops to their homes for Thanksgiving dinner, and me and two of my buddies ended up at the Drakes' horse farm." He paused, as if remembering those long-ago days. "A few months later I was sent overseas. We emailed as much as we could and she sent me funny cards and packages." He continued in a softer voice. "We married right after I got back." He glanced at Holly. "I had a hard time coming back to the States, getting used to the…differences. She understood. Her dad was a Vietnam vet. Maybe that helped." He smiled. "Maybe the mint juleps helped, too."

Holly glanced up but in the darkness she couldn't read his expression. "Go on."

"Remember how I said I was different when I came home?" Mac shook his head. "We have so much stuff in this country and everybody goes about their business, in their own little bubble with no idea what's happening on the other side of the world. Feeling secure, adapting to this life again, well, takes a while." He stopped and when Holly continued on he reached out and grabbed her coat. "Anne understood. And then the baby… My daughter gave me something to live for. I needed that."

Holly put her hands on his shoulders. "I understand. She was your first love and I don't want to replace her, either in your life or in Riley's life."

"No, Holly, you don't understand. Anne was the woman I needed when I came home.

She brought me back to life, back to myself. But you were my first love, Holly. I fell in love with you the day your brother brought me home."

"Mac, you were the first boy I ever kissed and the next day you left for boot camp. Why did you wait so long?"

Mac grimaced, still clutching his daughter. "Remember watching Wendy talking to Ms. King?"

Holly turned and started walking slowly down the sidewalk. "Yes." They passed the yellow-and-brown Go Bear Meadows sign in Mrs. Hershberger's yard.

"Remember the look in Wendy's eyes?" Mac's voice grew soft. "You had that look."

Holly realized Mac had stopped in front of Mrs. Hershberger's house and came back. "What are you talking about? What does Wendy have to do with anything?"

"That look, the one that says you can't wait to get out into the world and explore. You had that look, Holly. You'd been talking about traveling the world ever since I knew you. You and Chris always said you weren't marrying right out of high school like your brothers did. I didn't want to be the one to keep you here, to prevent you from living your dream."

The thought that Mac had waited so she could live her dream had never entered her head. Deep inside a pressure lifted. She thought back to Louise's ice cream in the microwave analogy and shook her head. "And now? Why did you wait so long?"

Mac barked a laugh. "I felt guilty, being the one left. Riley would have been better off losing me than her mother, so I tried to replace Anne."

Holly fingered the latch on the gate of Mrs. Hershberger's white picket fence. "You can't replace her."

Mac had continued to the end of the block and his voice carried in the crisp night air. "No, I can't. All I can do is surround Riley with as much love and support as possible."

Holly caught up to Mac just as he turned the corner toward his house. She slipped her arm through his. "So did you just say you love me?"

Mac shifted Riley to the other shoulder, then leaned down and kissed her forehead. "I love you, Holly Hoffman. I wouldn't be courting you if I didn't."

Holly tilted her head. "You're courting me?"

"That's what Hawkeye said."

"Well, he should know." They continued on in silence, finally coming to Mac's childhood home. "Riley said you usually go to North Carolina for Thanksgiving..." The comment hung in the crisp air.

Mac ascended the porch steps. A single light burned by the door. He turned and gave her a smile. "Holly?"

"Mac?"

He held up a finger. "Hold that thought."

As Mac disappeared into the house, Holly climbed the steps and settled onto the swing.

When he returned, he sat and wrapped an arm around her shoulders. "Maybe you could come along this year."

"I'd like that." Holly leaned into him. "Maybe I'll buy a horse while I'm there."

Mac threw back his head and laughed. "I have a feeling being married to you will be a heck of a ride."

"Well, hang on, McAndrews." Holly pressed a hand to his cheek and touched her lips to his. Memories of their first kiss flooded her mind, when the warmth of the sun and the smell of hay surrounded them. The scent of fall leaves and the chill of the autumn night replaced the memory, but the kiss was just as sweet.

"Mac?" Holly glimpsed a scattering of stars through the chains of the swing.

"Holly?" Mac's breath fanned her cheek as he dropped kisses along her jaw and down her neck.

"Did you just ask me to marry you?"

EPILOGUE

"HOLLY HOFFMAN. Is that you, back again?"

Latching the gate on Frosty's stall, Holly turned. "Tiffany?"

When the redheaded woman caught sight of the bulge at Holly's tummy she gasped. Tiffany sauntered up to them, hands on hips. "Does this mean that good-lookin' hunk is more than just a friend of the family this year?"

Holly laughed and threaded her arm through Mac's. "I believe it does, Tiffany. We were married on Christmas Eve."

Tiffany looked Mac up and down, her lips pursed. "Well, congratulations." Farther down the aisle, her daughter unsaddled her horse. "I better go help my girl. Good luck."

Holly waved. "Same to you." She turned to Mac. "We better go, too." Hand in hand, they walked down to the arena, where ten horses and their riders waited for the peewee class. Second in line, Frosty and Riley waited patiently. Picking a spot on the rail next to the gate, Holly caught Riley's eye and gave her a wink.

Riley smiled, flashing two big front teeth.

Mac brushed a strand of hair behind her ear. "Do you want to sit with the others?"

Holly scrutinized the crowd on the bleachers, where her parents and Mac's mother sat, talking animatedly. Her father flashed her a thumbs-up and she waved back. Sitting next to Rose were Liz and Rick Drake, their gazes glued on their granddaughter. "No, I'm fine here."

The Drakes had become part of their family, visiting often. Fritz and Rick were building a swing set together in Mac's backyard. If they hadn't insisted Frosty move north with Riley, would any of this have happened?

Holly reflected on the way families grew, picking up people like a snowball rolling downhill.

A finger tapped her shoulder. Her belly stretching a maternity shirt, Louise pointed at Riley. "She looks great. The navy print shirt and matching blanket really set off her blond hair and the white horse." Louise narrowed her eyes at Holly. "You might actually be developing some fashion sense in your old age."

"What are you doing here?" Holly asked. Moose stood close by, solid as a tree, his adoring gaze on his wife. "Aren't you afraid she'll go into labor?"

Louise waved a hand in the air. "He's a policeman. They know how to deliver babies."

Mac rolled his eyes. "We watch a movie, Louise."

Louise shrugged. "We had to be here. If not for Moose and me, none of this cute McAndrews family drama would be happening."

"What are you taking about?"

"Did you think I couldn't come in until nine on Saturday mornings? Pul-leaz. I've always been an early riser."

Holly's mouth dropped. The older she got, the less she knew.

"Oh, look," Louise said, "they're starting."

Mac wrapped his arms around Holly and she leaned into his solid frame. Louise had survived her tragedy. She planned to return to part-time work at the hospital in the spring.

Holly returned her attention to the ring. Riley and Frosty executed the commands effortlessly, moving as if they were one. The feet of the white horse with the black mane and tail barely touched the ground.

"Thank you for this." Mac dipped his head toward the arena. He whispered in her ear. "I love you, Holly. I always have."

Holly gazed into smiling blue eyes and light brown hair bleached blond by the summer sun. Deep inside she felt a flutter, a tickle, like an exploding seedpod. She would show her child the speckled jewelweed and tell the story of how his parents fell in love. Just as her grandmother had, Holly would pass along a shared memory, the joy of living, the beauty of nature exhibited so gracefully in the touch-me-not.

* * * * *

LARGER-PRINT BOOKS!

GET 2 FREE
LARGER-PRINT NOVELS
PLUS 2 FREE
MYSTERY GIFTS

Love Inspired®

SUSPENSE
RIVETING INSPIRATIONAL ROMANCE

Larger-print novels are now available...

YES! Please send me 2 FREE LARGER-PRINT Love Inspired® Suspense novels and my 2 FREE mystery gifts (gifts are worth about $10). After receiving them, if I don't wish to receive any more books, I can return the shipping statement marked "cancel." If I don't cancel, I will receive 4 brand-new novels every month and be billed just $5.49 per book in the U.S. or $5.99 per book in Canada. That's a savings of at least 19% off the cover price. It's quite a bargain! Shipping and handling is just 50¢ per book in the U.S. and 75¢ per book in Canada.* I understand that accepting the 2 free books and gifts places me under no obligation to buy anything. I can always return a shipment and cancel at any time. Even if I never buy another book, the two free books and gifts are mine to keep forever.

110/310 IDN GH6P

Name	(PLEASE PRINT)
Address	Apt. #
City	State/Prov.	Zip/Postal Code

Signature (if under 18, a parent or guardian must sign)

Mail to the **Reader Service:**
IN U.S.A.: P.O. Box 1867, Buffalo, NY 14240-1867
IN CANADA: P.O. Box 609, Fort Erie, Ontario L2A 5X3

Are you a current subscriber to Love Inspired® Suspense books and want to receive the larger-print edition?
Call 1-800-873-8635 or visit www.ReaderService.com.

* Terms and prices subject to change without notice. Prices do not include applicable taxes. Sales tax applicable in N.Y. Canadian residents will be charged applicable taxes. Offer not valid in Quebec. This offer is limited to one order per household. Not valid for current subscribers to Love Inspired Suspense larger-print books. All orders subject to credit approval. Credit or debit balances in a customer's account(s) may be offset by any other outstanding balance owed by or to the customer. Please allow 4 to 6 weeks for delivery. Offer available while quantities last.

Your Privacy—The Reader Service is committed to protecting your privacy. Our Privacy Policy is available online at www.ReaderService.com or upon request from the Reader Service.

We make a portion of our mailing list available to reputable third parties that offer products we believe may interest you. If you prefer that we not exchange your name with third parties, or if you wish to clarify or modify your communication preferences, please visit us at www.ReaderService.com/consumerschoice or write to us at Reader Service Preference Service, P.O. Box 9062, Buffalo, NY 14240-9062. Include your complete name and address.

LISLP15

WESTERN WP PROMISES

YES! Please send me **The Western Promises Collection** in Larger Print. This collection begins with 3 FREE books and 2 FREE gifts (gifts valued at approx. $14.00 retail) in the first shipment, along with the other first 4 books from the collection! If I do not cancel, I will receive 8 monthly shipments until I have the entire 51-book Western Promises collection. I will receive 2 or 3 FREE books in each shipment and I will pay just $4.99 US/ $5.89 CDN for each of the other four books in each shipment, plus $2.99 for shipping and handling per shipment. *If I decide to keep the entire collection, I'll have paid for only 32 books, because 19 books are FREE! I understand that accepting the 3 free books and gifts places me under no obligation to buy anything. I can always return a shipment and cancel at any time. My free books and gifts are mine to keep no matter what I decide.

272 HCN 3070 472 HCN 3070

Name	(PLEASE PRINT)	
Address		Apt. #
City	State/Prov.	Zip/Postal Code

Signature (if under 18, a parent or guardian must sign)

Mail to the **Reader Service:**
IN U.S.A.: P.O. Box 1867, Buffalo, NY 14240-1867
IN CANADA: P.O. Box 609, Fort Erie, Ontario L2A 5X3

WPBPA16R

LARGER-PRINT BOOKS!
GET 2 FREE LARGER-PRINT NOVELS PLUS
2 FREE GIFTS!

HARLEQUIN®

super romance®

More Story...More Romance

YES! Please send me 2 FREE LARGER-PRINT Harlequin® Superromance® novels and my 2 FREE gifts (gifts are worth about $10). After receiving them, if I don't wish to receive any more books, I can return the shipping statement marked "cancel." If I don't cancel, I will receive 4 brand-new novels every month and be billed just $5.94 per book in the U.S. or $6.24 per book in Canada. That's a savings of at least 12% off the cover price! It's quite a bargain! Shipping and handling is just 50¢ per book in the U.S. or 75¢ per book in Canada.* I understand that accepting the 2 free books and gifts places me under no obligation to buy anything. I can always return a shipment and cancel at any time. Even if I never buy another book, the two free books and gifts are mine to keep forever.

132/332 HDN GHVC

Name _____ (PLEASE PRINT)

Address _____ Apt. #

City _____ State/Prov. _____ Zip/Postal Code

Signature (if under 18, a parent or guardian must sign)

Mail to the **Reader Service:**
IN U.S.A.: P.O. Box 1867, Buffalo, NY 14240-1867
IN CANADA: P.O. Box 609, Fort Erie, Ontario L2A 5X3

Want to try two free books from another line?
Call 1-800-873-8635 today or visit www.ReaderService.com.

* Terms and prices subject to change without notice. Prices do not include applicable taxes. Sales tax applicable in N.Y. Canadian residents will be charged applicable taxes. Offer not valid in Quebec. This offer is limited to one order per household. Not valid for current subscribers to Harlequin Superromance Larger-Print books. All orders subject to credit approval. Credit or debit balances in a customer's account(s) may be offset by any other outstanding balance owed by or to the customer. Please allow 4 to 6 weeks for delivery. Offer available while quantities last.

Your Privacy—The Reader Service is committed to protecting your privacy. Our Privacy Policy is available online at www.ReaderService.com or upon request from the Reader Service.

We make a portion of our mailing list available to reputable third parties that offer products we believe may interest you. If you prefer that we not exchange your name with third parties, or if you wish to clarify or modify your communication preferences, please visit us at www.ReaderService.com/consumerschoice or write to us at Reader Service Preference Service, P.O. Box 9062, Buffalo, NY 14240-9062. Include your complete name and address.

HSRLP15

READERSERVICE.COM

Manage your account online!
- Review your order history
- Manage your payments
- Update your address

> ### *We've designed the Reader Service website just for you.*

Enjoy all the features!
- Discover new series available to you, and read excerpts from any series.
- Respond to mailings and special monthly offers.
- Connect with favorite authors at the blog.
- Browse the Bonus Bucks catalog and online-only exculsives.
- Share your feedback.

Visit us at:
ReaderService.com